KU-481-068

Also by Jerry Pournelle with Larry Niven:

THE MOTE IN GOD'S EYE

Jerry Pournelle

The Mercenary

Futura Publications Limited
An Orbit Book

An Orbit Book

First published in Great Britain by
Futura Publications Limited in 1977

Copyright © 1977 by Jerry Pournelle

ISBN 0 8600 7972 4
Printed in Great Britain by
Hazell Watson & Viney Ltd
Aylesbury, Bucks

Futura Publications Limited
110 Warner Road
Camberwell, London SE5

TO: Sergeant Herman Liech, Regular Army, U.S.A.;
and Second Lieutenant Zeneke Asfaw,
Kagnew Battalion, Imperial Guard of Ethiopia.

Acknowledgments

The battle in Chapter XIX is based in large part on the actual experience of Lieutenant Zeneke Asfaw, Ethiopian Imperial Guard, during the Korean War.

Author's Note

This novel is part of the series of "future histories" in which *The Mote in God's Eye* takes place, and it gives the early history of the events in that novel.

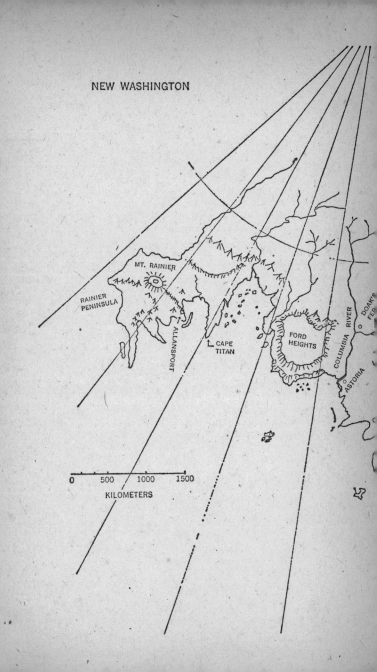

NEW WASHINGTON

MT. RAINIER

RAINIER
PENINSULA

ALLANSPORT

CAPE
TITAN

FORD
HEIGHTS

COLUMBIA RIVER

DOAK'S
FERRY

ASTORIA

0   500   1000   1500
KILOMETERS

Chronology

1969   Neil Armstrong sets foot on Earth's Moon.

1990   Series of treaties between U.S. and Soviet Union creates the CoDominium. Military research and development outlawed.

1996   French Foreign Legion forms the basic element of the CoDominium Armed Services.

2004   Alderson Drive perfected at Cal Tech.

2008   First Alderson Drive exploratory ships leave the Solar System.

2010–2100   CoDominium Intelligence Services engage in serious effort to suppress all research into technologies with military applications. They are aided by zero-growth organizations. Most scientific research ceases.

2010   Inhabitable planets discovered. Commercial exploitation begins.

2020   First interstellar colonies are founded. The CoDominium Space Navy and Marines are created, absorbing the original CoDominium Armed Services.

2020	Great Exodus period of colonization begins. First colonists are dissidents, malcontents, and voluntary adventurers.
2030	Sergei Lermontov is born in Moscow.
2040	Bureau of Relocation begins mass outsystem shipment of involuntary colonists.
2043	John Christian Falkenberg is born in Rome, Italy.
2060	Beginnings of nationalistic revival movements.

Prologue

AN OILY, ACRID smell assaulted him, and the noise was incessant. Hundreds of thousands had passed through the spaceport. Their odor floated through the embarcation hall to blend with the yammer of the current victims crammed into the enclosure.

The room was long and narrow. White painted concrete walls shut out bright Florida sunshine; but the walls were dingy with film and dirt that had been smeared about and not removed by the Bureau of Relocation's convict laborers. Cold luminescent panels glowed brightly above.

The smell and sounds and glare blended with his own fears. He didn't belong here, but no one would listen. No one wanted to. Anything he said was lost in the brutal totality of shouted orders, growls of surly trustee guards in their wire pen running the full length of the long hall; screaming children; the buzz of frightened humanity.

They marched onward, toward the ship that would take them out of the solar system and toward an unknown fate. A few colonists blustered and argued. Some suppressed rage until it might be of use. Most were ashen-faced, shuffling forward without visible emotion, beyond fear.

There were red lines painted on the concrete floor, and the colonists stayed carefully inside them. Even the children had learned to cooperate with BuRelock's guards. The colonists had a sameness about them: shabbily dressed in Welfare Issue clothing sprinkled with finery cast off by taxpayers and gleaned from Reclamation Stores or by begging or from a Welfare District Mission.

John Christian Falkenberg knew he didn't look much like a typical colonist. He was a gangland youth, already at fifteen approaching six feet in height and thin because he hadn't yet filled out to his latest spurt of growth. No one would take him for a man, no matter how hard he tried to act like one.

A forelock of sand-colored hair fell across his forehead and threatened to blind him, and he automatically brushed it aside with a nervous gesture. His bearing and posture set him apart from the others, as did his almost comically serious expression. His clothing was also unusual: it was new, and fit well, and obviously not reclaimed. He wore a brocaded tunic of real wool and cotton, bright flared trousers, a new belt, and a tooled leather purse at his left hip. His clothes had cost more than his father could afford, but they did him little good here. Still he stood straight and tall, his lips set in defiance.

John stalked forward to keep his place in the long line. His bag, regulation space duffel without tags, lay in front of him and he kicked it forward rather than stoop to pick it up. He thought it would look undignified to bend over, and his dignity was all he had left.

Ahead of him was a family of five, three screaming children and their apathetic parents—or, possibly, he thought, not parents. Citizen families were never very stable. BuRelock agents often farmed out their quotas, and their superiors were seldom concerned about the precise identities of those scooped up.

The disorderly crowds moved inexorably toward the end of the room. Each line terminated at a wire cage containing a plastisteel desk. Each family group moved into a cage, the doors were closed, and their interviews began.

The bored trustee placement officers hardly listened to their clients, and the colonists did not know what to say to them. Most knew nothing about Earth's outsystem worlds. A few had heard that Tanith was hot, Fulson's World cold, and Sparta a hard place to live, but free. Some understood that Hadley had a good climate and was under the benign protection of American Express and the Colonial Office. For those sentenced to transportation without confinement, knowing that little could make a lot of difference to their futures; most didn't know and were shipped off to labor-hungry mining and agricultural worlds, or the hell of Tanith, where their lot would be hard labor, no matter what their sentences might read.

The fifteen-year-old boy—he liked to consider himself a man, but he knew many of his emotions were boyish no matter how hard he tried to control them—had almost reached the interview cage. He felt despair.

16

Once past the interview, he'd be packed into a BuRelock transportation ship. John turned again toward the gray-uniformed guard standing casually behind the large-mesh protective screen. "I keep trying to tell you, there's been a mistake! I shouldn't—"

"Shut up," the guard answered. He motioned threateningly with the bell-shaped muzzle of his sonic stunner. "It's a mistake for everybody, right? Nobody belongs here. Tell the interview officer, sonny."

John's lip curled, and he wanted to attack the guard, to make him listen. He fought to control the rising flush of hatred. "Damn you, I—"

The guard raised the weapon. The Citizen family in front of John huddled together, shoving forward to get away from this mad kid who could get them all tingled. John subsided and sullenly shuffled forward in the line.

Tri-V commentators said the stunners were painless, but John wasn't eager to have it tried on him. The Tri-V people said a lot of things. They said most colonists were volunteers, and they said transportees were treated with dignity by the Bureau of Relocation.

No one believed them. No one believed anything the government told them. They did not believe in the friendship among nations that had created the CoDominium, or in the election figures, or—

He reached the interview cage. The trustee wore the same uniform as the guards, but his gray coveralls had numbers stenciled across back and chest. There were wide gaps between the man's jaggedly pointed teeth, and the teeth showed yellow stains when he smiled. He smiled often, but there was no warmth in the expression.

"Whatcha got for me?" the trustee asked. "Boy dressed like you can afford anything he wants. Where you want to go, boy?"

"I'm not a colonist," John insisted. His anger rose. The trustee was no more than a prisoner himself—what right had he to speak this way? "I demand to speak with a CoDominium officer."

"One of those, huh?" The trustee's grin vanished. "Tanith for you." He pushed a button and the door on the opposite side of the cage opened. "Get on," he snapped. "Fore I call the guards." His finger poised menacingly over the small console on his desk.

John took papers out of an inner pocket of his tunic. "I have an appointment to CoDominium Navy Service," he said. "I was ordered to report to Canaveral Embarcation Station for transport by BuRelock ship to Luna Base."

"Get movin'—uh?" The trustee stopped himself and the grin reappeared. "Let me see that." He held out a grimy hand.

"No." John was more sure of himself now. "I'll show them to any CD officer, but you won't get your hands on them. Now call an officer."

"Sure." The trustee didn't move. "Cost you ten credits."

"What?"

"Ten credits. Fifty bucks if you ain't got CD credits. Don't give me that look, kid. You don't pay, you go on the Tanith ship. Maybe they'll put things straight there, maybe they won't, but you'll be late reporting. Best you slip me something."

John held out a twenty-dollar piece. "That all you got?" the trustee demanded. "O.K., O.K., have to do." He punched a code into the phone, and a minute later a petty officer in blue CoDominium Space Navy coveralls came into the cage

"What you need, Smiley?"

"Got one of yours. New middy. Got himself mixed up with the colonists." The trustee laughed as John struggled to control himself.

The petty officer eyed Smiley with distaste. "Your orders, sir?" he said.

John handed him the papers, afraid that he would never see them again. The Navy man glanced through them. "John Christian Falkenberg?"

"Yes."

"Thank you, sir." He turned to the trustee. "Gimme."

"Aw, he can afford it."

"Want me to call the Marines, Smiley?"

"Jesus, you hardnosed—" The trustee took the coin from his pocket and handed it over.

"This way, please, sir," the Navy man said. He bent to pick up John's duffel. "And here's your money, sir."

"Thanks. You keep it."

The petty officer nodded. "Thank you, sir. Smiley, you bite one of *our* people again and I'll have the Marines look you up when you're off duty. Let's go, sir."

John followed the spacer out of the cubicle. The petty officer was twice his age, and no one had ever called John "sir" before. It gave John Falkenberg a sense of belonging, a sense of having found something he had searched for all his life. Even the street gangs had been closed to him, and friends he had grown up with had always seemed part of someone else's life, not his own. Now, in seconds, he seemed to have found—found what, he wondered.

They went through narrow whitewashed corridors, then into the bright Florida sunshine. A narrow gangway led to the forward end of an enormous winged landing ship that floated at the end of a long pier crowded with colonists and cursing guards.

The petty officer spoke briefly to the Marine sentries at the officers' gangway, then carefully saluted the officer at the head of the boarding gangway. John wanted to do the same, but he knew that you didn't salute in civilian clothing. His father had made him read books on military history and the customs of the Service as soon as he decided to find John an appointment to the Academy.

Babble from the colonists filled the air until they were inside the ship. As the hatch closed behind him the last sounds he heard were the curses of the guards.

"If you please, sir. This way." The petty officer led him through a maze of steel corridors, airtight bulkheads, ladders, pipes, wire races, and other unfamiliar sights. Although the CD Navy operated it, most of the ship belonged to BuRelock, and she stank. There were no viewports and John was lost after several turns in the corridors.

The petty officer led on at a brisk pace until he came to a door that seemed no different from any other. He pressed a button on a panel outside it.

"Come in," the panel answered.

The compartment held eight tables, but only three men, all seated at a single booth. In contrast to the gray steel corridors outside, the compartment was almost cheerful, with paintings on the walls, padded furniture, and what seemed like carpets.

The CoDominium seal hung from the far wall—American eagle and Soviet sickle and hammer, red, white, and blue, white stars and red stars.

The three men held drinks and seemed relaxed. All wore civilian clothing not much different from John's except that the older man wore a more conservative tunic. The others seemed about John's age, perhaps a year older; no more.

"One of ours, sir," the petty officer announced. "New middy got lost with the colonists."

19

One of the younger men laughed, but the older cut him off with a curt wave. "All right, coxswain. Thank you. Come in, we don't bite."

"Thank you, sir," John said. He shuffled uncertainly in the doorway, wondering who these men were. Probably CD officers, he decided. The petty officer wouldn't act that way toward anyone else. Frightened as he was, his analytical mind continued to work, and his eyes darted around the compartment.

Definitely CD officers, he decided. Going back up to Luna Base after leave, or perhaps a duty tour in normal gravity. Naturally they'd worn civilian clothing. Wearing the CD uniform off duty earthside was an invitation to be murdered.

"Lieutenant Hartmann, at your service," the older man introduced himself. "And Midshipmen Rolnikov and Bates. Your orders, please?"

"John Christian Falkenberg, sir," John said. "Midshipman. Or I guess I'm a midshipman. But I'm not sure. I haven't been sworn in or anything."

All three men laughed at that. "You will be, Mister," Hartmann said. He took John's orders. "But you're one of the damned all the same, swearing in or no."

He examined the plastic sheet, comparing John's face to the photograph, then reading the bottom lines. He whistled. "Grand Senator Martin Grant. Appointed by the Navy's friend, no less. With him to bat for you, I wouldn't be surprised to see you outrank me in a few years."

"Senator Grant is a former student of my father's," John said.

"I see," Hartmann returned the orders and motioned John to sit with them. Then he turned to one of the other midshipmen. "As to you, Mister Bates, I fail to see the humor. What is so funny about one of your brother officers becoming lost among the colonists? You have never been lost?"

Bates squirmed uncomfortably. His voice was high-pitched, and John realized that Bates was no older than himself. "Why didn't he show the guards his taxpayer status card?" Bates demanded. "They would have taken him to an officer. Wouldn't they?"

Hartmann shrugged.

"I didn't have one," John said.

"Um." Hartmann seemed to withdraw, although he

didn't actually move. "Well," he said. "We don't usually get officers from Citizen families—"

"We are not Citizens," John said quickly. "My father is a CoDominium University professor, and I was born in Rome."

"Ah," Hartmann said. "Did you live there long?"

"No, sir. Father prefers to be a visiting faculty member. We have lived in many university towns." The lie came easily now, and John thought that Professor Falkenberg probably believed it after telling it so many times. John knew better: he had seen his father desperate to gain tenure, but always, always making too many enemies.

He is too blunt and too honest. One explanation. He is a revolting S.O.B. and can't get along with anyone. That's another. I've lived with the situation so long I don't care anymore. But, it would have been nice to have a home. I think.

Hartmann relaxed slightly. "Well, whatever the reason, Mister Falkenberg, you would have done better to arrange to be born a United States taxpayer. Or a Soviet party member. Unfortunately, you, like me, are doomed to remain in the lower ranks of the officer corps."

There was a trace of accent to Hartmann's voice, but John couldn't place it exactly. German, certainly; there were many Germans in the CD fighting services. This was not the usual German, though; John had lived in Heidelberg long enough to learn many shades of the German speech. East German? Possibly.

He realized the others were waiting for him to say something. "I thought, sir, I thought there was equality within the CD services."

Hartmann shrugged. "In theory, yes. In practice—the generals and admirals, even the captains who command ships, always seem to be Americans or Soviets. It is not the preference of the officer corps, Mister. We have no countries of origin among ourselves and no politics. Ever. The Fleet is our fatherland, and our only fatherland." He glanced at his glass. "Mister Bates, we need more to drink, and a glass for our new comrade. Hop it."

"Aye, aye, sir." The pudgy middy left the compartment, passing the unattended bar in the corner on his way. He returned a moment later with a full bottle of American whiskey and an empty glass.

Hartmann poured the glass full and pushed it toward John. "The Navy will teach you many things, Mister

21

Midshipman John Christian Falkenberg. One of them is to drink. We all drink too much. Another thing we will teach you is why we do, but before you learn why, you must learn to do it."

He lifted the glass. When John raised his and took only a sip, Hartmann frowned. "More," he said. The tone made it an order.

John drank half the whiskey. He had been drinking beer for years, but his father did not often let him drink spirits. It did not taste good, and it burned his throat and stomach.

"Now, why have you joined our noble band of brothers?" Hartmann asked. His voice carried a warning: he used bantering words, but under that was a more serious mood—perhaps he was not mocking the Service at all when he called it a band of brothers.

John hoped he was not. He had never had brothers. He had never had friends, or a home, and his father was a harsh schoolmaster, teaching him many things, but never giving him any affection—or friendship.

"I—"

"Honesty," Hartmann warned. "I will tell you a secret, the secret of the Fleet. We do not lie to our own." He looked at the other two midshipmen, and they nodded, Rolnikov slightly amused, Bates serious, as if in church.

"Out there," Hartmann said, "out there they lie, and they cheat, and they use each other. With us this is not true. We are used, yes. But we know that we are used, and we are honest with each other. That is why the men are loyal to us. And why we are loyal to the Fleet."

And that's significant, John thought, because Hartmann had glanced at the CoDominium banner on the wall, but he said nothing about the CD at all. Only the Fleet. "I'm here because my father wanted me out of the house and was able to get an appointment for me," John blurted.

"You will find another reason, or you will not stay with us," Hartmann said. "Drink up."

"Yes, sir."

"The proper response is 'aye aye, sir.'"

"Aye aye, sir." John drained the glass.

Hartmann smiled. "Very good." He refilled his glass, then the others. "What is the mission of the CoDominium Navy, Mister Falkenberg?"

"Sir? To carry out the will of the Grand Senate—"

"No. It is to exist. And by existing, to keep some mea-

22

sure of peace and order in this corner of the galaxy. To buy enough time for men to get far enough away from Earth that when the damned fools kill themselves they will not have killed the human race. And that is our only mission."

"Sir?" Midshipman Rolnikov spoke quietly and urgently. "Lieutenant, sir, should you drink so much?"

"Yes. I should," Hartmann replied. "I thank you for your concern, Mister Rolnikov. But as you see, I am, at present, a passenger. The Service has no regulation against drinking. None at all, Mister Falkenberg. There is a strong prohibition against being unfit for one's duties, but none against drinking. And I have no duties at the moment." He raised his glass. "Save one. To speak to you, Mister Falkenberg, and to tell you the truth, so that you will either run from us or be damned with us for the rest of your life, for we never lie to our own."

He fell silent for a moment, and Falkenberg wondered just how drunk Hartmann was. The officer seemed to be considering his words more carefully than his father ever had when he was drinking.

"What do you know of the history of the CoDominium Navy, Mister Falkenberg?" Hartmann demanded.

Probably more than you, John thought. Father's lecture on the growth of the CoDominium was famous. "It began with *détente,* and soon there was a web of formal treaties between the United States and the Soviet Union. The treaties did not end the basic enmity between these great powers, but their common interest was greater than their differences; for it was obviously better that there be only two great powers, than for there to be. . . ." No. Hartmann did not want to hear Professor Falkenberg's lecture. "Very little, sir."

"We were created out of the French Foreign Legion," Hartmann said. "A legion of strangers, to fight for an artificial alliance of nations that hate each other. How can a man give his soul and life to that, Mister Falkenberg? What heart has an alliance? What power to inspire men's loyalty?"

"I don't know, sir."

"Nor do they." Hartmann waved at the other middies, who were carefully leaning back in their seats, acting as if they were listening, as if they were not listening—John couldn't tell. Perhaps they thought Hartmann was crazy drunk. Yet it had been a good question.

"I don't know," John repeated.

"Ah. But no one knows, for there is no answer. Men cannot die for an alliance. Yet we do fight. And we do die."

"At the Senate's orders," Midshipman Rolnikov said quietly.

"But we do not love the Senate," Hartmann said. "Do you love the Grand Senate, Mister Rolnikov? Do you, Mister Bates? We know what the Grand Senate is. Corrupt, politicians who lie to each other, and who use us to gather wealth for themselves, power for their own factions. If they can. They do not use us as much as they once did. Drink, gentlemen. *Drink.*"

The whiskey had taken its effect, and John's head buzzed. He felt sweat break out at his temples and in his armpits, and his stomach rebelled, but he lifted the glass and drank again, in unison with Rolnikov and Bates, and it was more meaningful than the Communion cup had ever been. He tried to ask himself why, but there was only emotion, no thought. He belonged here, with this man, with these men, and he was a man with them.

As if he had read John's thoughts, Lieutenant Hartmann put his arms out, across the shoulders of the three boys, two on his left, John alone on his right, and he lowered his voice to speak to all of them. "No. We are here because the Fleet is our only fatherland, and our brothers in the Service are our only family. And if the Fleet should ever demand our lives, we give them as men because we have no other place to go."

I

Twenty-seven years later . . .

EARTH FLOATED ETERNALLY lovely above bleak lunar mountains. Daylight lay across California and most of the Pacific, and the glowing ocean made an impossibly blue background for a vortex of bright clouds swirling in a massive tropical storm. Beyond the lunar crags, man's home was a fragile ball amidst the black star-studded velvet of space; a ball that a man might reach out to grasp and crush in his bare hands.

Grand Admiral Sergei Lermontov looked at the bright viewscreen image and thought how easy it would be for Earth to die. He kept her image on the viewscreen to remind himself of that every time he looked up.

"That's all we can get you, Sergei." His visitor sat with hands carefully folded in his lap. A photograph would have shown him in a relaxed position, seated comfortably in the big visitor's chair covered with leathers from animals that grew on planets a hundred lightyears from Earth. Seen closer, the real man was not relaxed at all. He looked that way from his long experience as a politician.

"I wish it could be more." Grand Senator Martin Grant shook his head slowly from side to side. "At least it's something."

"We will lose ships and disband regiments. I cannot operate the Fleet on that budget." Lermontov's voice was flat and precise. He adjusted his rimless spectacles to a comfortable position on his thin nose. His gestures, like his voice, were precise and correct, and it was said in Navy wardrooms that the Grand Admiral practiced in front of a mirror.

"You'll have to do the best you can. It's not even certain

the United Party can survive the next election. God knows we won't be able to if we give any more to the Fleet."

"But there is enough money for national armies." Lermontov looked significantly at Earth's image on the viewscreen. "Armies that can destroy Earth. Martin, how can we keep the peace if you will not let us have ships and men?"

"You can't keep the peace if there's no CoDominium."

Lermontov frowned. "Is there a real chance that the United Party will lose, then?"

Martin Grant's head bobbed in an almost imperceptible movement. "Yes."

"And the United States will withdraw from the CD." Lermontov thought of all that would mean, for Earth and for the nearly hundred worlds where men lived. "Not many of the colonies will survive without us. It is too soon. If we did not suppress science and research it might be different, but there are so few independent worlds— Martin, we are spread thin across the colony worlds. The CoDominium must help them. We created their problems with our colonial governments. We gave them no chances at all to live without us. We cannot let them go suddenly."

Grant sat motionless, saying nothing.

"Yes, I am preaching to the converted. But it is the Navy that gave Grand Senate this power over the colonies. I cannot help feeling responsible."

Senator Grant's head moved slightly again, either a nod or a tremor. "I would have thought there was a lot you could do, Sergei. The Fleet obeys you, not the Senate. I know my nephew has made that clear enough. The warriors respect another warrior, but they've only contempt for us politicians."

"You are inviting treason?"

"No. Certainly I'm not suggesting that the Fleet try running the show. Military rule hasn't worked very well for us, has it?" Senator Grant turned his head slightly to indicate the globe behind him. Twenty nations on Earth were governed by armies, none of them very well.

On the other hand, the politicians aren't doing a much better job, he thought. Nobody is. "We don't seem to have any goals, Sergei. We just hang on, hoping that things will get better. Why should they?"

"I have almost ceased to hope for better conditions," Lermontov replied. "Now I only pray they do not get worse." His lips twitched slightly in a thin smile. "Those prayers are seldom answered."

"I spoke with my brother yesterday," Grant said. "He's threatening to retire again. I think he means it this time."

"But he cannot do that!" Lermontov shuddered. "Your brother is one of the few men in the U.S. government who understands how desperate is our need for time."

"I told him that."

"And?"

Grant shook his head. "It's the rat race, Sergei. John doesn't see any end to it. It's all very well to play rear guard, but for what?"

"Isn't the survival of civilization a worthwhile goal?"

"If that's where we're headed, yes. But what assurance do we have that we'll achieve even that?"

The Grand Admiral's smile was wintry. "None, of course. But we may be sure that *nothing* will survive if we do not have more time. A few years of peace, Martin. Much can happen in a few years. And if nothing does— why, we will have had a few years."

The wall behind Lermontov was covered with banners and plaques. Centered among them was the CoDominium Seal, American eagle, Soviet sickle and hammer, red stars and white stars. Beneath it was the Navy's official motto: PEACE IS OUR PROFESSION.

We chose that motto for them, Grant thought. The Senate made the Navy adopt it. Except for Lermontov I wonder how many Fleet officers believe it? What would they have chosen if left to themselves?

There are always the warriors, and if you don't give them something worthwhile to fight for. . . . But we can't live without them, because there comes a time when you have to have warriors. Like Sergei Lermontov.

But do we have to have politicians like me? "I'll talk to John again. I've never been sure how serious he is about retiring anyway. You get used to power, and it's hard to lay it down. It only takes a little persuasion, some argument to let you justify keeping it. Power's more addicting than opiates."

"But you can do nothing about our budget."

"No. Fact is, there's more problems. We need Bronson's votes, and he's got demands."

Lermontov's eyes narrowed, and his voice was thick with distaste. "At least we know how to deal with men like Bronson." And it was strange, Lermontov thought, that

27

despicable creatures like Bronson should be so small as problems. They could be bribed. They expected to be bought.

It was the men of honor who created the real problems. Men like Harmon in the United States and Kaslov in the Soviet Union, men with causes they would die for—they had brought mankind to this.

But I would rather know Kaslov and Harmon and their friends than Bronson's people who support us.

"You won't like some of what he's asked for," Grant said. "Isn't Colonel Falkenberg a special favorite of yours?"

"He is one of our best men. I use him when the situation seems desperate. His men will follow him anywhere, and he does not waste lives in achieving our objectives."

"He's apparently stepped on Bronson's toes once too often. They want him cashiered."

"No." Lermontov's voice was firm.

Martin Grant shook his head. Suddenly he felt very tired, despite the low gravity of the moon. "There's no choice, Sergei. It's not just personal dislike, although there's a lot of that too. Bronson's making up to Harmon, and Harmon thinks Falkenberg's dangerous."

"Of course he is dangerous. He is a warrior. But he is a danger only to enemies of the CoDominium. . . ."

"Precisely." Grant sighed again. "Sergei, I *know*. We're robbing you of your best tools and then expecting you to do the work without them."

"It is more than that, Martin. How do you control warriors?"

"I beg your pardon?"

"I asked, 'How do you control warriors?' " Lermontov adjusted his spectacles with the tips of the fingers of both hands. "By earning their respect, of course. But what happens if that respect is forfeit? There will be no controlling him; and you are speaking of one of the best military minds alive. You may live to regret this decision, Martin."

"Can't be helped. Sergei, do you think I like telling you to dump a good man for a snake like Bronson? But it doesn't matter. The Patriot Party's ready to make a big thing out of this, and Falkenberg couldn't survive that kind of political pressure anyway, you know that. No officer can. His career's finished no matter what."

"You have always supported him in the past."

28

"God damn it, Sergei, I appointed him to the Academy in the first place. I cannot support him, and you can't either. He goes, or we lose Bronson's vote on the budget."

"But why?" Lermontov demanded. "The real reason."

Grant shrugged. "Bronson's or Harmon's? Bronson has hated Colonel Falkenberg ever since that business on Kennicott. The Bronson family lost a lot of money there, and it didn't help that Bronson had to vote in favor of giving Falkenberg his medals either. I doubt there's any more to it than that.

"Harmon's a different matter. He really believes that Falkenberg might lead his troops against Earth. And once he asks for Falkenberg's scalp as a favor from Bronson—"

"I see. But Harmon's reasons are ludicrous. At least at the moment they are ludicrous—"

"If he's that damned dangerous, kill him," Grant said. He saw the look on Lermontov's face. "I don't really mean that, Sergei, but you'll have to do something."

"I will."

"Harmon thinks you might order Falkenberg to march on Earth."

Lermontov looked up in surprise.

"Yes. It's come to that. Not even Bronson's ready to ask for *your* scalp. Yet. But it's another reason why your special favorites have to take a low profile right now."

"You speak of our best men."

Grant's look was full of pain and sadness. "Sure. Anyone who's effective scares hell out of the Patriots. They want the CD eliminated entirely, and if they can't get that, they'll weaken it. They'll keep chewing away, too, getting rid of our most competent officers, and there's not a lot we can do. Maybe in a few years things will be better."

"And perhaps they will be worse," Lermontov said.

"Yeah. There's always that, too."

Sergei Lermontov stared at the viewscreen long after Grand Senator Grant had left the office. Darkness crept slowly across the Pacific, leaving Hawaii in shadow, and still Lermontov sat without moving, his fingers drumming restlessly on the polished wood desk top.

I knew it would come to this, he thought. Not so soon, though, not so soon. There is still so much to do before we can let go.

And yet it will not be long before we have no choice. Perhaps we should act now.

Lermontov recalled his youth in Moscow, when the Generals controlled the Presidium, and shuddered. No, he thought. The military virtues are useless for governing civilians. But the politicians are doing no better.

If we had not suppressed scientific research. But that was done in the name of the peace. Prevent development of new weapons. Keep control of technology in the hands of the government, prevent technology from dictating policy to all of us; it had seemed so reasonable, and besides, the policy was very old now. There were few trained scientists, because no one wanted to live under the restrictions of the Bureau of Technology.

What is done is done, he thought, and looked around the office. Open cabinets held shelves covered with the mementos of a dozen worlds. Exotic shells lay next to reptilian stuffed figures and were framed by gleaming rocks that could bring fabulous prices if he cared to sell.

Impulsively he reached toward the desk console and turned the selector switch. Images flashed across the viewscreen until he saw a column of men marching through a great open bubble of rock. They seemed dwarfed by the enormous cave.

A detachment of CoDominium Marines marching through the central area of Luna Base. Senate chamber and government offices were far below the cavern, buried so deeply into rock that no weapon could destroy the CoDominium's leaders by surprise. Above them were the warriors who guarded, and this group was marching to relieve the guard.

Lermontov turned the sound pickup but heard no more than the precise measured tramp of marching boots. They walked carefully in low gravity, their pace modified to accommodate their low weight; and they would, he knew, be just as precise on a high-gravity world.

They wore uniforms of blue and scarlet, with gleaming buttons of gold, badges of the dark rich bronze alloys found on Kennicott, berets made from some reptile that swam in Tanith's seas. Like the Grand Admiral's office, the CoDominium Marines showed the influence of worlds lightyears away.

"Sound off!"

The order came through the pickup so loud that it

startled the Admiral, and he turned down the volume as the men began to sing.

Lermontov smiled to himself. That song was officially forbidden, and it was certainly not an appropriate choice for the guard mount about to take posts outside the Grand Senate chambers. It was also very nearly the official marching song of the Marines. And that, Admiral Lermontov thought, ought to tell something to any Senator listening.

If Senators ever listened to anything from the military people.

The measured verses came through, slowly, in time with the sinister gliding step of the troops.

"We've left blood in the dirt of twenty-five worlds,
we've built roads on a dozen more,
and all that we have at the end of our hitch,
buys a night with a second-class whore.

"The Senate decrees, the Grand Admiral calls,
the orders come down from on high,
It's 'On Full Kits' and sound 'Board Ships,'
We're sending you where you can die.

"The lands that we take, the Senate gives back,
rather more often than not,
so the more that are killed, the less share the loot,
and we won't be back to this spot.

"We'll break the hearts of your women and girls,
we may break your arse as well,
Then the Line Marines with their banners unfurled,
will follow those banners to Hell.

"We know the devil, his pomps and his works,
Ah yes! we know them well!
When we've served out our hitch as Line Marines,
we can bugger the Senate of Hell!

"Then we'll drink with our comrades and lay down our
        packs,
we'll rest ten years on the flat of our backs,
then it's 'On Full Kits' and 'Out of Your Racks,'
you must build a new road through Hell!

"The Fleet is our country, we sleep with a rifle,
no one ever begot a son on his rifle,
they pay us in gin and curse when we sin,

there's not one that can stand us unless we're down
    wind,
we're shot when we lose and turned out when we win,
but we bury our comrades wherever they fall,
and there's none that can face us though we've nothing
    at all."

The verse ended with a flurry of drums, and Lermontov gently changed the selector back to the turning Earth.

Perhaps, he thought. Perhaps there's hope, but only if we have time.

Can the politicians buy enough time?

II

The Honorable John Rogers Grant laid a palm across a winking light on his desk console and it went out, shutting off the security phone to Luna Base. His face held an expression of pleasure and distaste, as it always did when he was through talking with his brother.

I don't think I've ever won an argument with Martin, he thought. Maybe it's because he knows me better than I know myself.

Grant turned toward the Tri-V, where the speaker was in full form. The speech had begun quietly as Harmon's speeches always did, full of resonant tones and appeals to reason. The quiet voice had asked for attention, but now it had grown louder and demanded it.

The background behind him changed as well, so that Harmon stood before the stars and stripes covering the hemisphere, with an American eagle splendid over the capitol. Harmon was working himself into one of his famous frenzies, and his face was contorted with emotion.

"Honor? It is a word that Lipscomb no longer understands! Whatever he might have been—and my friends, we all know how great he once was—he is no longer one of us! His cronies, the dark little men who whisper to him, have corrupted even as great a man as President Lipscomb!

"And our nation bleeds! She bleeds from a thousand wounds! People of America, hear me! She bleeds from the running sores of these men and their CoDominium!

"They say that if we leave the CoDominium it will mean war. I pray God it will not, but if it does, why these are hard times. Many of us will be killed, but we would die as men! Today our friends and allies, the people of Hungary, the people of Rumania, the Czechs, the Slovaks, the

Poles, all of them groan under the oppression of their Communist masters. Who keeps them there? We do! Our CoDominium!

"We have become no more than slavemasters. Better to die as men.

"But it will not come to that. The Russians will never fight. They are soft, as soft as we, their government is riddled with the same corruptions as ours. People of America, hear me! People of America, listen!"

Grant spoke softly and the Tri-V turned itself off. A walnut panel slid over the darkened screen, and Grant spoke again.

The desk opened to offer a small bottle of milk. There was nothing he could do for his ulcer despite the advances in medical science. Money was no problem, but there was never time for surgery and weeks with the regeneration stimulators.

He leafed through papers on his desk. Most were reports with bright red security covers, and Grant closed his eyes for a moment. Harmon's speech was important and would probably affect the upcoming elections. The man is getting to be a nuisance, Grant thought.

I should do something about him.

He put the thought aside with a shudder. Harmon had been a friend, once. Lord, what have we come to? He opened the first report.

There had been a riot at the International Federation of Labor convention. Three killed and the smooth plans for the re-election of Matt Brady thrown into confusion. Grant grimaced again and drank more milk. The Intelligence people had assured him this one would be easy.

He dug through the reports and found that three of Harvey Bertram's child crusaders were responsible. They'd bugged Brady's suite. The idiot hadn't known better than to make deals in his room. Now Bertram's people had enough evidence of sell-outs to inflame floor sentiment in a dozen conventions.

The report ended with a recommendation that the government drop Brady and concentrate support on Mac-Knight, who had a good reputation and whose file in the CIA building bulged with information. MacKnight would be easy to control. Grant nodded to himself and scrawled his signature on the action form.

He threw it into the "Top Secret: Out" tray and watched it vanish. There was no point in wasting time. Then he wondered idly what would happen to Brady. Matt Brady had been a good United Party man; blast Bertram's people anyway.

He took up the next file, but before he could open it his secretary came in. Grant looked up and smiled, glad of his decision to ignore the electronics. Some executives never saw their secretaries for weeks at a time.

"Your appointment, sir," she said. "And it's time for your nerve tonic."

He grunted. "I'd rather die." But he let her pour a shotglass of evil-tasting stuff, and he tossed it off and chased it with milk. Then he glanced at his watch, but that wasn't necessary. Miss Ackridge knew the travel time to every Washington office. There'd be no time to start another report, which suited Grant fine.

He let her help him into his black coat and brush off a few silver hairs. He didn't feel sixty-five, but he looked it now. It happened all at once. Five years ago he could pass for forty. John saw the girl in the mirror behind him and knew that she loved him, but it wouldn't work.

And why the hell not? he wondered. It isn't as if you're pining away for Priscilla. By the time she died you were praying it would happen, and we married late to begin with. So why the hell do you act as if the great love of your life has gone out forever? All you'd have to do is turn around, say five words, and—and what? She wouldn't be the perfect secretary any longer, and secretaries are harder to find than mistresses. Let it alone.

She stood there a moment longer, then moved away. "Your daughter wants to see you this evening," she told him. "She's driving down this afternoon and says it's important."

"Know why?" Grant asked. Ackridge knew more about Sharon than Grant did. Possibly a lot more.

"I can guess. I think her young man has asked her."

John nodded. It wasn't unexpected, but still it hurt. So soon, so soon. They grow so fast when you're an old man. John Jr. was a commander in the CoDominium Navy, soon to be a captain with a ship of his own. Frederick was dead in the same accident as his mother. And now Sharon, the baby, had found another life . . . not that they'd been close since he'd taken this job.

"Run his name through CIA, Flora. I meant to do that months ago. They won't find anything, but we'll need it for the records."

"Yes, sir. You'd better be on your way now. Your drivers are outside."

He scooped up his briefcase. "I won't be back tonight. Have my car sent around to the White House, will you? I'll drive myself home tonight."

He acknowledged the salutes of the driver and armed mechanic with a cheery wave and followed them to the elevator at the end of the long corridor. Paintings and photographs of ancient battles hung along both sides of the hall, and there was carpet on the floor, but otherwise it was like a cave. Blasted Pentagon, he thought for the hundredth time. Silliest building ever constructed. Nobody can find anything, and it can't be guarded at any price. Why couldn't someone have bombed it?

They took a surface car to the White House. A flight would have been another detail to worry about, and besides, this way he got to see the cherry trees and flower beds around the Jefferson. The Potomac was a sludgy brown mess. You could swim in it if you had a strong stomach, but the Army Engineers had "improved" it a few administrations back. They'd given it concrete banks. Now they were ripping them out, and it brought down mudslides.

They drove through rows of government buildings, some abandoned. Urban renewal had given Washington all the office space the Government would ever need, and more, so that there were these empty buildings as relics of the time when D.C. was the most crime-ridden city in the world. Sometime in Grant's youth, though, they'd hustled everyone out of Washington who didn't work there, with bulldozers quickly following to demolish the tenements. For political reasons the offices had gone in as quickly as the other buildings were torn down.

They passed the Population Control Bureau and drove around the Elipse and past Old State to the gate. The guard carefully checked his identity and made him put his palm on the little scanning plate. Then they entered the tunnel to the White House basement.

The President stood when Grant entered the Oval Office, and the others shot to their feet as if they had ejection charges under them. Grant shook hands around but looked closely at Lipscomb. The President was feeling the strain, no question about it. Well, they all were.

The secretary of defense wasn't there, but then he never was. The secretary was a political hack who controlled a bloc of Aerospace Guild votes and an even larger bloc of aerospace industry stocks. As long as government contracts kept his companies busy employing his men, he didn't give a damn about policy. He could sit in on formal Cabinet sessions where nothing was ever said, and no one would know the difference. John Grant was Defense as much as he was CIA.

Few of the men in the Oval Office were well known to the public. Except for the President any one of them could have walked the streets of any city except Washington without fear of recognition. But the power they controlled, as assistants and deputies, was immense, and they all knew it. There was no need to pretend here.

The servitor brought drinks and Grant accepted Scotch. Some of the others didn't trust a man who wouldn't drink with them. His ulcer would give him hell, and his doctor more, but doctors and ulcers didn't understand the realities of power. Neither, thought Grant, do I or any of us, but we've got it.

"Mr. Karins, would you begin?" the President asked. Heads swiveled to the west wall where Karins stood at the briefing screen. To his right a polar projection of Earth glowed with lights showing the status of the forces that the President ordered, but Grant controlled.

Karins stood confidently, his paunch spilling out over his belt. The fat was an obscenity in so young a man. Herman Karins was the second youngest man in the room, assistant director of the office of management and budget, and said to be one of the most brilliant economists Yale had ever produced. He was also the best political technician in the country, but he hadn't learned that at Yale.

He activated the screen to show a set of figures. "I have the latest poll results," Karins said too loudly. "This is the real stuff, not the slop we give the press. It stinks."

Grant nodded. It certainly did. The Unity Party was hovering around thirty-eight percent, just about evenly divided between the Republican and Democratic wings. Harmon's Patriot Party had just over twenty-five. Millington's violently left wing Liberation Party had its usual ten, but the real shocker was Bertram's Freedom Party. Bertram's popularity stood at an unbelievable twenty percent of the population.

"These are figures for those who have an opinion and might vote," Karins said. "Of course there's the usual gang that doesn't give a damn, but we know how they split off. They go to whomever got to 'em last anyway. You see the bad news."

"You're sure of this?" the assistant postmaster general asked. He was the leader of the Republican wing of Unity, and it hadn't been six months since he had told them they could forget Bertram.

"Yes, sir," Karins said. "And it's growing. Those riots at the labor convention probably gave 'em another five points we don't show. Give Bertram six months and he'll be ahead of us. How you like them apples, boys and girls?"

"There is no need to be flippant, Mr. Karins," the President said.

"Sorry, Mr. President." Karins wasn't sorry at all and he grinned at the assistant postmaster general with triumph. Then he flipped the switches to show new charts.

"Soft and hard," Karins said. "You'll notice Bertram's vote is pretty soft, but solidifying. Harmon's is so hard you couldn't get 'em away from him without you use nukes. And ours is a little like butter. Mr. President, I can't even guarantee we'll be the largest party after the election, much less that we can hold a majority."

"Incredible," the chairman of the joint chiefs muttered.

"Worse than incredible." The commerce rep shook her head in disbelief. "A disaster. Who will win?"

Karins shrugged. "Toss-up, but if I had to say, I'd pick Bertram. He's getting more of our vote than Harmon."

"You've been quiet, John," the President said. "What are your thoughts here?"

"Well, sir, it's fairly obvious what the result will be no matter who wins as long as it isn't us." Grant lifted his Scotch and sipped with relish. He decided to have another and to hell with the ulcer. "If Harmon wins, he pulls out of the CoDominium, and we have war. If Bertram takes over, he relaxes security, Harmon drives him out with his storm troopers, and we have war anyway."

Karins nodded. "I don't figure Bertram could hold power more'n a year, probably not that long. Man's too honest."

The President sighed loudly. "I can recall a time when men said that about me, Mr. Karins."

"It's still true, Mr. President." Karins spoke hurriedly. "But you're realistic enough to let us do what we have to do. Bertram wouldn't."

38

"So what do we do about it?" the President asked gently.

"Rig the election," Karins answered quickly. "I give out the popularity figures here." He produced a chart indicating a majority popularity for Unity. "Then we keep pumping out more faked stuff while Mr. Grant's people work on the vote-counting computers. Hell, it's been done before."

"Won't work this time." They turned to look at the youngest man in the room. Larry Moriarty, assistant to the President, and sometimes called the "resident heretic," blushed at the attention. "The people know better. Bertram's people are already taking jobs in the computer centers, aren't they, Mr. Grant? They'll see it in a minute."

Grant nodded. He'd sent the report over the day before; interesting that Moriarty had already digested it.

"You make this a straight rigged election, and you'll have to use CoDominium Marines to keep order," Moriarty continued.

"The day I need CoDominium Marines to put down riots in the United States is the day I resign," the President said coldly. "I may be a realist, but there are limits to what I will do. You'll need a new chief, gentlemen."

"That's easy to say, Mr. President," Grant said. He wanted his pipe, but the doctors had forbidden it. To hell with them, he thought, and took a cigarette from a pack on the table. "It's easy to say, but you can't do it."

The President frowned. "Why not?"

Grant shook his head. "The Unity Party supports the CoDominium, and the CoDominium keeps the peace. An ugly peace, but by God, peace. I wish we hadn't got support for the CoDominium treaties tied so thoroughly to the Unity Party, but it is and that's that. And you know damn well that even in the Party it's only a thin majority that supports the CoDominium. Right, Harry?"

The assistant postmaster general nodded. "But don't forget, there's support for the CD in Bertram's group."

"Sure, but they hate our guts," Moriarty said. "They say we're corrupt. And they're right."

"So flipping what if they're right?" Karins snapped. "We're in, they're out. Anybody who's in for long is corrupt. If he isn't, he's not in."

"I fail to see the point of this discussion," the President interrupted. "I for one do not enjoy being reminded of all the things I have done to keep this office. The question is,

39

what are we going to do? I feel it only fair to warn you that nothing could make me happier than to have Mr. Bertram sit in this chair. I've been President for a long time, and I'm tired. I don't want the job anymore."

III

EVERYONE SPOKE AT once, shouting to the President, murmuring to their neighbors, until Grant cleared his throat loudly. "Mr. President," he said, using the tone of command he'd been taught during his brief tour in the Army Reserve. "Mr. President, if you will pardon me, that is a ludicrous suggestion. There is no one else in the Unity Party who has even a ghost of a chance of winning. You alone remain popular. Even Mr. Harmon speaks as well of you as he does of anyone not in his group. You cannot resign without dragging the Unity Party with you, and you cannot give that chair to Mr. Bertram because he couldn't hold it six months."

"Would that be so bad?" President Lipscomb leaned toward Grant with the confidential manner he used in his fireside chats to the people. "Are we really so sure that only we can save the human race, John? Or do we only wish to keep power?"

"Both, I suppose," Grant said. "Not that I'd mind retiring myself."

"Retire!" Karins snorted. "You let Bertram's clean babies in the files for two hours, and none of us will retire to anything better'n a CD prison planet. You got to be kidding, retire."

"That may be true," the President said.

"There's other ways," Karins suggested. "General, what happens if Harmon takes power and starts his war?"

"Mr. Grant knows better than I do," General Carpenter said. When the others stared at him, Carpenter continued. "No one has ever fought a nuclear war. Why should the uniform make me more of an expert than you? Maybe we could win. Heavy casualties, very heavy, but our defenses are good."

41

Carpenter gestured at the moving lights on the wall projection. "We have better technology than the Russki's. Our laser guns ought to get most of their missiles. CD Fleet won't let either of us use space weapons. We might win."

"We might." Lipscomb was grim. "John?"

"We might not win. We might kill more than half the human race. We might get more. How in God's name do I know what happens when we throw nuclear weapons around?"

"But the Russians aren't prepared," Commerce said. "If we hit them without warning—people never change governments in the middle of a war."

President Lipscomb sighed. "I am not going to start a nuclear war to retain power. Whatever I have done, I have done to keep peace. That is my last excuse. I could not live with myself if I sacrifice peace to keep power."

Grant cleared his throat gently. "We couldn't do it anyway. If we start converting defensive missiles to offensive, CoDominium Intelligence would hear about it in ten days. The Treaty prevents that, you know."

He lit another cigarette. "We aren't the only threat to the CD, anyway. There's always Kaslov."

Kaslov was a pure Stalinist, who wanted to liberate Earth for Communism. Some called him the last Communist, but of course he wasn't the last. He had plenty of followers. Grant could remember a secret conference with Ambassador Chernikov only weeks ago.

The Soviet was a polished diplomat, but it was obvious that he wanted something desperately. He wanted the United States to keep the pressure on, not relax her defenses at the borders of the U.S. sphere of influence, because if the Communist probes ever took anything from the U.S. without a hard fight, Kaslov would gain more influence at home. He might even win control of the Presidium.

"Nationalism everywhere," the President sighed. "Why?"

No one had an answer to that. Harmon gained power in the U.S. and Kaslov in the Soviet Union; while a dozen petty nationalist leaders gained power in a dozen other countries. Some thought it started with Japan's nationalistic revival.

"This is all nonsense," said the Assistant Postmaster General. "We aren't going to quit and we aren't starting any wars. Now what does it take to get the support away

42

from Mr. Clean Bertram and funnel it back to us where it belongs? A good scandal, right? Find Bertram's dirtier than we are, right? Worked plenty of times before. You can steal people blind if you scream loud enough about how the other guy's a crook."

"Such as?" Karins prompted.

"Working with the Japs. Giving the Japs nukes, maybe. Supporting Meiji's independence movement. I'm sure Mr. Grant can arrange something."

Karins nodded vigorously. "That might do it. Disillusion his organizers. The pro-CoDominium people in his outfit would come to us like a shot."

Karins paused and chuckled. "Course some of them will head for Millington's bunch, too."

They all laughed. No one worried about Millington's Liberation Party. His madmen caused riots and kept the taxpayers afraid, and made a number of security arrangements highly popular. The Liberation Party gave the police some heads to crack, nice riots for Tri-V to keep the Citizens amused and the taxpayers happy.

"I think we can safely leave the details to Mr. Grant." Karins grinned broadly.

"What will you do, John?" the President asked.

"Do you really want to know, Mr. President?" Moriarty interrupted. "I don't."

"Nor do I, but if I can condone it, I can at least find out what it is. What will you do, John?"

"Frame-up, I suppose. Get a plot going, then uncover it."

"That?" Moriarty shook his head. "It's got to be good. The people are beginning to wonder about all these plots."

Grant nodded. "There will be evidence. Hard-core evidence. A secret arsenal of nuclear weapons."

There was a gasp. Then Karins grinned widely again. "Oh, man, that's tore it. Hidden nukes. Real ones, I suppose?"

"Of course." Grant looked with distaste at the fat youth. What would be the point of fake nuclear weapons? But Karins lived in a world of deception, so much so that fake weapons might be appropriate in it.

"Better have lots of cops when you break that story," Karins said. "People hear that, they'll tear Bertram apart."

True enough, Grant thought. It was a point he'd have to remember. Protection of those kids wouldn't be easy. Not since one militant group atom-bombed Bakersfield,

California, and a criminal syndicate tried to hold Seattle for a hundred million ransom. People no longer thought of private stocks of atomic weapons as something to laugh at.

"We won't involve Mr. Bertram personally," the President said grimly. "Not under any circumstances. Is that understood?"

"Yes, sir," John answered quickly. He hadn't liked the idea either. "Just some of his top aides." Grant stubbed out the cigarette. It, or something, had left a foul taste in his mouth. "I'll have them end up with the CD for final custody. Sentenced to transportation. My brother can arrange it so they don't have hard sentences."

"Sure. They can be independent planters on Tanith if they'll cooperate," Karins said. "You can see they don't suffer."

Like hell, Grant thought. Life on Tanith was no joy under the best conditions.

"There's one more thing," the President said. "I understand Grand Senator Bronson wants something from the CD. Some officer was a little too efficient at uncovering the Bronson family deals, and they want him removed." The President looked as if he'd tasted sour milk. "I hate this, John. I hate it, but we need Bronson's support. Can you speak to your brother?"

"I already have," Grant said. "It will be arranged."

Grant left the meeting a few minutes later. The others could continue in endless discussion, but Grant saw no point to them. The action needed was clear, and the longer they waited the more time Bertram would have to assemble his supporters and harden his support. If something were to be done, it should be now.

Grant had found all his life that the wrong action taken decisively and in time was better than the right action taken later. After he reached the Pentagon he summoned his deputies and issued orders. It took no more than an hour to set the machinery in motion.

Grant's colleagues always said he was rash, too quick to take action without examining the consequences. They also conceded that he was lucky. To Grant it wasn't luck, and he did consider the consequences; but he anticipated events rather than reacted to crisis. He had known that Bertram's support was growing alarmingly for weeks and

44

had made contingency plans long before going to the conference with the President.

Now it was clear that action must be taken immediately. Within days there would be leaks from the conference. Nothing about the actions to be taken, but there would be rumors about the alarm and concern. A secretary would notice that Grant had come back to the Pentagon after dismissing his driver. Another would see that Karins chuckled more than usual when he left the Oval Office, or that two political enemies came out together and went off to have a drink. Another would hear talk about Bertram, and soon it would be all over Washington: the President was worried about Bertram's popularity.

Since the leaks were inevitable, he should act while this might work. Grant dismissed his aides with a sense of satisfaction. He had been ready, and the crisis would be over before it began. It was only after he was alone that he crossed the paneled room to the teak cabinet and poured a double Scotch.

The Maryland countryside slipped past far below as the Cadillac cruised on autopilot. A ribbon antenna ran almost to Grant's house, and he watched the twilight scene with as much relaxation as he ever achieved lately. House lights blinked below, and a few surface cars ran along the roads. Behind him was the sprawling mass of Columbia Welfare Island where most of those displaced from Washington had gone. Now the inhabitants were third generation and had never known any other life.

He grimaced. Welfare Islands were lumps of concrete buildings and roof parks, containers for the seething resentment of useless lives kept placid by Government furnished supplies of Tanith hashpot and borloi and American cheap booze. A man born in one of those complexes could stay there all his life, and many did.

Grant tried to imagine what it would be like there, but he couldn't. Reports from his agents gave an intellectual picture, but there was no way to identify with those people. He could not feel the hopelessness and dulled senses, burning hatreds, terrors, bitter pride of street gangs.

Karins knew, though. Karins had begun his life in a Welfare Island somewhere in the midwest. Karins clawed his way through the schools to a scholarship and a ticket out forever. He'd resisted stimulants and dope and Tri-V. Was it worth it? Grant wondered. And of course there

45

was another way out of Welfare, as a voluntary colonist; but so few took that route now. Once there had been a lot of them.

The speaker on the dash suddenly came to life cutting off Beethoven in mid bar. "WARNING. YOU ARE APPROACHING A GUARDED AREA. UNAUTHORIZED CRAFT WILL BE DESTROYED WITHOUT FURTHER WARNING. IF YOU HAVE LEGITIMATE ERRANDS IN THIS RESTRICTED AREA, FOLLOW THE GUIDE BEAM TO THE POLICE CHECK STATION. THIS IS A FINAL WARNING."

The Cadillac automatically turned off course to ride the beam down to State Police headquarters, and Grant cursed. He activated the mike and spoke softly. "This is John Grant of Peachem's Bay. Something seems to be wrong with my transponder."

There was a short pause, then a soft feminine voice came from the dash speaker. "We are very sorry, Mr. Grant. Your signal is correct. Our identification unit is out of order. Please proceed to your home."

"Get that damned thing fixed before it shoots down a taxpayer," Grant said. Ann Arundel County was a Unity stronghold. How long would that last after an accident like that? He took the manual controls and cut across country, ignoring regulations. They could only give him a ticket now that they knew who he was, and his banking computer would pay it without bothering to tell him of it.

It brought a grim smile to his face. Traffic regulations were broken, computers noted it and levied fines, other computers paid them, and no human ever became aware of them. It was only if there were enough tickets accumulated to bring a warning of license suspension that a taxpayer learned of the things—unless he liked checking his bank statements himself.

His home lay ahead, a big rambling early twentieth-century place on the cove. His yacht was anchored offshore, and it gave him a guilty twinge. She wasn't neglected, but she was too much in the hands of paid crew, too long without attention from her owner.

Carver, the chauffeur, rushed out to help Grant down from the Cadillac. Hapwood was waiting in the big library with a glass of sherry. Prince Bismark, shivering in the presence of his god, put his Doberman head on Grant's lap, ready to leap into the fire at command.

There was irony in the situation, Grant thought. At

46

home he enjoyed the power of a feudal lord, but it was limited by how strongly the staff wanted to stay out of Welfare. But he only had to lift the Security phone in the corner, and his real power, completely invisible and limited only by what the President wanted to find out, would operate. Money gave him the visible power, heredity gave him the power over the dog; what gave him the real power of the Security phone?

"What time would you like dinner, sir?" Hapwood asked. "And Miss Sharon is here with a guest."

"A guest?"

"Yes, sir. A young man, Mr. Allan Torrey, sir."

"Have they eaten?"

"Yes, sir. Miss Ackridge called to say that you would be late for dinner."

"All right, Hapwood. I'll eat now and see Miss Grant and her guest afterwards."

"Very good, sir. I will inform the cook." Hapwood left the room invisibly.

Grant smiled again. Hapwood was another figure from Welfare and had grown up speaking a dialect Grant would never recognize. For some reason he had been impressed by English butlers he'd seen on Tri-V and cultivated their manner—and now he was known all over the county as the perfect household manager.

Hapwood didn't know it, but Grant had a record of every cent his butler took in: kickbacks from grocers and caterers, contributions from the gardeners, and the surprisingly well-managed investment portfolio. Hapwood could easily retire to his own house and live the life of a taxpayer investor.

Why? Grant wondered idly. Why does he stay on? It makes life easier for me, but why? It had intrigued Grant enough to have his agents look into Hapwood, but the man had no politics other than staunch support for Unity. The only suspicious thing about his contacts was the refinement with which he extracted money from every transaction involving Grant's house. Hapwood had no children, and his sexual needs were satisfied by infrequent visits to the fringe areas around Welfare.

Grant ate mechanically, hurrying to be through and see his daughter, yet he was afraid to meet the boy she had brought home. For a moment he thought of using the Security phone to find out more about him, but he shook his head angrily. Too much security thinking wasn't good.

For once he was going to be a parent, meeting his daughter's intended and nothing more.

He left his dinner unfinished without thinking how much the remnants of steak would have cost, or that Hapwood would probably sell them somewhere, and went to the library. He sat behind the massive Oriental fruitwood desk and had a brandy.

Behind him and to both sides the walls were lined with book shelves, immaculate dust-free accounts of the people of dead empires. It had been years since he had read one. Now all his reading was confined to reports with bright red covers. The reports told live stories about living people, but sometimes, late at night, Grant wondered if his country were not as dead as the empires in his books.

Grant loved his country but hated her people, all of them: Karins and the new breed, the tranquilized Citizens in their Welfare Islands, the smug taxpayers grimly holding on to their privileges. What, then, do I love? he wondered. Only our history, and the greatness that once was the United States, and that's found only in those books and in old buildings, never in the security reports.

Where are the patriots? All of them have become Patriots, stupid men and women following a leader toward nothing. Not even glory.

Then Sharon came in. She was a lovely girl, far prettier than her mother had ever been, but she lacked her mother's poise. She ushered in a tall boy in his early twenties.

Grant studied the newcomer as they came toward him. Nice-looking boy. Long hair, neatly trimmed, conservative mustache for these times. Blue and violet tunic, red scarf . . . a little flashy, but even John Jr. went in for flashy clothes when he got out of CD uniform.

The boy walked hesitantly, almost timidly, and Grant wondered if it were fear of him and his position in the government, or only the natural nervousness of a young man about to meet his fiancée's wealthy father. The tiny diamond on Sharon's hand sparkled in the yellow light from the fireplace, and she held the hand in an unnatural position.

"Daddy, I . . . I've talked so much about him, this is Allan. He's just asked me to marry him!" She sparkled, Grant saw; and she spoke trustingly, sure of his approval, never thinking he might object. Grant wondered if Sharon weren't the only person in the country who didn't fear him. Except for John Jr., who didn't have to be afraid.

John was out of the reach of Grant's Security phone. The CD Fleet takes care of its own.

At least he's asked her to marry him. He might have simply moved in with her. Or has he already? Grant stood and extended his hand. "Hello, Allan."

Torrey's grip was firm, but his eyes avoided Grant's. "So you want to marry my daughter." Grant glanced pointedly at her left hand. "It appears that she approves the idea."

"Yes, sir. Uh, sir, she wanted to wait and ask you, but I insisted. It's my fault, sir." Torrey looked up at him this time, almost in defiance.

"Yes." Grant sat again. "Well, Sharon, as long as you're home for the evening, I wish you'd speak to Hapwood about Prince Bismark. I do not think the animal is properly fed."

"You mean right now?" she asked. She tightened her small mouth into a pout. "Really, Daddy, this is Victorian! Sending me out of the room while you talk to my fiancé!"

"Yes, it is, isn't it?" Grant said nothing else, and finally she turned away.

Then: "Don't let him frighten you, Allan. He's about as dangerous as that—as that moosehead in the trophy room!" She fled before there could be any reply.

IV

THEY SAT AWKWARDLY. Grant left his desk to sit near the
fire with Torrey. Drinks, offer of a smoke, all the usual
amenities—he did them all; but finally Hapwood had
brought their refreshments and the door was closed.

"All right, Allan," John Grant began. "Let us be trite
and get it over with. How do you intend to support her?"

Torrey looked straight at him this time. His eyes danced
with what Grant was certain was concealed amusement. "I
expect to be appointed to a good post in the Department
of the Interior. I'm a trained engineer."

"Interior?" Grant thought for a second. The answer
surprised him—he hadn't thought the boy was another
office seeker. "I suppose it can be arranged."

Torrey grinned. It was an infectious grin, and Grant
liked it. "Well, sir, it's already arranged. I wasn't asking
for a job."

"Oh?" Grant shrugged. "I hadn't heard."

"Deputy Assistant Secretary for Natural Resources. I
took a master's in ecology."

"That's interesting, but I would have thought I'd have
heard of your coming appointment."

"It won't be official yet, sir. Not until Mr. Bertram is
elected President. For the moment I'm on his staff." The
grin was still there, and it was friendly, not hostile. The
boy thought politics was a game. He wanted to win, but
it was only a game.

And he's seen real polls, Grant thought. "Just what do
you do for Mr. Bertram, then?"

Allan shrugged. "Write speeches, carry the mail, run
the Xerox—you've been in campaign headquarters. I'm the
guy who gets the jobs no one else wants."

Grant laughed. "I did start as a gopher, but I soon

hired my own out of what I once contributed to the Party. They did not try that trick again with me. I don't suppose that course is open to you."

"No, sir. My father's a taxpayer, but paying taxes is pretty tough just now—"

"Yes." Well, at least he wasn't from a Citizen family. Grant would learn the details from Ackridge tomorrow, for now the important thing was to get to know the boy.

It was difficult. Allan was frank and relaxed, and Grant was pleased to see that he refused a third drink, but there was little to talk about. Torrey had no conception of the realities of politics. He was one of Bertram's child crusaders, and he was out to save the United States from people like John Grant, although he was too polite to say so.

And I was once that young, Grant thought. I wanted to save the world, but it was so different then. No one wanted to end the CoDominium when I was young. We were too happy to have the Second Cold War over with. What happened to the great sense of relief when we could stop worrying about atomic wars? When I was young that was all we thought of, that we would be the last generation. Now they take it for granted that we'll have peace forever. Is peace such a little thing?

"There's so much to do," Torrey was saying. "The Baja Project, thermal pollution of the Sea of Cortez! They're killing off a whole ecology just to create estates for the taxpayers.

"I know it isn't your department, sir, you probably don't even know what they're doing. But Lipscomb has been in office too long! Corruption, special interests, it's time we had a genuine two-party system again instead of things going back and forth between the wings of Unity. It's time for a change, and Mr. Bertram's the right man, I know he is."

Grant's smile was thin, but he managed it. "You'll hardly expect me to agree with you," Grant said.

"No, sir."

Grant sighed. "But perhaps you're right at that. I must say I wouldn't mind retiring, so that I could live in this house instead of merely visiting it on weekends."

What was the point? Grant wondered. He'd never convince this boy, and Sharon wanted him. Torrey would drop Bertram after the scandals broke.

And what explanations were there anyway? The Baja

51

Project was developed to aid a syndicate of taxpayers in the six states of the old former Republic of Mexico. The Government needed them, and they didn't care about whales and fish. Shortsighted, yes, and Grant had tried to argue them into changing the project, but they wouldn't, and politics is the art of the possible.

Finally, painfully, the interview ended. Sharon came in, grinning sheepishly because she was engaged to one of Bertram's people, but she understood that no better than Allan Torrey. It was only a game. Bertram would win and Grant would retire, and no one would be hurt.

How could he tell them that it didn't work that way any longer? Unity wasn't the cleanest party in the world, but at least it had no fanatics—and all over the world the causes were rising again. The Friends of the People were on the move, and it had all happened before, it was all told time and again in those aseptically clean books on the shelves above him.

BERTRAM AIDES ARRESTED BY INTER-CONTINENTAL BUREAU OF INVESTIGA-TION!! IBI RAIDS SECRET WEAPONS CACHE IN BERTRAM HEADQUARTERS. NUCLEAR WEAPONS HINTED!!!

Chicago, May 15, (UPI)—IBI agents here have arrested five top aides to Senator Harvey Bertram in what government officials call one of the most despicable plots ever discovered. . . .

Grant read the transcript on his desk screen without satisfaction. It had all gone according to plan, and there was nothing left to do, but he hated it.

At least it was clean. The evidence was there. Bertram's people could have their trial, challenge jurors, challenge judges. The Government would waive its rights under the Thirty-first Amendment and let the case be tried under the old adversary rules. It wouldn't matter.

Then he read the small type below. "Arrested were Grigory Kalamintor, nineteen, press secretary to Bertram; Timothy Giordano, twenty-two, secretary; Allan Torrey, twenty-two, executive assistant—" The page blurred, and Grant dropped his face into his hands.

"My God, what have we done?"

He hadn't moved when Miss Ackridge buzzed. "Your daughter on four, sir. She seems upset."

"Yes." Grant punched savagely at the button. Sharon's face swam into view. Her makeup was ruined by long streaks of tears. She looked older, much like her mother during one of their—

"Daddy! They've arrested Allan! And I know it isn't true, he wouldn't have anything to do with nuclear weapons! A lot of Mr. Bertram's people said there would never be an honest election in this country. They said John Grant would see to that! I told him they were wrong, but they weren't, were they? You've done this to stop the election, haven't you?"

There was nothing to say because she was right. But who might be listening? "I don't know what you're talking about. I've only seen the Tri-V casts about Allan's arrest, nothing more. Come home, kitten, and we'll talk about it."

"Oh no! You're not getting me where Dr. Pollard can give me a nice friendly little shot and make me forget about Allan! No! I'm staying with my friends, and I won't be home, Daddy. And when I go to the newspapers, I think they'll listen to me. I don't know what to tell them yet, but I'm sure Mr. Bertram's people will think of something. How do you like that, Mr. God?"

"Anything you tell the press will be lies, Sharon. You know nothing." One of his assistants had come in and now left the office.

"Lies? Where did I learn to lie?" The screen went blank.

And is it that thin? he wondered. All the trust and love, could it vanish that fast, was it that thin?

"Sir?" It was Hartman, his assistant.

"Yes?"

"She was calling from Champaign, Illinois. A Bertram headquarters they think we don't know about. The phone had one of those guaranteed no-trace devices."

"Trusting lot, aren't they?" Grant said. "Have some good men watch that house, but leave her alone." He stood and felt a wave of nausea so strong that he had to hold the edge of the desk. "MAKE DAMNED SURE THEY LEAVE HER ALONE. DO YOU UNDERSTAND?" he shouted.

Hartman went as pale as Grant. The chief hadn't raised his voice to one of his own people in five years. "Yes, sir, I understand."

"Then get out of here." Grant spoke carefully, in low tones, and the cold mechanical voice was more terrifying than the shout.

He sat alone and stared at the telephone. What use was its power now?

What can we do? It wasn't generally known that Sharon was engaged to the boy. He'd talked them out of a formal engagement until the banns could be announced in the National Cathedral and they could hold a big social party. It had been something to do for them at the time, but . . .

But what? He couldn't have the boy released. Not that boy. He wouldn't keep silent as the price of his own freedom. He'd take Sharon to a newspaper within five minutes of his release, and the resulting headlines would bring down Lipscomb, Unity, the CoDominium—and the peace. Newsmen would listen to the daughter of the top secret policeman in the country.

Grant punched a code on the communicator, then another. Grand Admiral Lermontov appeared on the screen.

"Yes, Mr. Grant?"

"Are you alone?"

"Yes."

The conversation was painful, and the long delay while the signals reached the moon and returned didn't make it easier.

"When is the next CD warship going outsystem? Not a colony ship, and most especially not a prison ship. A warship."

Another long pause, longer even than the delay. "I suppose anything could be arranged," the Admiral said. "What do you need?"

"I want . . ." Grant hesitated, but there was no time to be lost. No time at all. "I want space for two very important political prisoners. A married couple. The crew is not to know their identity, and anyone who does learn their identity must stay outsystem for at least five years. And I want them set down on a good colony world, a decent place. Sparta, perhaps. No one ever returns from Sparta. Can you arrange that?"

Grant could see the changes in Lermontov's face as the words reached him. The Admiral frowned. "It can be done if it is important enough. It will not be easy."

"It's important enough. My brother Martin will explain everything you'll need to know later. The prisoners will be delivered tonight, Sergei. Please have the ship ready. And —and it better not be *Saratoga*. My son's in that one and he—he will know one of the prisoners." Grant swallowed hard. "There should be a chaplain aboard. The kids will be getting married."

Lermontov frowned again, as if wondering if John Grant had gone insane. Yet he needed the Grants, both of them, and certainly John Grant would not ask such a favor if it were not vital.

"It will be done," Lermontov said.

"Thank you. I'll also appreciate it if you will see they have a good estate on Sparta. They are not to know who arranged it. Just have it taken care of and send the bill to me."

It was all so very simple. Direct his agents to arrest Sharon and conduct her to CD Intelligence. He wouldn't want to see her first. The attorney general would send Torrey to the same place and announce that he had escaped.

It wasn't as neat as having all of them convicted in open court, but it would do, and having one of them a fugitive from justice would even help. It would be an admission of guilt.

Something inside him screamed again and again that this was his little girl, the only person in the world who wasn't afraid of him, but Grant refused to listen. He leaned back in the chair and almost calmly dictated his orders.

He took the flimsy sheet from the writer and his hand didn't tremble at all as he signed it.

All right, Martin, he thought. All right. I've bought the time you asked for, you and Sergei Lermontov. Now can you do something with it?

V

2087 A.D.

THE LANDING BOAT fell away from the orbiting warship.
When it had drifted to a safe distance, retros fired, and
after it had entered the thin reaches of the planet's upper
atmosphere, scoops opened in the bows. The thin air was
drawn in and compressed until the stagnation temperature
in the ramjet chamber was high enough for ignition.

The engines lit with a roar of flame. Wings swung out
to provide lift at hypersonic speeds, and the spaceplane
turned to streak over empty ocean toward the continental
land mass two thousand kilometers away.

The ship circled over craggy mountains twelve kilometers high, then dropped low over thickly forested plains.
It slowed until it was no longer a danger to the thin strip
of inhabited lands along the ocean shores. The planet's
great ocean was joined to a smaller sea by a nearly land-
locked channel no more than five kilometers across at its
widest point, and nearly all of the colonists lived near the
junction of the waters.

Hadley's capital city nestled on a long peninsula at the
mouth of that channel, and the two natural harbors, one
in the sea, the other in the ocean, gave the city the fitting
name of Refuge. The name suggested a tranquility the city
no longer possessed.

The ship extended its wings to their fullest reach and
floated low over the calm water of the channel harbor. It
touched and settled in. Tugboats raced across clear blue
water. Sweating seamen threw lines and towed the landing
craft to the dock where they secured it.

A long line of CoDominium Marines in garrison uniform marched out of the boat. They gathered on the gray

56

concrete piers into neat brightly colored lines. Two men in civilian clothing followed the Marines from the flyer.

They blinked at the unaccustomed blue-white of Hadley's sun. The sun was so far away that it would have been only a small point if either of them were foolish enough to look directly at it. The apparent small size was only an illusion caused by distance; Hadley received as much illumination from its hotter sun as Earth does from Sol.

Both men were tall and stood as straight as the Marines in front of them, so that except for their clothing they might have been mistaken for a part of the disembarking battalion. The shorter of the two carried luggage for both of them, and stood respectfully behind; although older he was obviously a subordinate. They watched as two younger men came uncertainly along the pier. The newcomers' unadorned blue uniforms contrasted sharply with the bright reds and golds of the CoDominium Marines milling around them. Already the Marines were scurrying back into the flyer to carry out barracks bags, weapons, and all the other personal gear of a light infantry battalion.

The taller of the two civilians faced the uniformed newcomers. "I take it you're here to meet us?" he asked pleasantly. His voice rang through the noise on the pier, and it carried easily although he had not shouted. His accent was neutral, the nearly universal English of non-Russian officers in the CoDominium Service, and it marked his profession almost as certainly as did his posture and the tone of command.

The newcomers were uncertain even so. There were a lot of ex-officers of the CoDominium Space Navy on the beach lately. CD budgets were lower every year. "I think so," one finally said. "Are you John Christian Falkenberg?"

His name was actually John Christian Falkenberg III, and he suspected that his grandfather would have insisted on the distinction. "Right. And Sergeant Major Calvin."

"Pleasure to meet you, sir. I'm Lieutenant Banners, and this is Ensign Mowrer. We're on President Budreau's staff." Banners looked around as if expecting other men, but there were none except the uniformed Marines. He gave Falkenberg a slightly puzzled look, then added, "We have transportation for you, but I'm afraid your men will have to walk. It's about eleven miles."

"Miles." Falkenberg smiled to himself. This *was* out in the boondocks. "I see no reason why ten healthy mercenaries can't march eighteen kilometers, Lieutenant." He turned to face the black shape of the landing boat's entry port and called to someone inside. "Captain Fast. There is no transportation, but someone will show you where to march the men. Have them carry all gear."

"Uh, sir, that won't be necessary," the lieutenant protested. "We can get—well, we have horse-drawn transport for baggage." He looked at Falkenberg as if he expected him to laugh.

"That's hardly unusual on colony worlds," Falkenberg said. Horses and mules could be carried as frozen embryos, and they didn't require high-technology industries to produce more, nor did they need an industrial base to fuel them.

"Ensign Mowrer will attend to it," Lieutenant Banners said. He paused again and looked thoughtful as if uncertain how to tell Falkenberg something. Finally he shook his head. "I think it would be wise if you issued your men their personal weapons, sir. There shouldn't be any trouble on their way to barracks, but—anyway, ten armed men certainly won't have any problems."

"I see. Perhaps I should go with my troops, Lieutenant. I hadn't known things were quite this bad on Hadley." Falkenberg's voice was calm and even, but he watched the junior officers carefully.

"No, sir. They aren't, really. . . . But there's no point in taking chances." He waved Ensign Mowrer to the landing craft and turned back to Falkenberg. A large black shape rose from the water outboard of the landing craft. It splashed and vanished. Banners seemed not to notice, but the Marines shouted excitedly. "I'm sure the ensign and your officers can handle the disembarkation, and the President would like to see you immediately, sir."

"No doubt. All right, Banners, lead on. I'll bring Sergeant Major Calvin with me." He followed Banners down the pier.

There's no point to this farce, Falkenberg thought. Anyone seeing ten armed men conducted by a Presidential ensign will know they're mercenary troops, civilian clothes or not. Another case of wrong information.

Falkenberg had been told to keep the status of himself and his men a secret, but it wasn't going to work. He wondered if this would make it more difficult to keep his own secrets.

Banners ushered them quickly through the bustling
58

CoDominium Marine barracks, past bored guards who half-saluted the Presidential Guard uniform. The Marine fortress was a blur of activity, every open space crammed with packs and weapons; the signs of a military force about to move on to another station.

As they were leaving the building, Falkenberg saw an elderly Naval officer. "Excuse me a moment, Banners." He turned to the CoDominium Navy captain. "They sent someone for me. Thanks, Ed."

"No problem. I'll report your arrival to the Admiral. He wants to keep track of you. Unofficially, of course. Good luck, John. God knows you need some right now. It was a rotten deal."

"It's the way it goes."

"Yeah, but the Fleet used to take better care of its own than that. I'm beginning to wonder if anyone is safe. Damn Senator—"

"Forget it," Falkenberg interrupted. He glanced back to be sure Lieutenant Banners was out of earshot. "Pay my respects to the rest of your officers. You run a good ship."

The captain smiled thinly. "Thanks. From you that's quite a compliment." He held out his hand and gripped John's firmly. "Look, we pull out in a couple of days, no more than that. If you need a ride on somewhere I can arrange it. The goddam Senate won't have to know. We can fix you a hitch to anywhere in CD territory."

"Thanks, but I guess I'll stay."

"Could be rough here," the captain said.

"And it won't be everywhere else in the CoDominium?" Falkenberg asked. "Thanks again, Ed." He gave a half-salute and checked himself.

Banners and Calvin were waiting for him, and Falkenberg turned away. Calvin lifted three personal effects bags as if they were empty and pushed the door open in a smooth motion. The CD captain watched until they had left the building, but Falkenberg did not look back.

"Damn them," the captain muttered. "Damn the lot of them."

"The car's here." Banners opened the rear door of a battered ground effects vehicle of no discoverable make. It had been cannibalized from a dozen other machines, and some parts were obviously cut-and-try jobs done by an uncertain machinist. Banners climbed into the driver's seat and started the engine. It coughed twice, then ran smoothly, and they drove away in a cloud of black smoke.

They drove past another dock where a landing craft with wings as large as the entire Marine landing boat was unloading an endless stream of civilian passengers. Children screamed, and long lines of men and women stared about uncertainly until they were ungently hustled along by guards in uniforms matching Banners'. The sour smell of unwashed humanity mingled with the crisp clean salt air from the ocean beyond. Banners rolled up the windows with an expression of distaste.

"Always like that," Calvin commented to no one in particular. "Water discipline in them CoDominium prison ships bein' what it is, takes weeks dirtside to get clean again."

"Have you ever been in one of those ships?" Banners asked.

"No, sir," Calvin replied. "Been in Marine assault boats just about as bad, I reckon. But I can't say I fancy being stuffed into no cubicle with ten, fifteen thousand civilians for six months."

"We may all see the inside of one of those," Falkenberg said. "And be glad of the chance. Tell me about the situation here, Banners."

"I don't even know where to start, sir," the lieutenant answered. "I—do you know about Hadley?"

"Assume I don't," Falkenberg said. May as well see what kind of estimate of the situation the President's officers can make, he thought. He could feel the Fleet Intelligence report bulging in an inner pocket of his tunic, but those reports always left out important details; and the attitudes of the Presidential Guard could be important to his plans.

"Yes, sir. Well, to begin with, we're a long way from the nearest shipping lanes—but I guess you knew that. The only real reason we had any merchant trade was the mines. Thorium, richest veins known anywhere for a while, until they started to run out.

"For the first few years that's all we had. The mines are up in the hills, about eighty miles over that way." He pointed to a thin blue line just visible at the horizon.

"Must be pretty high mountains," Falkenberg said. "What's the diameter of Hadley? About eighty percent of Earth? Something like that. The horizon ought to be pretty close."

"Yes, sir. They are high mountains. Hadley is small, but we've got bigger and better everything here." There was pride in the young officer's voice.

"Them bags seem pretty heavy for a planet this small," Calvin said.

"Hadley's very dense," Banners answered. "Gravity nearly ninety percent standard. Anyway, the mines are over there, and they have their own spaceport at a lake nearby. Refuge—that's this city—was founded by the American Express Company. They brought in the first colonists, quite a lot of them."

"Volunteers?" Falkenberg asked.

"Yes. All volunteers. The usual misfits. I suppose my father was typical enough, an engineer who couldn't keep up with the rat race and was tired of Bureau of Technology restrictions on what he could learn. They were the first wave, and they took the best land. They founded the city and got an economy going. American Express was paid back all advances within twenty years." Banners' pride was evident, and Falkenberg knew it had been a difficult job.

"That was, what, fifty years ago?" Falkenberg asked.

"Yes."

They were driving through crowded streets lined with wooden houses and a few stone buildings. There were rooming houses, bars, sailors' brothels, all the usual establishments of a dock street, but there were no other cars on the road. Instead the traffic was all horses and oxen pulling carts, bicycles, and pedestrians.

The sky above Refuge was clear. There was no trace of smog or industrial wastes. Out in the harbor tugboats moved with the silent efficiency of electric power, and there were also wind-driven sailing ships, lobster boats powered by oars, even a topsail schooner lovely against clean blue water. She threw up white spume as she raced out to sea. A three-masted, full-rigged ship was drawn up to a wharf where men loaded her by hand with huge bales of what might have been cotton.

They passed a wagonload of melons. A gaily dressed young couple waved cheerfully at them, then the man snapped a long whip at the team of horses that pulled their wagon. Falkenberg studied the primitive scene and said, "It doesn't look like you've been here fifty years."

"No." Banners gave them a bitter look. Then he swerved to avoid a group of shapeless teen-agers lounging in the

61

dockside street. He had to swerve again to avoid the barricade of paving stones that they had masked. The car jounced wildly. Banners gunned it to lift it higher and headed for a low place in the barricade. It scraped as it went over the top, then he accelerated away.

Falkenberg took his hand from inside his shirt jacket. Behind him Calvin was inspecting a submachine gun that had appeared from the oversized barracks bag he'd brought into the car with him. When Banners said nothing about the incident, Falkenberg frowned and leaned back in his seat, listening. The Intelligence reports mentioned lawlessness, but this was as bad as a Welfare Island on Earth.

"No, we're not much industrialized," Banners continued. "At first there wasn't any need to develop basic industries. The mines made everyone rich, so we imported everything we needed. The farmers sold fresh produce to the miners for enormous prices. Refuge was a service industry town. People who worked here could soon afford farm animals, and they scattered out across the plains and into the forests."

Falkenberg nodded. "Many of them wouldn't care for cities."

"Precisely. They didn't want industry, they'd come here to escape it." Banners drove in silence for a moment. "Then some blasted CoDominium bureaucrat read the ecology reports about Hadley. The Population Control Bureau in Washington decided this was a perfect place for involuntary colonization. The ships were coming here for the thorium anyway, so instead of luxuries and machinery they were ordered to carry convicts. Hundreds of thousands of them, Colonel Falkenberg. For the last ten years there have been better than fifty thousand people a year dumped in on us."

"And you couldn't support them all," Falkenberg said gently.

"No, sir." Banners' face tightened. He seemed to be fighting tears. "God knows we try. Every erg the fusion generators can make goes into converting petroleum into basic protocarb just to feed them. But they're not like the original colonists! They don't know anything, they won't *do* anything! Oh, not really, of course. Some of them work. Some of our best citizens are transportees. But there are so many of the other kind."

"Why'n't you tell 'em to work or starve?" Calvin asked

62

bluntly. Falkenberg gave him a cold look, and the sergeant nodded slightly and sank back into his seat.

"Because the CD wouldn't let us!" Banners shouted. "Damn it, we didn't have self-government. The CD Bureau of Relocation people told us what to do. They ran everything . . ."

"We know," Falkenberg said gently. "We've seen the results of Humanity League influence over BuRelock. My sergeant major wasn't asking you a question, he was expressing an opinion. Nevertheless, I am surprised. I would have thought your farms could support the urban population."

"They should be able to, sir." Banners drove in grim silence for a long minute. "But there's no transportation. The people are here, and most of the agricultural land is five hundred miles inland. There's arable land closer, but it isn't cleared. Our settlers wanted to get away from Refuge and BuRelock. We have a railroad, but bandit gangs keep blowing it up. We can't rely on Hadley's produce to keep Refuge alive. There are a million people on Hadley, and half of them are crammed into this one ungovernable city."

They were approaching an enormous bowl-shaped structure attached to a massive square stone fortress. Falkenberg studied the buildings carefully, then asked what they were.

"Our stadium," Banners replied. There was no pride in his voice now. "The CD built it for us. We'd rather have had a new fusion plant, but we got a stadium that can hold a hundred thousand people."

"Built by the GLC Construction and Development Company, I presume," Falkenberg said.

"Yes . . . how did you know?"

"I think I saw it somewhere." He hadn't, but it was an easy guess: GLC was owned by a holding company that was in turn owned by the Bronson family. It was easy enough to understand why aid sent by the CD Grand Senate would end up used for something GLC might participate in.

"We have very fine sports teams and racehorses," Banners said bitterly. "The building next to it is the Presidential Palace. Its architecture is quite functional."

The Palace loomed up before them, squat and massive; it looked more fortress than capital building.

The city was more thickly populated as they approached

the Palace. The buildings here were mostly stone and poured concrete instead of wood. Few were more than three stories high, so that Refuge sprawled far along the shore. The population density increased rapidly beyond the stadium-palace complex. Banners was watchful as he drove along the wide streets, but he seemed less nervous than he had been at dockside.

Refuge was a city of contrasts. The streets were straight and wide, and there was evidently a good waste-disposal system, but the lower floors of the buildings were open shops, and the sidewalks were clogged with market stalls. Clouds of pedestrians moved through the kiosks and shops.

There was still no motor traffic and no moving pedways. Horse troughs and hitching posts had been constructed at frequent intervals along with starkly functional street lights and water distribution towers. The few signs of technology contrasted strongly with the general primitive air of the city.

A contingent of uniformed men thrust their way through the crowd at a street crossing. Falkenberg looked at them closely, then at Banners. "Your troops?"

"No, sir. That's the livery of Glenn Foster's household. Officially they're unorganized reserves of the President's Guard, but they're household troops all the same." Banners laughed bitterly. "Sounds like something out of a history book, doesn't it? We're nearly back to feudalism, Colonel Falkenberg. Anyone rich enough keeps hired bodyguards. They *have* to. The criminal gangs are so strong the police don't try to catch anyone under organized protection, and the judges wouldn't punish them if they were caught."

"And the private bodyguards become gangs in their own right, I suppose,"

Banners looked at him sharply. "Yes, sir. Have you seen it before?"

"Yes. I've seen it before." Banners was unable to make out the expression on Falkenberg's lips.

VI

THEY DROVE INTO the Presidential Palace and received the salutes of the blue uniformed troopers. Falkenberg noted the polished weapons and precise drill of the Presidential Guard. There were well-trained men on duty here, but the unit was small. Falkenberg wondered if they could fight as well as stand guard. They were local citizens, loyal to Hadley, and would be unlike the CoDominium Marines he was accustomed to.

He was conducted through a series of rooms in the stone fortress. Each had heavy metal doors, and several were guardrooms. Falkenberg saw no signs of government activity until they had passed through the outer layers of the enormous palace into an open courtyard, and through that to an inner building.

Here there was plenty of activity. Clerks bustled through the halls, and girls in the draped togas fashionable years before on Earth sat at desks in offices. Most seemed to be packing desk contents into boxes, and other people scurried through the corridors. Some offices were empty, their desks covered with fine dust, and there were plastiboard moving boxes stacked outside them.

There were two anterooms to the President's office. President Budreau was a tall, thin man with a red pencil mustache and quick gestures. As they were ushered into the overly ornate room the President looked up from a sheaf of papers, but his eyes did not focus immediately on his visitors. His face was a mask of worry and concentration.

"Colonel John Christian Falkenberg, sir," Lieutenant Banners said. "And Sergeant Major Calvin."

Budreau got to his feet. "Pleased to see you, Falkenberg." His expression told them differently; he looked at his

65

visitors with faint distaste and motioned Banners out of the room. When the door closed he asked, "How many men did you bring with you?"

"Ten, Mr. President. All we could bring aboard the carrier without arousing suspicion. We were lucky to get that many. The Grand Senate had an inspector at the loading docks to check for violation of the antimercenary codes. If we hadn't bribed a port official to distract him we wouldn't be here at all. Calvin and I would be on Tanith as involuntary colonists."

"I see." From his expression he wasn't surprised. John thought Budreau would have been more pleased if the inspector had caught them. The President tapped the desk nervously. "Perhaps that will be enough. I understand the ship you came with also brought the Marines who have volunteered to settle on Hadley. They should provide the nucleus of an excellent constabulary. Good troops?"

"It was a demobilized battalion," Falkenberg replied. "Those are the troops the CD didn't want anymore. Could be the scrapings of every guardhouse on twenty planets. We'll be lucky if there's a real trooper in the lot."

Budreau's face relaxed into its former mask of depression. Hope visibly drained from him.

"Surely you have troops of your own," Falkenberg said.

Budreau picked up a sheaf of papers. "It's all here. I was just looking it over when you came in." He handed the report to Falkenberg. "There's little encouragement in it, Colonel. I have never thought there was any military solution to Hadley's problems, and this confirms that fear. If you have only ten men plus a battalion of forced-labor Marines, the military answer isn't even worth considering."

Budreau returned to his seat. His hands moved restlessly over the sea of papers on his desk. "If I were you, Falkenberg, I'd get back on that Navy boat and forget Hadley."

"Why don't you?"

"Because Hadley's my home! No rabble is going to drive me off the plantation my grandfather built with his own hands. They will not make me run out." Budreau clasped his hands together until the knuckles were white with the strain, but when he spoke again his voice was calm. "You have no stake here. I do."

Falkenberg took the report from the desk and leafed through the pages before handing it to Calvin. "We've come a long way, Mr. President. You may as well tell me what the problem is before I leave."

Budreau nodded sourly. The red mustache twitched and he ran the back of his hand across it. "It's simple enough. The ostensible reason you're here, the reason we gave the Colonial Office for letting us recruit a planetary constabulary, is the bandit gangs out in the hills. No one knows how many of them there are, but they are strong enough to raid farms. They also cut communications between Refuge and the countryside whenever they want to."

"Yes." Falkenberg stood in front of the desk because he hadn't been invited to sit. If that bothered him it did not show. "Guerrilla gangsters have no real chance if they've no political base."

Budreau nodded. "But, as I am sure Vice President Bradford told you, they are not the real problem." The President's voice was strong, but there was a querulous note in it, as if he was accustomed to having his conclusions argued against and was waiting for Falkenberg to begin. "Actually, we could live with the bandits, but they get political support from the Freedom Party. My Progressive Party is larger than the Freedom Party, but the Progressives are scattered all over the planet. The FP is concentrated right here in Refuge, and they have God knows how many voters and about forty thousand loyalists they can concentrate whenever they want to stage a riot."

"Do you have riots very often?" John asked.

"Too often. There's not much to control them with. I have three hundred men in the Presidential Guard, but they're CD recruited and trained like young Banners. They're not much use at riot control, and they're loyal to the job, not to me anyway. The FP's got men inside the guard."

"So we can scratch the President's Guard when it comes to controlling the Freedom Party," John observed.

"Yes." Budreau smiled without amusement. "Then there's my police force. My police were all commanded by CD officers who are pulling out. My administrative staff was recruited and trained by BuRelock, and all the competent people have been recalled to Earth."

"I can see that would create a problem."

"Problem? It's impossible," Budreau said. "There's nobody left with skill enough to govern, but I've got the job and everybody else wants it. I might be able to scrape up a thousand Progressive partisans and another fifteen thousand party workers who would fight for us in a pinch, but they have no training. How can they face the FP's forty thousand?"

"You seriously believe the Freedom Party will revolt?"

"As soon as the CD's out, you can count on it. They've demanded a new constitutional convention to assemble just after the CoDominium Governor leaves. If we don't give them the convention they'll rebel and carry a lot of undecided with them. After all, what's unreasonable about a convention when the colonial governor has gone?"

"I see."

"And if we do give them the convention they want, they'll drag things out until there's nobody left in it but their people. My Party is composed of working voters. How can they stay on day after day? The FP's unemployed will sit it out until they can throw the Progressives out of office. Once they get in they'll ruin the planet. Under the circumstances I don't see what a military man can do for us, but Vice President Bradford insisted that we hire you."

"Perhaps we can think of something," Falkenberg said smoothly. "I've no experience in administration as such, but Hadley is not unique. I take it the Progressive Party is mostly old settlers?"

"Yes and no. The Progressive Party wants to industrialize Hadley, and some of our farm families oppose that. But we want to do it slowly. We'll close most of the mines and take out only as much thorium as we have to sell to get the basic industrial equipment. I want to keep the rest for our own fusion generators, because we'll need it later.

"We want to develop agriculture and transport, and cut the basic citizen ration so that we'll have the fusion power available for our new industries. I want to close out convenience and consumer manufacturing and keep it closed until we can afford it." Budreau's voice rose and his eyes shone; it was easier to see why he had become popular. He believed in his cause.

"We want to build the tools of a self-sustaining world and get along without the CoDominium until we can rejoin the human race as equals!" Budreau caught himself and frowned. "Sorry. Didn't mean to make a speech. Have a seat, won't you?"

"Thank you." Falkenberg sat in a heavy leather chair and looked around the room. The furnishings were ornate, and the office decor had cost a fortune to bring from Earth; but most of it was tasteless—spectacular rather than elegant. The Colonial Office did that sort of thing a lot, and Falkenberg wondered which Grand Senator owned the firm that supplied office furnishings. "What does the opposition want?"

"I suppose you really do need to know all this." Budreau frowned and his mustache twitched nervously. He made an effort to relax, and John thought the President had probably been an impressive man once. "The Freedom Party's slogan is 'Service to the People.' Service to them means consumer goods now. They want strip mining. That's got the miners' support, you can bet. The FP will rape this planet to buy goods from other systems, and to hell with how they're paid for. Runaway inflation will be only one of the problems they'll create."

"They sound ambitious."

"Yes. They even want to introduce internal combustion engine economy. God knows how, there's no support technology here, but there's oil. We'd have to buy all that from off planet, there's no heavy industry here to make engines even if the ecology could absorb them, but that doesn't matter to the FP. They promise cars for everyone. Instant modernization. More food, robotic factories, entertainment, in short, paradise and right now."

"Do they mean it, or is that just slogans?"

"I think most of them mean it," Budreau answered. "It's hard to believe, but I think they do."

"Where do they *say* they'll get the money?"

"Soaking the rich, as if there were enough wealthy people here to matter. Total confiscation of everything everyone owns wouldn't pay for all they promise. Those people have no idea of the realities of our situation, and their leaders are ready to blame anything that's wrong on the Progressive Party, CoDominium administrators, anything but admit that what they promise just isn't possible. Some of the Party leaders may know better, but they don't admit it if they do."

"I take it that program has gathered support."

"Of course it has," Budreau fumed. "And every Bu-Relock ship brings thousands more ready to vote the FP line."

Budreau got up from his desk and went to a cabinet on the opposite wall. He took out a bottle of brandy and three glasses and poured, handing them to Calvin and Falkenberg. Then he ignored the sergeant but waited for Falkenberg to lift his glass.

"Cheers." Budreau drained the glass at one gulp. "Some of the oldest families on Hadley have joined the damned Freedom Party. They're worried about the taxes *I've* proposed! The FP won't leave them anything at all, but they still join the opposition in hopes of making deals. You don't look surprised."

"No, sir. It's a story as old as history, and a military man reads history."

Budreau looked up in surprise. "Really?"

"A smart soldier wants to know the causes of wars. Also how to end them. After all, war is the normal state of affairs, isn't it? Peace is the name of the ideal we deduce from the fact that there have been interludes between wars." Before Budreau could answer, Falkenberg said, "No matter. I take it you expect armed resistance immediately after the CD pulls out."

"I hoped to prevent it. Bradford thought you might be able to do something, and I'm gifted at the art of persuasion." The President sighed. "But it seems hopeless. They don't want to compromise. They think they can get a total victory."

"I wouldn't think they'd have much of a record to run on," Falkenberg said.

Budreau laughed. "The FP partisans claim credit for driving the CoDominium out, Colonel."

They laughed together. The CoDominium was leaving because the mines were no longer worth enough to make it pay to govern Hadley. If the mines were as productive as they'd been in the past, no partisans would drive the Marines away.

Budreau nodded as if reading his thoughts. "Well, they have people believing it anyway. There was a campaign of terrorism for years, nothing very serious. It didn't threaten the mine shipments, or the Marines would have put a stop to it. But they have demoralized the capital police. Out in the bush people administer their own justice, but here in Refuge the FP gangs control a lot of the city."

Budreau pointed to a stack of papers on one corner of the desk. "Those are resignations from the force. I don't even know how many police I'll have left when the CD pulls out." Budreau's fist tightened as if he wanted to pound on the desk, but he sat rigidly still. "Pulls out. For years they ran everything, and now they're leaving us to clean up. I'm President by courtesy of the CoDominium. They put me in office, and now they're leaving."

"At least you're in charge," Falkenberg said. "The BuRelock people wanted someone else. Bradford talked them out of it."

"Sure. And it cost us a lot of money. For what? Maybe it would have been better the other way."

"I thought you said their policies would ruin Hadley."

"I did say that. I believe it. But the policy issues came after the split, I think." Budreau was talking to himself as much as to John. "Now they hate us so much they oppose anything we want out of pure spite. And we do the same thing."

"Sounds like CoDominium politics. Russkis and US in the Grand Senate. Just like home." There was no humor in the polite laugh that followed.

Budreau opened a desk drawer and took out a parchment. "I'll keep the agreement, of course. Here's your commission as commander of the constabulary. But I still think you might be better off taking the next ship out. Hadley's problems can't be solved by military consultants."

Sergeant Major Calvin snorted. The sound was almost inaudible, but Falkenberg knew what he was thinking. Budreau shrank from the bald term "mercenary," as if "military consultant" were easier on his conscience. John finished his drink and stood.

"Mr. Bradford wants to see you," Budreau said. "Lieutenant Banners will be outside to show you to his office."

"Thank you, sir." Falkenberg strode from the big room. As he closed the door he saw Budreau going back to the liquor cabinet.

Vice President Ernest Bradford was a small man with a smile that never seemed to fade. He worked at being liked, but it didn't always work. Still, he had gathered a following of dedicated party workers, and he fancied himself an accomplished politician.

When Banners showed Falkenberg into the office, Bradford smiled even more broadly, but he suggested that Banners should take Calvin on a tour of the Palace guardrooms. Falkenberg nodded and let them go.

The Vice President's office was starkly functional. The desks and chairs were made of local woods with an indifferent finish, and a solitary rose in a crystal vase provided the only color. Bradford was dressed in the same manner, shapeless clothing bought from a cheap store.

"Thank God you're here," Bradford said when the door

71

was closed. "But I'm told you only brought ten men. We can't do anything with just ten men! You were supposed to bring over a hundred men loyal to us!" He bounced up excitedly from his chair, then sat again. "Can you do something?"

"There were ten men in the Navy ship with me," Falkenberg said. "When you show me where I'm to train the regiment I'll find the rest of the mercenaries."

Bradford gave him a broad wink and beamed. "Then you did bring more! We'll show them—all of them. We'll win yet. What did you think of Budreau?"

"He seems sincere enough. Worried, of course. I think I would be in his place."

Bradford shook his head. "He can't make up his mind. About anything! He wasn't so bad before, but lately he's had to be forced into making every decision. Why did the Colonial Office pick him? I thought you were going to arrange for me to be President. We gave you enough money."

"One thing at a time," Falkenberg said. "The Undersecretary couldn't justify you to the Minister. We can't get to everyone, you know. It was hard enough for Professor Whitlock to get them to approve Budreau, let alone you. We sweated blood just getting them to let go of having a Freedom Party President."

Bradford's head bobbed up and down like a puppet's. "I knew I could trust you," he said. His smile was warm, but despite all his efforts to be sincere it did not come through. "You have kept your part of the bargain, anyway. And once the CD is gone—"

"We'll have a free hand, of course."

Bradford smiled again. "You are a very strange man, Colonel Falkenberg. The talk was that you were utterly loyal to the CoDominium. When Dr. Whitlock suggested that you might be available I was astounded."

"I had very little choice," Falkenberg reminded him.

"Yes." Bradford didn't say that Falkenberg had little more now, but it was obvious that he thought it. His smile expanded confidentially. "Well, we have to let Mr. Hamner meet you now. He's the Second Vice President. Then we can go to the Warner estate. I've arranged for your troops to be quartered there, it's what you wanted for a training ground. No one will bother you. You can say your other men are local volunteers."

Falkenberg nodded. "I'll manage. I'm getting rather good at cover stories lately."

"Sure." Bradford beamed again. "By God, we'll win this yet." He touched a button on his desk. "Ask Mr. Hamner to come in, please." He winked at Falkenberg and said, "Can't spend too long alone. Might give someone the idea that we have a conspiracy."

"How does Hamner fit in?" Falkenberg asked.

"Wait until you see him. Budreau trusts him, and he's dangerous. He represents the technology people in the Progressive Party. We can't do without him, but his policies are ridiculous. He wants to turn loose of everything. If he has his way, there won't be any government. And his people take credit for everything—as if technology was all there was to government. He doesn't know the first thing about governing. All the people we have to keep happy, the meetings, he thinks that's all silly, that you can build a party by working like an engineer."

"In other words, he doesn't understand the political realities," Falkenberg said. "Just so. I suppose he has to go, then."

Bradford nodded, smiling again. "Eventually. But we do need his influence with the technicians at the moment. And of course, he knows nothing about any arrangements you and I have made."

"Of course." Falkenberg sat easily and studied maps until the intercom announced that Hamner was outside. He wondered idly if the office were safe to talk in. Bradford was the most likely man to plant devices in other people's offices, but he couldn't be the only one who'd benefit from eavesdropping, and no place could be absolutely safe.

There isn't much I can do if it is, Falkenberg decided. And it's probably clean.

George Hamner was a large man, taller than Falkenberg and even heavier than Sergeant Major Calvin. He had the relaxed movements of a big man, and much of the easy confidence that massive size usually wins. People didn't pick fights with George Hamner. His grip was gentle when they shook hands, but he closed his fist relentlessly, testing Falkenberg carefully. As he felt answering pressure he looked surprised, and the two men stood in silence for a long moment before Hamner relaxed and waved to Bradford.

"So you're our new colonel of constabulary," Hamner

73

said. "Hope you know what you're getting into. I should say I hope you *don't* know. If you know about our problems and take the job anyway, we'll have to wonder if you're sane."

"I keep hearing about how severe Hadley's problems are," Falkenberg said. "If enough of you keep saying it, maybe I'll believe it's hopeless, but right now I don't see it. So we're outnumbered by the Freedom Party people. What kind of weapons do they have to make trouble with?"

Hamner laughed. "Direct sort of guy, aren't you? I like that. There's nothing spectacular about their weapons, just a lot of them. Enough small problems make a big problem, right? But the CD hasn't permitted any big stuff. No tanks or armored cars, hell, there aren't enough cars of any kind to make any difference. No fuel or power distribution net ever built, so no way cars would be useful. We've got a subway, couple of monorails for in-city stuff, and what's left of the railroad . . . you didn't ask for a lecture on transportation, did you."

"No."

Hamner laughed. "It's my pet worry at the moment. We don't have enough. Let's see, weapons. . . ." The big man sprawled into a chair. He hooked one leg over the arm and ran his fingers through thick hair just receding from his large brows. "No military aircraft, hardly any aircraft at all except for a few choppers. No artillery, machine guns, heavy weapons in general. Mostly light-caliber hunting rifles and shotguns. Some police weapons. Military rifles and bayonets, a few, and we have almost all of them. Out in the streets you can find anything, Colonel, and I mean literally anything. Bows and arrows, knives, swords, axes, hammers, you name it."

"He doesn't need to know about obsolete things like that," Bradford said. His voice was heavy with contempt, but he still wore his smile.

"No weapon is ever really obsolete," Falkenberg said. "Not in the hands of a man who'll use it. What about body armor? How good a supply of Nemourlon do you have?"

Hamner looked thoughtful for a second. "There's some body armor in the streets, and the police have some. The President's Guard doesn't use the stuff. I can supply you with Nemourlon, but you'll have to make your own armor out of it. Can you do that?"

Falkenberg nodded. "Yes. I brought an excellent tech-

74

nician and some tools. Gentlemen, the situation's about what I expected. I can't see why everyone is so worried. We have a battalion of CD Marines, not the best Marines perhaps, but they're trained soldiers. With the weapons of a light infantry battalion and the training I can give the recruits we'll add to the battalion, I'll undertake to face your forty thousand Freedom Party people. The guerrilla problem will be somewhat more severe, but we control all the food distribution in the city. With ration cards and identity papers it should not be difficult to set up controls."

Hamner laughed. It was a bitter laugh. "You want to tell him, Ernie?"

Bradford looked confused. "Tell him what?"

Hamner laughed again. "Not doing your homework. It's in the morning report for a couple of days ago. The Colonial Office has decided, on the advice of BuRelock, that Hadley does not need any military weapons. The CD Marines will be lucky to keep their rifles and bayonets. All the rest of their gear goes out with the CD ships."

"But this is insane," Bradford protested. He turned to Falkenberg. "Why would they do that?"

Falkenberg shrugged. "Perhaps some Freedom Party manager got to a Colonial Office official. I assume they are not above bribery?"

"Of course not," Bradford said. "We've got to do something!"

"If we can. I suspect it will not be easy." Falkenberg pursed his lips into a tight line. "I hadn't counted on this. It means that if we tighten up control through food rationing and identity documents, we face armed rebellion. How well organized are these FP partisans, anyway?"

"Well organized and well financed," Hamner said. "And I'm not so sure about ration cards being the answer to the guerrilla problem anyway. The CoDominium was able to put up with a lot of sabotage because they weren't interested in anything but the mines, but we can't live with the level of terror we have right now in this city. Some way or other we have to restore order—and justice, for that matter."

"Justice isn't something soldiers ordinarily deal with," Falkenberg said. "Order's another matter. *That* I think we can supply."

"With a few hundred men?" Hamner's voice was incredulous. "But I like your attitude. At least you don't sit around and whine for somebody to help you. Or sit and think and never make up your mind."

"We will see what we can do," Falkenberg said.

"Yeah." Hamner got up and went to the door. "Well, I wanted to meet you, Colonel. Now I have. *I've* got work to do. I'd think Ernie does too, but I don't notice him doing much of it." He didn't look at them again, but went out, leaving the door open.

"You see," Bradford said. He closed the door gently. His smile was knowing. "He is useless. We'll find someone to deal with the technicians as soon as you've got everything else under control."

"He seemed to be right on some points," Falkenberg said. "For example, he knows it won't be easy to get proper police protection established. I saw an example of what goes on in Refuge on the way here, and if it's that bad all over—"

"You'll find a way," Bradford said. He seemed certain. "You can recruit quite a large force, you know. And a lot of the lawlessness is nothing more than teen-age street gangs. They're not loyal to anything, Freedom Party, us, the CD, or anything else. They merely want to control the block they live on."

"Sure. But they're hardly the whole problem."

"No. But you'll find a way. And forget Hamner. His whole group is rotten. They're not real Progressives, that's all." His voice was emphatic, and his eyes seemed to shine. Bradford lowered his voice and leaned forward. "Hamner used to be in the Freedom Party, you know. He claims to have broken with them over technology policies, but you can never trust a man like that."

"I see. Fortunately, I don't have to trust him."

Bradford beamed. "Precisely. Now let's get you started. You have a lot of work, and don't forget now, you've already agreed to train some party troops for me."

VII

THE ESTATE WAS large, nearly five kilometers on a side, located in low hills a day's march from the city of Refuge. There was a central house and barns, all made of local wood that resembled oak. The buildings nestled in a wooded bowl in the center of the estate.

"You're sure you won't need anything more?" Lieutenant Banners asked.

"No, thank you," Falkenberg said. "The few men we have with us carry their own gear. We'll have to arrange for food and fuel when the others come, but for now we'll make do."

"All right, sir," Banners said. "I'll go back with Mowrer and leave you the car, then. And you've the animals. . . ."

"Yes. Thank you, Lieutenant."

Banners saluted and got into the car. He started to say something else, but Falkenberg had turned away and Banners drove off the estate.

Calvin watched him leave. "That's a curious one," he said. "Reckon he'd like to know more about what we're doing."

Falkenberg's lips twitched into a thin smile. "I expect he would at that. You will see to it that he learns no more than we want him to."

"Aye aye, sir. Colonel, what was that Mr. Bradford was saying about Party troopers? We going to have many of them?"

"I think so." Falkenberg walked up the wide lawn toward the big ranch house. Captain Fast and several of the others were waiting on the porch, and there was a bottle of whiskey on the table.

Falkenberg poured a drink and tossed it off. "I think we'll have quite a few Progressive Party loyalists here once we start, Calvin. I'm not looking forward to it, but they were inevitable."

"Sir?" Captain Fast had been listening quietly.

Falkenberg gave him a half-smile. "Do you really think the governing authorities are going to hand over a monopoly of military force to us?"

"You think they don't trust us."

"Amos, would *you* trust us?"

"No sir," Captain Fast said. "But we could hope."

"We will not accomplish our mission on hope, Captain. Sergeant Major."

"Sir."

"I have an errand for you later this evening. For the moment, find someone to take me to my quarters and then see about our dinner."

"Sir."

Falkenberg woke to a soft rapping on the door of his room. He opened his eyes and put his hand on the pistol under his pillow, but made no other movement.

The rap came again. "Yes," Falkenberg called softly.

"I'm back, Colonel," Calvin answered.

"Right. Come in." Falkenberg swung his feet out of his bunk and pulled on his boots. He was fully dressed otherwise.

Sergeant Major Calvin came in. He was dressed in the light leather tunic and trousers of the CD Marine battledress. The total black of a night combat coverall protruded from the war bag slung over his shoulder. He wore a pistol on his belt, and a heavy trench knife was slung in a holster on his left breast.

A short wiry man with a thin brown mustache came in with Calvin.

"Glad to see you," Falkenberg said. "Have any trouble?"

"Gang of toughs tried to stir up something as we was coming through the city, Colonel," Calvin replied. He grinned wolfishly. "Didn't last long enough to set any records."

"Anyone hurt?"

"None that couldn't walk away."

"Good. Any problem at the relocation barracks?"

"No, sir," Calvin replied. "They don't guard them places. Anybody wants to get away from BuRelock's charity, they let 'em go. Without ration cards, of course. This was just involuntary colonists, not convicts."

As he took Calvin's report, Falkenberg was inspecting the man who had come in with him. Major Jeremy Savage looked tired and much older than his forty-five years. He was thinner than John remembered him.

"Bad as I've heard?" Falkenberg asked him.

"No picnic," Savage replied in the clipped accents he'd learned when he grew up on Churchill. "Didn't expect it to be. We're here, John Christian."

"Yes, and thank God. Nobody spotted you? The men behave all right?"

"Yes, sir. We were treated no differently from any other involuntary colonists. The men behaved splendidly, and a week or two of hard exercise should get us all back in shape. Sergeant Major tells me the battalion arrived intact."

"Yes. They're still at Marine barracks. That's our weak link, Jeremy. I want them out here where we control who they talk to, and as soon as possible."

"You've got the best ones. I think they'll be all right."

Falkenberg nodded. "But keep your eyes open, Jerry, and be careful with the men until the CD pulls out. I've hired Dr. Whitlock to check things for us. He hasn't reported in yet, but I assume he's on Hadley."

Savage acknowledged Falkenberg's wave and sat in the room's single chair. He took a glass of whiskey from Calvin with a nod of thanks.

"Going all out hiring experts, eh? He's said to be the best available. . . . My, that's good. They don't have anything to drink on those BuRelock ships."

"When Whitlock reports in we'll have a full staff meeting," Falkenberg said. "Until then, stay with the plan. Bradford is supposed to send the battalion out tomorrow, and soon after that he'll begin collecting volunteers from his party. We're supposed to train them. Of course, they'll all be loyal to Bradford. Not to the Party and certainly not to us."

Savage nodded and held out the glass to Calvin for a refill.

"Now tell me a bit about those toughs you fought on the way here, Sergeant Major," Falkenberg said.

"Street gang, Colonel. Not bad at individual fightin', but no organization. Hardly no match for near a hundred of us."

"Street gang." John pulled his lower lip speculatively,

then grinned. "How many of our battalion used to be punks just like them, Sergeant Major?"

"Half anyway, sir. Includin' me."

Falkenberg nodded. "I think it might be a good thing if the Marines got to meet some of those kids, Sergeant Major. Informally, you know."

"Sir!" Calvin's square face beamed with anticipation.

"Now," Falkenberg continued. "Recruits will be our real problem. You can bet some of them will try to get chummy with the troops. They'll want to pump the men about their backgrounds and outfits. And the men will drink, and when they drink they talk. How will you handle that, Top Soldier?"

Calvin looked thoughtful. "Won't be no trick for a while. We'll keep the recruits away from the men except drill instructors, and DI's don't talk to recruits. Once they've passed basic it'll get a bit stickier, but hell, Colonel, troops like to lie about their campaigns. We'll just encourage 'em to fluff it up a bit. The stories'll be so tall nobody'll believe 'em."

"Right. I don't have to tell both of you we're skating on pretty thin ice for a while."

"We'll manage, Colonel." Calvin was positive. He'd been with Falkenberg a long time, and although any man can make mistakes, it was Calvin's experience that Falkenberg would find a way out of any hole they dropped into.

And if they didn't—well, over every CD orderly room door was a sign. It said, "You are Marines in order to die, and the Fleet will send you where you can die." Calvin had walked under that sign to enlist, and thousands of times since.

"That's it, then, Jeremy," Falkenberg said.

"Yes, sir," Savage said crisply. He stood and saluted. "Damned if it doesn't feel good to be doing this again, sir." Years fell away from his face.

"Good to have you back aboard," Falkenberg replied. He stood to return the salute. "And thanks, Jerry. For everything. . . ."

The Marine battalion arrived the next day. They were marched to the camp by regular CD Marine officers, who turned them over to Falkenberg. The captain in charge of the detail wanted to stay around and watch, but Falkenberg found an errand for him and sent Major Savage along to keep him company. An hour later there was no one in the camp but Falkenberg's people.

Two hours later the troops were at work constructing their own base camp.

Falkenberg watched from the porch of the ranch house. "Any problems, Sergeant Major?" he asked.

Calvin fingered the stubble on his square jaw. He shaved twice a day on garrison duty, and at the moment he was wondering if he needed his second. "Nothing a trooper's blast won't cure, Colonel. With your permission I'll draw a few barrels of whiskey tonight and let 'em tie one on before the recruits come in."

"Granted."

"They won't be fit for much before noon tomorrow, but we're on schedule now. The extra work'll be good for 'em."

"How many will run?"

Calvin shrugged. "Maybe none, Colonel. We got enough to keep 'em busy, and they don't know this place very well. Recruits'll be a different story, and once they get in we may have a couple take off."

"Yes. Well, see what you can do. We're going to need every man. You heard President Budreau's assessment of the situation."

"Yes, sir. That'll make the troops happy. Sounds like a good fight comin' up."

"I think you can safely promise the men some hard fighting, Sergeant Major. They'd also better understand that there's no place to go if we don't win this one. No pickups on this tour."

"No pickups on half the missions we've been on, Colonel. I better see Cap'n Fast about the brandy. Join us about midnight, sir? The men would like that."

"I'll be along, Sergeant Major."

Calvin's prediction was wrong: the troops were useless throughout the entire next day. The recruits arrived the day after.

The camp was a flurry of activity. The Marines relearned lessons of basic training. Each maniple of five men cooked for itself, did its own laundry, made its own shelters from woven synthetics and rope, and contributed men for work on the encampment revetments and palisades.

The recruits did the same kind of work under the supervision of Falkenberg's mercenary officers and NCO's.

Most of the men who had come with Savage on the Bu-Relock colony transport were officers, centurions, sergeants, and technicians, while there was an unusual number of monitors and corporals within the Marine battalion. Between the two groups there were enough leaders for an entire regiment.

The recruits learned to sleep in their military great-cloaks, and to live under field conditions with no uniform but synthi-leather battledress and boots. They cooked their own food and constructed their own quarters and depended on no one outside the regiment. After two weeks they were taught to fashion their own body armor from Nemourlon. When it was completed they lived in it, and any man who neglected his duties found his armor weighted with lead. Maniples, squads, and whole sections of recruits and veterans on punishment marches became a common sight after dark.

The volunteers had little time to fraternize with the Marine veterans. Savage and Calvin and the other cadres relentlessly drove them through drills, field problems, combat exercises, and maintenance work. The recruit formations were smaller each day as men were driven to leave the service, but from somewhere there was a steady supply of new troops.

These were all younger men who came in small groups directly to the camp. They would appear before the regimental orderly room at reveille, and often they were accompanied by Marine veterans. There was attrition in their formations as well as among the Party volunteers, but far fewer left the service—and they were eager for combat training.

After six weeks Vice President Bradford visited the camp. He arrived to find the entire regiment in formation, the recruits on one side of a square, the veterans on the other.

Sergeant Major Calvin was reading to the men.

"Today is April 30 on Earth." Calvin's voice boomed out; he had no need for a bullhorn. "It is Camerone Day. On April 30, 1863, Captain Jean Danjou of the Foreign Legion, with two officers and sixty-two legionnaires, faced two thousand Mexicans at the farmhouse of Camerone.

"The battle lasted all day. The legionnaires had no food or water, and their ammunition was low. Captain Danjou was killed. His place was taken by Lieutenant Villain. He also was killed.

"At five in the afternoon all that remained were Lieutenant Clément Maudet and four men. They had one cartridge each. At the command each man fired his last round and charged the enemy with the bayonet.

"There were no survivors."

The troops were silent. Calvin looked at the recruits. They stood at rigid attention in the hot sun. Finally Calvin spoke. "I don't expect none of you to ever get it. Not the likes of you. But maybe one of you'll someday know what Camerone is all about.

"Every man will draw an extra wine ration tonight. Combat veterans will also get a half-liter of brandy. Now attention to orders."

Falkenberg took Bradford inside the ranch house. It was now fitted out as the Officers' Mess, and they sat in one corner of the lounge. A steward brought drinks.

"And what was all that for?" Bradford demanded. "These aren't Foreign Legionnaires! You're supposed to be training a planetary constabulary."

"A constabulary that has one hell of a fight on its hands," Falkenberg reminded him. "True, we don't have any continuity with the Legion in this outfit, but you have to remember that our basic cadre are CD Marines. Or were. If we skipped Camerone Day, we'd have a mutiny."

"I suppose you know what you're doing." Bradford sniffed. His face had almost lost the perpetual half-smile he wore, but there were still traces of it. "Colonel, I have a complaint from the men we've assigned as officers. My Progressive Party people have been totally segregated from the other troops, and they don't like it. I don't like it."

Falkenberg shrugged. "You chose to commission them before training, Mr. Bradford. That makes them officers by courtesy, but they don't know anything. They would look ridiculous if I mixed them with the veterans, or even the recruits, until they've learned military basics."

"You've got rid of a lot of them, too—"

"Same reason, sir. You have given us a difficult assignment. We're outnumbered and there's no chance of outside support. In a few weeks we'll face forty thousand Freedom Party men, and I won't answer for the consequences if we hamper the troops with incompetent officers."

"All right. I expected that. But it isn't just the officers, Colonel. The Progressive volunteers are being driven out as well. Your training is too hard. Those are loyal men, and loyalty is important here!"

Falkenberg smiled softly. "Agreed. But I'd rather have one battalion of good men I can trust than a regiment of troops who might break under fire. After I've a bare minimum of first-class troops, I'll consider taking on others for garrison duties. Right now the need is for men who can fight."

"And you don't have them yet—those Marines seemed well disciplined."

"In ranks, certainly. But do you really think the CD would let go of reliable troops?"

"Maybe not," Bradford conceded. "O.K. You're the expert. But where the hell are you getting the other recruits? Jailbirds, kids with police records. You keep them while you let my Progressives run!"

"Yes, sir." Falkenberg signaled for another round of drinks. "Mr. Vice President—"

"Since when have we become that formal?" Bradford asked. His smile was back.

"Sorry. I thought you were here to read me out."

"No, of course not. But I've got to answer to President Budreau, you know. And Hamner. I've managed to get your activities assigned to my department, but it doesn't mean I can tell the Cabinet to blow it."

"Right," Falkenberg said. "Well, about the recruits. We take what we can get. It takes time to train green men, and if the street warriors stand up better than your party toughs, I can't help it. You can tell the Cabinet that when we've a cadre we can trust, we'll be easier on volunteers. We can even form some kind of part-time militia. But right now the need is for men tough enough to win this fight coming up, and I don't know any better way to do it."

After that Falkenberg found himself summoned to report to the Palace every week. Usually he met only Bradford and Hamner; President Budreau had made it clear that he considered the military force as an evil whose necessity was not established, and only Bradford's insistence kept the regiment supplied.

At one conference Falkenberg met Chief Horgan of the Refuge police.

"The Chief's got a complaint, Colonel," President Budreau said.

"Yes sir?" Falkenberg asked.

84

"It's those damned Marines," Horgan said. He rubbed the point of his chin. "They're raising hell in the city at night. We've never hauled any of them in because Mr. Bradford wants us to go easy, but it's getting rough."

"What are they doing?" Falkenberg asked.

"You name it. They've taken over a couple of taverns and won't let anybody in without their permission, for one thing. And they have fights with street gangs every night.

"We could live with all that, but they go to other parts of town, too. Lots of them. They go into taverns and drink all night, then say they can't pay. If the owner gets sticky, they wreck the place. . . ."

"And they're gone before your patrols get there," Falkenberg finished for him. "It's an old tradition. They call it System D, and more planning effort goes into that operation than I can ever get them to put out in combat. I'll try to put a stop to System D, anyway."

"It would help. Another thing. Your guys go into the toughest parts of town and start fights whenever they can find anyone to mix with."

"How are they doing?" Falkenberg asked interestedly.

Horgan grinned, then caught himself after a stern look from Budreau. "Pretty well. I understand they've never been beaten. But it raises hell with the citizens, Colonel. And another trick of theirs is driving people crazy! They march through the streets fifty strong at all hours of the night playing bagpipes! Bagpipes in the wee hours, Colonel, can be a frightening thing."

Falkenberg thought he saw a tiny flutter in Horgan's left eye, and the police chief was holding back a wry smile.

"I wanted to ask you about that, Colonel," Second Vice President Hamner said. "This is hardly a Scots outfit, why do they have bagpipes anyway?"

Falkenberg shrugged. "Pipes are standard with many Marine regiments. Since the Russki CD outfits started taking up Cossack customs, the Western bloc regiments adopted their own. After all, the Marines were formed out of a number of old military units. Foreign Legion, Highlanders—a lot of men like the pipes. I'll confess I do myself."

"Sure, but not in my city in the middle of the night," Horgan said.

John grinned openly at the chief of police. "I'll try to

keep the pipers off the streets at night. I can imagine they're not good for civilian morale. But as to keeping the Marines in camp, how do I do it? We need every one of them, and they're volunteers. They can get on the CD carrier and ship out when the rest go, and there's not one damned thing we can do about it."

"There's less than a month until they haul down that CoDominium flag," Bradford added with satisfaction. He glanced at the CD banner on its staff outside. Eagle with red shield and black sickle and hammer on its breast; red stars and blue stars around it. Bradford nodded in satisfaction. It wouldn't be long.

That flag meant little to the people of Hadley. On Earth it was enough to cause riots in nationalistic cities in both the U.S. and the Soviet Union, while in other countries it was a symbol of the alliance that kept any other nation from rising above second-class status. To Earth the Co-Dominium Alliance represented peace at a high price, too high for many.

For Falkenberg it represented nearly thirty years of service ended by court martial.

Two weeks to go. Then the CoDominium Governor would leave, and Hadley would be officially independent. Vice President Bradley visited the camp to speak to the recruits.

He told them of the value of loyalty to the government, and the rewards they would all have as soon as the Progressive Party was officially in power. Better pay, more liberties, and the opportunity for promotion in an expanding army; bonuses and soft duty. His speech was full of promises, and Bradford was quite proud of it.

When he had finished, Falkenberg took the Vice President into a private room in the Officers' Mess and slammed the door.

"Damn you, you don't *ever* make offers to my troops without my permission." John Falkenberg's face was cold with anger.

"I'll do as I please with my army, Colonel," Bradford replied smugly. The little smile on his face was completely without warmth. "Don't get snappy with me, *Colonel* Falkenberg. Without my influence Budreau would dismiss you in an instant."

Then his mood changed, and Bradford took a flask of

brandy from his pocket. "Here, Colonel, have a drink."
The little smile was replaced with something more genuine. "We have to work together, John. There's too much
to do, even with both of us working it won't all get done.
Sorry, I'll ask your advice in future, but don't you think
the troops should get to know me? I'll be President soon."
He looked to Falkenberg for confirmation.

"Yes, sir." John took the flask and held it up for a
toast. "To the new President of Hadley. I shouldn't have
snapped at you, but don't make offers to troops who
haven't proved themselves. If you give men reason to think
they're good when they're not, you'll never have an army
worth its pay."

"But they've done well in training. You said so."

"Sure, but you don't tell *them* that. Work them until
they've nothing more to give, and let them know that's
just barely satisfactory. Then one day they'll give you more
than they knew they had in them. That's the day you can
offer rewards, only by then you won't need to."

Bradford nodded grudging agreement. "If you say so.
But I wouldn't have thought—"

"Listen," Falkenberg said. A party of recruits and their
drill masters marched past outside.

"Listen," Falkenberg said.
A party of recruits and their drill masters marched past
outside. They were singing and their words came in the
open window.

> "When you've blue'd your last tosser,
> on the brothel and the booze,
> and you're out in the cold on your ear,
> you hump your bundle on the rough,
> and tell the sergeant that you're tough,
> and you'll do him the favor of his life.
> He will cry and he will scream,
> and he'll curse his rotten luck,
> and he'll ask why he was ever born.
> If you're lucky he will take you,
> and he'll do his best to break you,
> and they'll feed you rotten monkey on a knife."

"Double time, heaow!" The song broke off as the men
ran across the central parade ground.

Bradford turned away from the window. "That sort of
thing is all very well for the jailbirds, Colonel, but I

insist on keeping my loyalists as well. In future you will dismiss no Progressive without my approval. Is that understood?"

Falkenberg nodded. He'd seen this coming for some time. "In that case, sir, it might be better to form a separate battalion. I will transfer all of your people into the Fourth Battalion and put them under the officers you've appointed. Will that be satisfactory?"

"If you'll supervise their training, yes."

"Certainly," Falkenberg said.

"Good." Bradford's smile broadened, but it wasn't meant for Falkenberg. "I will also expect you to consult me about any promotions in that battalion. You agree to that, of course."

"Yes, sir. There may be some problems about finding locals to fill the senior NCO slots. You've got potential monitors and corporals, but they've not the experience to be sergeants and centurions."

"You'll find a way, I'm sure," Bradford said carefully. "I have some rather, uh, special duties for the Fourth Battalion, Colonel. I'd prefer it to be entirely staffed by Party loyalists of my choosing. Your men should only be there to supervise training, not as their commanders. Is this agreed?"

"Yes, sir."

Bradford's smile was genuine as he left the camp.

Day after day the troops sweated in the bright blue-tinted sunlight. Riot control, bayonet drill, use of armor in defense and attacks against men with body armor, and more complex exercises as well. There were forced marches under the relentless direction of Major Savage, the harsh shouts of sergeants and centurions, Captain Amos Fast with his tiny swagger stick and biting sarcasm. . . .

Yet the number leaving the regiment was smaller now, and there was still a flow of recruits from the Marines' nocturnal expeditions. The recruiting officers could even be selective, although they seldom were. The Marines, like the Legion before it, took anyone willing to fight; and Falkenberg's officers were all Marine trained.

Each night groups of Marines sneaked past sentries to drink and carouse with the field hands of nearby ranchers. They gambled and shouted in local taverns, and they paid little attention to their officers. There were many complaints, and Bradford's protests became stronger.

Falkenberg always gave the same answer. "They always come back, and they don't have to stay here. How do you suggest I control them? Flogging?"

The constabulary army had a definite split personality, with recruits treated harsher than veterans. Meanwhile the Fourth Battalion grew larger each day.

VIII

GEORGE HAMNER TRIED to get home for dinner every night, no matter what it might cost him in night work later. He thought he owed at least that to his family.

His walled estate was just outside the Palace district. It had been built by his grandfather with money borrowed from American Express. The old man had been proud of paying back every cent before it was due. It was a big comfortable place which cunningly combined local materials and imported luxuries, and George was always glad to return there.

At home he felt he was master of something, that at least one thing was under his control. It was the only place in Refuge where he could feel that way.

In less than a week the CoDominium Governor would leave. Independence was near, and it should be a time of hope, but George Hamner felt only dread. Problems of public order were not officially his problem. He held the Ministry of Technology, but the breakdown in law and order couldn't be ignored. Already half of Refuge was untouched by government.

There were large areas where the police went only in squads or not at all, and maintenance crews had to be protected or they couldn't enter. For now the CoDominium Marines escorted George's men, but what would it be like when the Marines were gone?

George sat in the paneled study and watched lengthening shadows in the groves outside. They made dancing patterns through the trees and across neatly clipped lawns. The outside walls spoiled the view of Raceway Channel below, and Hamner cursed them.

Why must we have walls? Walls and a dozen armed men to patrol them. I can remember when I sat in this

90

room with my father, I was no more than six, and we could watch boats in the Channel. And later, we had such big dreams for Hadley. Grandfather telling why he had left Earth, and what we could do here. Freedom and plenty. We had a paradise, and Lord, Lord, what have we done with it?

He worked for an hour, but accomplished little. There weren't any solutions, only chains of problems that led back into a circle. Solve one and all would fall into place, but none were soluble without the others. And yet, if we had a few years, he thought. A few years, but we aren't going to get them.

In a few years the farms will support the urban population if we can move people out of the agricultural interior and get them working—but they won't leave Refuge, and we can't make them do it.

If we could, though. If the city's population could be thinned, the power we divert to food manufacture can be used to build a transport net. Then we can get more to live in the interior, and we can get more food into the city. We could make enough things to keep country life pleasant, and people will want to leave Refuge. But there's no way to the first step. The people don't want to move and the Freedom Party promises they won't have to.

George shook his head. Can Falkenberg's army make them leave? If he gets enough soldiers can he forcibly evacuate part of the city? Hamner shuddered at the thought. There would be resistance, slaughter, civil war. Hadley's independence can't be built on a foundation of blood. No.

His other problems were similar. The government was bandaging Hadley's wounds, but that's all. Treating symptoms because there was never enough control over events to treat causes.

He picked up a report on the fusion generators. They needed spare parts, and he wondered how long even this crazy standoff would last. He couldn't really expect more than a few years even if everything went well. A few years, and then famine because the transport net couldn't be built fast enough. And when the generators failed, the city's food supplies would be gone, sanitation services crippled . . . famine and plague. Were those horsemen better than conquest and war?

He thought of his interview with the Freedom Party leaders. They didn't care about the generators because they were sure that Earth wouldn't allow famines on Hadley. They thought Hadley could use her own helplessness as a weapon to extract payments from the CoDominium.

George cursed under his breath. They were wrong. Earth didn't care, and Hadley was too far away to interest anyone. But even if they were right they were selling Hadley's independence, and for what? Didn't real independence mean anything to them?

Laura came in with a pack of shouting children.

"Already time for bed?" he asked. The four-year-old picked up his pocket calculator and sat on his lap, punching buttons and watching the numbers and lights flash.

George kissed them all and sent them out, wondering as he did what kind of future they had.

I should get out of politics, he told himself. I'm not doing any good, and I'll get Laura and the kids finished along with me. But what happens if we let go? What future will they have then?

"You look worried." Laura was back after putting the children to bed. "It's only a few days—"

"Yeah."

"And what really happens then?" she asked. "Not the promises we keep hearing. What really happens when the CD leaves? It's going to be bad, isn't it?"

He pulled her to him, feeling her warmth, and tried to draw comfort from her nearness. She huddled against him for a moment, then pulled away.

"George, shouldn't we take what we can and go east? We wouldn't have much, but you'd be alive."

"It won't be *that* bad," he told her. He tried to chuckle, as if she'd made a joke, but the sound was hollow. She didn't laugh with him.

"There'll be time for that later," he told her. "If things don't work. But it should be all right at first. We've got a planetary constabulary. It should be enough to protect the government—but I'm moving all of you into the palace in a couple of days."

"The army," she said with plenty of contempt. "Some army, Georgie. Bradford's volunteers who'd kill you—and don't think he wouldn't like to see you dead, either. And those Marines! You said yourself they were the scum of space."

"I said it. I wonder if I believe it. There's something strange happening here, Laura. Something I don't understand."

She sat on the couch near his desk and curled her legs under herself. He'd always liked that pose. She looked up, her eyes wide with interest. She never looked at anyone else that way.

"I went to see Major Karantov today," George said. "Thought I'd presume on an old friend to get a little information about this man Falkenberg. Boris wasn't in his office, but one of the junior lieutenants, fellow named Kleist—"

"I've met him," Laura said. "Nice boy. A little young."

"Yes. Anyway, we got into a conversation about what happens after independence. We discussed street fighting, and the mob riots, you know, and I said I wished we had some reliable Marines instead of the demobilized outfit they were leaving here. He looked funny and asked just what did I want, the Grand Admiral's Guard?"

"That's strange."

"Yes, and when Boris came in and I asked what Kleist meant, Boris said the kid was new and didn't know what he was talking about."

"And you think he did?" Laura asked. "Boris wouldn't lie to you. Stop that!" she added hastily. "You have an appointment."

"It can wait."

"With only a couple of dozen cars on this whole planet and one of them coming for you, you will not keep it waiting while you make love to your wife, George Hamner!" Her eyes flashed, but not with anger. "Besides, I want to know what Boris told you." She danced away from him, and he went back to the desk.

"It's not just that," George said. "I've been thinking about it. Those troops don't look like misfits to me. Off duty they drink, and they've got the field hands locking their wives and daughters up, but you know, come morning they're out on that drill field. And Falkenberg doesn't strike me as the type who'd put up with undisciplined men."

"But—"

He nodded. "But it doesn't make sense. And there's the matter of the officers. He's got too many, and they're not from Hadley. That's why I'm going out there tonight, without Bradford."

"Have you asked Ernie about it?"

"Sure. He says he's got some Party loyalists training as officers. I'm a little slow, Laura, but I'm not that stupid. I may not notice everything, but if there were fifty Progressives with military experience I'd know. Bradford is lying, and why?"

Laura looked thoughtful and pulled her lower lip in a gesture that Hamner hardly noticed now, although he'd kidded her about it before they were married. "He lies for practice," she said. "But his wife has been talking about independence, and she let something slip about when Ernie would be President she'd make some changes."

"Well, Ernie expects to succeed Budreau."

"No," Laura said. "She acted like it would be soon. Very soon."

George Hamner shook his massive head. "He hasn't the guts for a coup," he said firmly. "And the technicians would walk out in a second. They can't stand him and he knows it."

"Ernest Bradford has never recognized any limitations," Laura said. "He really believes he can make anyone like him if he'll just put out the effort. No matter how many times he's kicked a man, he thinks a few smiles and apologies will fix it. But what did Boris tell you about Falkenberg?"

"Said he was as good as we can get. A top Marine commander, started as a Navy man and went over to Marines because he couldn't get fast enough promotions in the Navy."

"An ambitious man. How ambitious?"

"Don't know."

"Is he married?"

"I gather he once was, but not for a long time. I got the scoop on the court martial. There weren't any slots open for promotion. But when a review board passed Falkenberg over for a promotion that the admiral couldn't have given him in the first place, Falkenberg made such a fuss about it that he was dismissed for insubordination."

"Can you trust him, then?" Laura asked. "His men may be the only thing keeping you alive—"

"I know. And you, and Jimmy, and Christie, and Peter. . . . I asked Boris that, and he said there's no better man available. You can't hire CD men from active duty. Boris recommends him highly. Says troops love him, he's a brilliant tactician, has experience in troop command and staff work as well—"

"Sounds like quite a catch."

"Yes. But Laura, if he's all that valuable, why did they boot him out? My God, it all sounds so trivial—"

The interphone buzzed, and Hamner answered it absently. It was the butler to announce that his car and driver were waiting. "I'll be late, sweetheart. Don't wait up for me. But you might think about it . . . I swear Falkenberg is the key to something, and I wish I knew what."

"Do you like him?" Laura asked.

"He isn't a man who tries to be liked."

"I asked if *you* like him."

"Yes. And there's no reason to. I like him, but can I trust him?"

As he went out he thought about that. Could he trust Falkenberg? With Laura's life . . . and the kids . . . and for that matter, with a whole planet that seemed headed for hell and no way out.

The troops were camped in an orderly square. Earth ramparts had been thrown up around the perimeter, and the tents were pitched in lines that might have been laid with a transit.

The equipment was scrubbed and polished, blanket rolls were tight, each item in the same place inside the two-man tents . . . but the men were milling about, shouting, gambling openly in front of the campfires. There were plenty of bottles in evidence even from the outer gates.

"Halt! Who's there?"

Hamner started. The car had stopped at the barricaded gate, but Hamner hadn't seen the sentry. This was his first visit to the camp at night, and he was edgy. "Vice President Hamner," he answered.

A strong light played on his face from the opposite side of the car. Two sentries, then, and both invisible until he'd come on them. "Good evening, sir," the first sentry said. "I'll pass the word you're here."

He raised a small communicator to his lips. "Corporal of the Guard, Post Number Five." Then he shouted the same thing, the call ringing clear in the night. A few heads around campfires turned toward the gate, then went back to their other activities.

Hamner was escorted across the camp to officers' row. The huts and tent stood across a wide parade ground from the densely packed company streets of the troops and had their own guards.

Over in the company area the men were singing, and Hamner paused to listen.

"I've a head like a concertina, and I think I'm ready
    to die,
and I'm here in the clink for a thundrin' drink and
    blacking the Corporal's eye,
With another man's cloak underneath of my head
and a beautiful view of the yard,
it's the crapaud for me, and no more System D,
I was Drunk and Resistin' the Guard!
Mad drunk and resistin' the guard!
   It's the crapaud for me, and no more System D,
   I was Drunk and Resistin' the Guard."

Falkenberg came out of his hut. "Good evening, sir. What brings you here?"

I'll just bet you'd like to know, Hamner thought. "I have a few things to discuss with you, Colonel. About the organization of the constabulary."

"Certainly." Falkenberg was crisp and seemed slightly nervous. Hamner wondered if he were drunk. "Shall we go to the Mess?" Falkenberg asked. "More comfortable there, and I haven't got my quarters made up for visitors."

Or you've got something here I shouldn't see, George thought. Something or someone. Local girl? What difference does it make? God, I wish I could trust this man.

Falkenberg led the way to the ranch house in the center of officers' row. The troops were still shouting and singing, and a group was chasing each other on the parade ground. Most were dressed in the blue and yellow garrison uniforms Falkenberg had designed, but others trotted past in synthileather battledress. They carried rifles and heavy packs.

"Punishment detail," Falkenberg explained. "Not as many of those as there used to be."

Sound crashed from the Officers' Mess building: drums and bagpipes, a wild sound of war mingled with shouted laughter. Inside, two dozen men sat at a long table as white-coated stewards moved briskly about with whiskey bottles and glasses.

Kilted bandsmen marched around the table with pipes. Drummers stood in one corner. The deafening noise stopped as Falkenberg entered, and everyone got to his feet. Some were quite unsteady.

"Carry on," Falkenberg said, but no one did. They eyed

96

Hamner nervously, and at a wave from the mess president at the head of the table the pipers and drummers went outside. Several stewards with bottles followed them. The other officers sat and talked in low tones. After all the noise the room seemed very quiet.

"We'll sit over here, shall we?" the colonel asked. He led Hamner to a small table in one corner. A steward brought two glasses of whiskey and set them down.

The room seemed curiously bare to Hamner. A few banners, some paintings; very little else. Somehow, he thought, there ought to be more. As if they're waiting. But that's ridiculous.

Most of the officers were strangers, but George recognized half a dozen Progressives, the highest rank a first lieutenant. He waved at the ones he knew and received brief smiles that seemed almost guilty before the Party volunteers turned back to their companions.

"Yes, sir?" Falkenberg prompted.

"Just who are these men?" George demanded. "I know they're not native to Hadley. Where did they come from?"

"CoDominium officers on the beach," Falkenberg answered promptly. "Reduction in force. Lots of good men got riffed into early retirement. Some of them heard I was coming here and chose to give up their reserve ranks. They came out on the colony ship on the chance I'd hire them."

"And you did."

"Naturally I jumped at the chance to get experienced men at prices we could afford."

"But why all the secrecy? Why haven't I heard about them before?"

Falkenberg shrugged. "We've violated several of the Grand Senate's regulations on mercenaries, you know. It's best not to talk about these things until the CD has definitely gone. After that, the men are committed. They'll have to stay loyal to Hadley." Falkenberg lifted his whiskey glass. "Vice President Bradford knew all about it."

"I'll bet he did." Hamner lifted his own glass. "Cheers."

"Cheers."

And I wonder what else that little snake knows about, Hamner wondered. Without his support Falkenberg would be out of here in a minute . . . and what then? "Colonel, your organization charts came to my office yesterday. You've kept all the Marines in one battalion with these newly hired officers. Then you've got three battalions of locals, but all the Party stalwarts are in the Fourth. The Second and Third are local recruits, but under your own men."

"That's a fair enough description, yes, sir," Falkenberg said.

And you know my question, George thought. "Why, Colonel? A suspicious man would say that you've got your own little army here, with a structure set so that you can take complete control if there's ever a difference of opinion between you and the government."

"A suspicious man might say that," Falkenberg agreed. He drained his glass and waited for George to do the same. A steward came over with freshly filled glasses.

"But a practical man might say something else," Falkenberg continued. "Do you expect me to put green officers in command of those guardhouse troops? Or your good-hearted Progressives in command of green recruits?"

"But you've done just that—"

"On Mr. Bradford's orders I've kept the Fourth Battalion as free of my mercenaries as possible. That isn't helping their training, either. But Mr. Bradford seems to have the same complaint as you."

"I haven't complained."

"I thought you had," Falkenberg said. "In any event, you have your Party force, if you wish to use it to control me. Actually you have all the control you need anyway. You hold the purse strings. Without supplies to feed these men and money to pay them, I couldn't hold them an hour."

"Troops have found it easier to rob the paymaster than fight for him before now," Hamner observed. "Cheers." He drained the glass, then suppressed a cough. The stuff was strong, and he wasn't used to drinking neat whiskey. He wondered what would happen if he ordered something else, beer, or a mixed drink. Somehow it didn't seem to go with the party.

"I might have expected that remark from Bradford," Falkenberg said.

Hamner nodded. Bradford was always suspicious of something. There were times when George wondered if the First Vice President were quite sane, but that was silly. Still, when the pressure was on, Ernie Bradford did manage to get on people's nerves with his suspicions, and he would rather see nothing done than give up control of anything.

"How am I supposed to organize this coup?" Falkenberg demanded. "I have a handful of men loyal to me. The rest are mercenaries, or your locals. You've paid a lot to bring me and my staff here. You want us to fight impossible odds with nonexistent equipment. If you also insist on your own organization of forces, I cannot accept the responsibility."

"I didn't say that."

Falkenberg shrugged. "If President Budreau so orders, and he would on your recommendation, I'll turn command over to anyone he names."

And he'd name Bradford, Hamner thought. I'd rather trust Falkenberg. Whatever Falkenberg does will at least be competently done; with Ernie there was no assurance he wasn't up to something, and none that he'd be able to accomplish anything if he wasn't.

But. "What do you want out of this, Colonel Falkenberg?"

The question seemed to surprise the colonel. "Money, of course," Falkenberg answered. "A little glory, perhaps, although that's not a word much used nowadays. A position of responsibility commensurate with my abilities. I've always been a soldier, and I know nothing else."

"And why didn't you stay with the CD?"

"It is in the record," Falkenberg said coldly. "Surely you know."

"But I don't." Hamner was calm, but the whiskey was enough to make him bolder than he'd intended to be, even in this camp surrounded by Falkenberg's men. "I don't know at all. It makes no sense as I've been told it. You had no reason to complain about promotion, and the Admiral had no reason to prefer charges. It looks as if you had yourself cashiered."

Falkenberg nodded. "You're nearly correct. Astute of you." The soldier's lips were tight and his gray eyes bored into Hamner. "I suppose you are entitled to an answer. Grand Senator Bronson has sworn to ruin me for reasons you needn't know. If I hadn't been dismissed for a trivial charge of technical insubordination, I'd have faced a series of trumped-up charges. At least this way I'm out with a clean record."

A clean record and a lot of bitterness. "And that's all there is to it?"

"That's all."

It was plausible. So was everything else Falkenberg said.

99

Yet Hamner was sure that Falkenberg was lying. Not lying directly, but not telling everything either. Hamner felt that if he knew the right questions he could get the answers, but there weren't any questions to ask.

And, Hamner thought, I must either trust this man or get rid of him; and to irritate him while keeping him is the stupidest policy of all.

The pipers came back in, and the mess president looked to Falkenberg. "Something more?" Falkenberg asked.

"No."

"Thank you." The colonel nodded to the junior officer. The mess president waved approval to the pipe major. Pipe major raised his mace, and the drums crashed. The pipers began, standing in place at first, then marching around the table. Officers shouted, and the room was filled with martial cries. The party was on again.

George looked for one of his own appointees and discovered that every Progressive officer in the room was one of his own. There wasn't a single man from Bradford's wing of the Party. Was that significant?

He rose and caught the eye of a Progressive lieutenant. "I'll let Farquhar escort me out, Colonel," Hamner said.

"As you please."

The noise followed them out of the building and along the regimental street. There were more sounds from the parade ground and the camp beyond. Fires burned brightly in the night.

"All right, Jamie, what's going on here?" Hamner demanded.

"Going on, sir? Nothing that I know of. If you mean the party, we're celebrating the men's graduation from basic training. Tomorrow they'll start advanced work."

"Maybe I meant the party," Hamner said. "You seem pretty friendly with the other officers."

"Yes, sir." Hamner noted the enthusiasm in Jamie Farquhar's voice. The boy was young enough to be caught up in the military mystique, and George felt sorry for him. "They're good men," Jamie said.

"Yes, I suppose so. Where are the others? Mr. Bradford's people?"

"They had a field problem that kept them out of camp until late," Farquhar said. "Mr. Bradford came around about dinner time and asked that they be sent to a meeting somewhere. He spends a lot of time with them."

"I expect he does," Hamner said. "Look, you've been around the Marines, Jamie. Where are those men from? What CD outfits?"

"I really don't know, sir. Colonel Falkenberg has forbidden us to ask. He says that the men start with a clean record here."

Hamner noted the tone Farquhar used when he mentioned Falkenberg. More than respect. Awe, perhaps. "Have any of them served with the colonel before?"

"I think so, yes, sir. They don't like him. Curse the colonel quite openly. But they're afraid of that big sergeant major of his. Calvin has offered to whip any two men in the camp, and they can choose the rules. A few of the newcomers tried it, but none of the Marines would. Not one."

"And you say the colonel's not popular with the men?"

Farquhar was thoughtful for a moment. "I wouldn't say he was *popular*, no sir."

Yet, Hamner thought, Boris had said he was. Whiskey buzzed in George's head. "Who is popular?"

"Major Savage, sir. The men like him. And Captain Fast, the Marines particularly respect him. He's the adjutant."

"All right. Look, can this outfit fight? Have we got a chance after the CD leaves?" They stood and watched the scenes around the campfires. Men were drinking heavily, shouting and singing and chasing each other through the camp. There was a fist fight in front of one tent, and no officer moved to stop it.

"Do you allow that?" Hamner demanded.

"We try not to interfere too much," Farquhar said. "The colonel says half an officer's training is learning what *not* to see. Anyway, the sergeants have broken up the fight, see?"

"But you let the men drink."

"Sir, there's no regulation against drinking. Only against being unfit for duty. And these men are tough. They obey orders and they can fight. I think we'll do rather well."

Pride. They've put some pride into Jamie Farquhar, and maybe into some of those jailbirds out there too. "All right, Jamie. Go back to your party. I'll find my driver."

As he was driven away, George Hamner felt better about Hadley's future, but he was still convinced something was wrong; and he had no idea what it was.

IX

The Stadium had been built to hold one hundred thousand people. There were at least that many jammed inside it now, and an equal number swarmed about the market squares and streets adjacent to it. The full CoDominium Marine garrison was on duty to keep order, but it wasn't needed.

The celebration was boisterous, but there wouldn't be any trouble today. The Freedom Party was as anxious to avoid an incident as the Marines on this, the greatest day for Hadley since Discovery. The CoDominium was turning over power to local authority and getting out; and nothing must spoil that.

Hamner and Falkenberg watched from the upper tiers of the Stadium. Row after row of plastisteel seats cascaded like a giant staircase down from their perch to the central grassy field below. Every seat was filled, so that the Stadium was a riot of color.

President Budreau and Governor Flaherty stood in the Presidential box directly across from Falkenberg and Hamner. The President's Guard, in blue uniforms, and the CoDominium Marines, in their scarlet and gold, stood at rigid attention around the officials.

The President's box was shared by Vice President Bradford, the Freedom Party opposition leaders, Progressive officials, officers of the retiring CoDominium government, and everyone else who could beg an invitation. George knew that some of them were wondering where he had got off to.

Bradford would particularly notice Hamner's absence. He might, George thought, even think the Second Vice President was out stirring up opposition or rebellion. Ernie Bradford had lately been accusing Hamner of every kind of disloyalty to the Progressive Party, and it wouldn't be long before he demanded that Budreau dismiss him.

To the devil with the little man! George thought. He hated crowds, and the thought of standing there and listening to all those speeches, of being polite to party officials whom he detested, was just too much. When he'd suggested watching from another vantage point, Falkenberg had quickly agreed. The soldier didn't seem to care too much for formal ceremonies either. Civilian ceremonies, Hamner corrected himself; Falkenberg seemed to like military parades.

The ritual was almost over. The CD Marine bands had marched through the field, the speeches had been made, presents delivered and accepted. A hundred thousand people had cheered, and it was an awesome sound. The raw power was frightening.

Hamner glanced at his watch. As he did the Marine band broke into a roar of drums. The massed drummers ceased to beat one by one until there was but a single drum roll that went on and on and on, until finally it too stopped. The entire Stadium waited.

One trumpet, no more. A clear call, plaintive but triumphant, the final salute to the CoDominium banner above the Palace. The notes hung in Hadley's air like something tangible, and slowly, deliberately, the crimson and blue banner floated down from the flagpole as Hadley's blazing gold and green arose.

Across the city uniformed men saluted these flags, one rising, the other setting. The blue uniforms of Hadley saluted with smiles, the red-uniformed Marines with indifference. The CoDominium banner rose and fell across two hundred lightyears and seventy worlds in this year of Grace; what difference would one minor planet make?

Hamner glanced at John Falkenberg. The colonel had no eyes for the rising banners of Hadley. His rigid salute was given to the CD flag, and as the last note of the final trumpet salute died away Hamner thought he saw Falkenberg wipe his eyes.

The gesture was so startling that George looked again, but there was nothing more to see, and he decided that he had been mistaken.

"That's it, then," Falkenberg snapped. His voice was strained. "I suppose we ought to join the party. Can't keep His Nibs waiting."

Hamner nodded. The Presidential box connected directly to the Palace, and the officials would arrive at the reception quickly while Falkenberg and Hamner had the entire width of the crowded Stadium to traverse. People were already streaming out to join the festive crowds on the grass in the center of the bowl.

"Let's go this way," George said. He led Falkenberg to the top of the Stadium and into a small alcove where he used a key to open an inconspicuous door. "Tunnel system takes us right into the Palace, across and under the Stadium," he told Falkenberg. "Not exactly secret, but we don't want the people to know about it because they'd demand we open it to the public. Built for maintenance crews, mostly." He locked the door behind them and waved expressively at the wide interior corridor. "Place was pretty well designed, actually."

The grudging tone of admiration wasn't natural to him. If a thing was well done, it was well done . . . but lately he found himself talking that way about CoDominium projects. He resented the whole CD administration and the men who'd dumped the job of governing after creating problems no one could solve.

They wound down stairways and through more passages, then up to another set of locked doors. Through those was the Palace courtyard. The celebrations were already under way, and it would be a long night.

George wondered what would come now. In the morning the last CD boat would rise, and the CoDominium would be gone. Tomorrow, Hadley would be alone with her problems.

"Tensh-Hut!" Sergeant Major Calvin's crisp command cut through the babble.

"Please be seated, gentlemen." Falkenberg took his place at the head of the long table in the command room of what had been the central headquarters for the CoDominium Marines.

Except for the uniforms and banners there were few changes from what people already called "the old days." The officers were seated in the usual places for a regimental staff meeting. Maps hung along one wall, and a computer output screen dominated another. Stewards in white coats brought coffee and discreetly retired behind the armed sentries outside.

Falkenberg looked at the familiar scene and knew the

104

constabulary had occupied the Marine barracks for two days; the Marines had been there twenty years.

A civilian lounged in the seat reserved for the regimental intelligence officer. His tunic was a riot of colors; he was dressed in current Earth fashions, with a brilliant cravat and baggy sleeves. A long sash took the place of a belt and concealed his pocket calculator. Hadley's upper classes were only just beginning to wear such finery.

"You all know why we're here," Falkenberg told the assembled officers. "Those of you who've served with me before know I don't hold many staff councils. They are customary among mercenary units, however. Sergeant Major Calvin will represent the enlisted personnel of the regiment."

There were faint titters. Calvin had been associated with John Falkenberg for eighteen standard years. Presumably they had differences of opinion, but no one ever saw them. The idea of the RSM opposing his colonel in the name of the troops was amusing. On the other hand, no colonel could afford to ignore the views of his sergeants' mess.

Falkenberg's frozen features relaxed slightly as if he appreciated his own joke. His eyes went from face to face. Everyone in the room was a former Marine, and all but a very few had served with him before. The Progressive officers were on duty elsewhere—and it had taken careful planning by the adjutant to accomplish that without suspicion.

Falkenberg turned to the civilian. "Dr. Whitlock, you've been on Hadley for sixty-seven days. That's not very long to make a planetary study, but it's about all the time we have. Have you reached any conclusions?"

"Yeah." Whitlock spoke with an exaggerated drawl that most agreed was affected. "Not much different from Fleet's evaluation, Colonel. Can't think why you went to the expense of bringin' me out here. Your Intelligence people know their jobs about as well as I know mine."

Whitlock sprawled back in his seat and looked very relaxed and casual in the midst of the others' military formality. There was no contempt in his manner. The military had one set of rules and he had another, and he worked well with soldiers.

"Your conclusions are similar to Fleet's, then," Falkenberg said.

"With the limits of analysis, yes, sir. Doubt any competent man could reach a different conclusion. This planet's headed for barbarism within a generation."

There was no sound from the other officers but several were startled. Good training kept them from showing it.

Whitlock produced a cigar from a sleeve pocket and inspected it carefully. "You want the analysis?" he asked.

"A summary, please." Falkenberg looked at each face again. Major Savage and Captain Fast weren't surprised; they'd known before they came to Hadley. Some of the junior officers and company commanders had obviously guessed.

"Simple enough," Whitlock said. "There's no self-sustaining technology for a population half this size. Without imports the standard of livin's bound to fall. Some places they could take that, but not here.

"Here, when they can't get their pretty gadgets, 'stead of workin' the people here in Refuge will demand the Government do something about it. Guv'mint's in no position to refuse, either. Not strong enough.

"So they'll have to divert investment capital into consumer goods. There'll be a decrease in technological efficiency, and then fewer goods, leadin' to more demands, and another cycle just like before. Hard to predict just what comes after that, but it can't be good.

"Afore long, then, they won't have the technological resources to cope even if they could get better organized. It's not a new pattern, Colonel. Fleet saw it comin' a while back. I'm surprised you didn't take their word for it."

Falkenberg nodded. "I did, but with something this important I thought I better get another opinion. You've met the Freedom Party leaders, Dr. Whitlock. Is there any chance they could keep civilization if they governed?"

Whitlock laughed. It was a long drawn-out laugh, relaxed, totally out of place in a military council. " 'Bout as much chance as for a 'gator to turn loose of a hog, Colonel. Even assumin' they know what to do, how can they do it? Suppose they get a vision and try to change their policies? Somebody'll start a new party along the lines of the Freedom Party's present thinkin'.

"Colonel, you will *never* convince all them people there's things the Guv'mint just *cain't* do. They don't want to believe it, and there's always goin' to be slick talkers willin' to say it's all a plot. Now, if the Progressive Party, which has the right ideas already, was to set up to rule strong, they might be able to keep something goin' a while longer."

"Do you think they can?" Major Savage asked.

"Nope. They might have fun tryin'," Whitlock answered. "Problem is that independent countryside. There's not enough support for what they'd have to do in city or country. Eventually that's all got to change, but the revolution that gives this country a real powerful government's going to be one bloody mess, I can tell you. A long drawn-out bloody mess at that."

"Haven't they any hope at all?" The questioner was a junior officer newly promoted to company commander.

Whitlock sighed. "Every place you look, you see problems. City's vulnerable to any sabotage that stops the food plants, for instance. And the fusion generators ain't exactly eternal, either. They're runnin' 'em hard without enough time off for maintenance. Hadley's operating on its capital, not its income, and pretty soon there's not goin' to be any capital to operate off of."

"And that's your conclusion," Falkenberg said. "It doesn't sound precisely like the perfect place for us to retire to."

"Sure doesn't," Whitlock agreed. He stretched elaborately. "Cut it any way you want to, this place isn't going to be self-sufficient without a lot of blood spilled."

"Could they ask for help from American Express?" the junior officer asked.

"They could ask, but they won't get it," Whitlock said. "Son, this planet was neutralized by agreement way back when the CD Governor came aboard. Now the Russians aren't going to let a U.S. company like AmEx take it back into the U.S. sphere, same as the U.S. won't let the Commies come in and set up shop. Grand Senate would order a quarantine on this system just like that." The historian snapped his fingers. "Whole purpose of the CoDominium."

"One thing bothers me," Captain Fast said. "You've been assuming that the CD will simply let Hadley revert to barbarism. Won't BuRelock and the Colonial Office come back if things get that desperate?"

"No."

"You seem rather positive," Major Savage observed.

"I'm positive," Dr. Whitlock said. "Budgets got cut again this year. They don't have the resources to take on a place like Hadley. BuRelock's got its own worries."

"But—" The lieutenant who'd asked the questions earlier

sounded worried. "Colonel, what could happen to the Bureau of Relocation?"

"As Dr. Whitlock says, no budget," Falkenberg answered. "Gentlemen, I shouldn't have to tell you about that. You've seen what the Grand Senate did to the Fleet. That's why you're demobilized. And Kaslov's people have several new seats on the Presidium next year, just as Harmon's gang has won some minor elections in the States. Both those outfits want to abolish the CD, and they've had enough influence to get everyone's appropriations cut to the bone."

"But population control has to ship people out, sir," the lieutenant protested.

"Yes." Falkenberg's face was grim; perhaps he was recalling his own experiences with population control's methods. "But they have to employ worlds closer to Earth, regardless of the problems that may cause for the colonists. Marginal exploitation ventures like Hadley's mines are being shut down. This isn't the only planet the CD's abandoning this year." His voice took on a note of thick irony. "Excuse me. Granting independence."

"So they can't rely on CoDominium help," Captain Fast said.

"No. If Hadley's going to reach takeoff, it's got to do it on its own."

"Which Dr. Whitlock says is impossible," Major Savage observed. "John, we've got ourselves into a cleft stick, haven't we?"

"I said it was unlikely, not that it was impossible," Whitlock reminded them. "It'll take a government stronger than anything Hadley's liable to get, though. And some smart people making the right moves. Or maybe there'll be some luck. Like a good, selective plague. Now that'd do it. Plague to kill off the right people—but if it got too many, there wouldn't be enough left to take advantage of the technology, so I don't suppose that's the answer either."

Falkenberg nodded grimly. "Thank you, Dr. Whitlock. Now, gentlemen, I want battalion commanders and headquarters officers to read Dr. Whitlock's report. Meanwhile, we have another item. Major Savage will shortly make a report to the Progressive Party Cabinet, and I want you to pay attention. We will have a critique after his presentation. Major?"

Savage stood and went to the readout screen. "Gentlemen." He used the wall console to bring an organization chart onto the screen.

"The regiment consists of approximately two thousand officers and men. Of these, five hundred are former Marines, and another five hundred are Progressive partisans organized under officers appointed by Mr. Vice President Bradford.

"The other thousand are general recruits. Some of them are passable mercenaries, and some are local youngsters who want to play soldier and would be better off in a national guard. All recruits have received basic training comparable to CD Marine ground basic without assault, fleet, or jump schooling. Their performance has been somewhat better than we might expect from a comparable number of Marine recruits in CD service.

"This morning, Mr. Bradford ordered the Colonel to remove the last of our officers and non-coms from the Fourth Battalion, and as of this P.M. the Fourth will be totally under the control of officers appointed by First Vice President Bradford. He has not informed us of the reason for this order."

Falkenberg nodded. "In your estimate, Major, are the troops ready for combat duties?" Falkenberg listened idly as he drank coffee. The briefing was rehearsed, and he knew what Savage would answer. The men were trained, but they did not as yet make up a combat unit. Falkenberg waited until Savage had finished the presentation. "Recommendations?"

"Recommend that the Second Battalion be integrated with the First, sir. Normal practice is to form each maniple with one recruit, three privates, and a monitor in charge. With equal numbers of new men and veterans we will have a higher proportion of recruits, but this will give us two battalions of men under our veteran NCO's, with Marine privates for leavening.

"We will thus break up the provisional training organization and set up the regiment with a new permanent structure, First and Second Battalions for combat duties, Third composed of locals with former Marine officers to be held in reserve. The Fourth will not be under our command."

"Your reasons for this organization?" Falkenberg asked.

"Morale, sir. The new troops feel discriminated against. They're under harsher discipline than the former Marines, and they resent it. Putting them in the same maniples with the Marines will stop that."

"Let's see the new structure."

Savage manipulated the input console and charts swam across the screen. The administrative structure was standard, based in part on the CD Marines and the rest on the national armies of Churchill. That wasn't the important part. It wasn't obvious, but the structure demanded that all the key posts be held by Falkenberg's mercenaries.

The best Progressive appointees were either in the Third or Fourth Battalions, and there were no locals with the proper experience in command; so went the justification. It looked good to Falkenberg, and there was no sound military reason to question it. Bradford would be so pleased about his new control of the Fourth that he wouldn't look at the rest; not yet, anyway. The others didn't know enough to question it.

Yes, Falkenberg thought. It ought to work. He waited until Savage was finished and thanked him, then addressed the others. "Gentlemen, if you have criticisms, let's hear them now. I want a solid front when we get to the Cabinet meeting tomorrow, and I want every one of you ready to answer any question. I don't have to tell you how important it is that they buy this."

They all nodded.

"And another thing," Falkenberg said. "Sergeant Major."

"Sir!"

"As soon as the Cabinet has bought off on this new organization plan, I want this regiment under normal discipline."

"Sir!"

"Break it to 'em hard, Top Soldier. Tell the Forty-second the act's over. From here on recruits and old hands get treated alike, and the next man who gives me trouble will wish he hadn't been born."

"Sir!" Calvin smiled happily. The last months had been a strain for everyone. Now the colonel was taking over again, thank God. The men had lost some of the edge, but he'd soon put it back again. It was time to take off the masks, and Calvin for one was glad of it.

X

THE SOUND OF fifty thousand people shouting in unison can be terrifying. It raises fears at a level below thought; creates a panic older than the fear of nuclear weapons and the whole panoply of technology. It is raw, naked power from a cauldron of sound.

Everyone in the Palace listened to the chanting crowd. The Government people were outwardly calm, but they moved quietly through the halls, and spoke in low tones—or shouted for no reason. The Palace was filled with a nameless fear.

The Cabinet meeting started at dawn and continued until late in the morning. It had gone on and on without settling anything. Just before noon Vice President Bradford stood at his place at the council table with his lips tight in rage. He pointed a trembling finger at George Hamner.

"It's your fault!" Bradford shouted. "Now the technicians have joined in the demand for a new constitution, and you control them. I've always said you were a traitor to the Progressive Party!"

"Gentlemen, please," President Budreau insisted. His voice held infinite weariness. "Come now, that sort of language—"

"Traitor?" Hamner demanded. "If your blasted officials would pay a little attention to the technicians, this wouldn't have happened. In three months you've managed to convert the techs from the staunchest supporters of this Party into allies of the rebels despite everything I could do."

"We need strong government," Bradford said. His voice was contemptuous, and the little half-smile had returned.

George Hamner made a strong effort to control his anger. "You won't get it this way. You've herded my techs around like cattle, worked them overtime for no extra pay, and set those damned soldiers of yours onto them when they protested. It's worth a man's life to have your constabulary mad at him."

"Resisting the police," Bradford said. "We can't permit that."

"You don't know what government is!" Hamner said. His control vanished and he stood, towering above Bradford. The little man retreated a step, and his smile froze. "You've got the nerve to call me a traitor after all you've done! I ought to break your neck!"

"Gentlemen!" Budreau stood at his place at the head of the table. "Stop it!" There was a roar from the Stadium. The Palace seemed to vibrate to the shouts of the constitutional convention.

The Cabinet room became silent for a moment. Wearily, Budreau continued. "This isn't getting us anywhere. I suggest we adjourn for half an hour to allow tempers to cool."

There was murmured agreement from the others.

"And I want no more of these accusations and threats when we convene again," President Budreau said. "Is that understood?"

Grudgingly the others agreed. Budreau left alone. Then Bradford, followed by a handful of his closest supporters. Other ministers rushed to be seen leaving with him, as if it might be dangerous to be thought in opposition to the First Vice President.

George Hamner found himself alone in the room. He shrugged, and went out. Ernest Bradford had been joined by a man in uniform. Hamner recognized Lieutenant Colonel Cordova, commander of the Fourth Battalion of constabulary, and a fanatic Bradford supporter. Hamner remembered when Bradford had first proposed a commission for Cordova, and how unimportant it had seemed then.

Bradford's group went down the hall. They seemed to be whispering something together and making a point of excluding the Second Vice President. Hamner merely shrugged.

"Buy you a coffee?" The voice came from behind and startled George. He turned to see Falkenberg.

"Sure. Not that it's going to do any good. We're in trouble, Colonel."

"Anything decided?" Falkenberg asked. "It's been a long wait."

"And a useless one. They ought to invite you into the

Cabinet meetings. You might have some good advice. There's sure as hell no reason to keep you waiting in an anteroom while we yell at each other. I've tried to change that policy, but I'm not too popular right now." There was another shout from the Stadium.

"Whole government's not too popular," Falkenberg said. "And when that convention gets through. . . ."

"Another thing I tried to stop last week," George told him. "But Budreau didn't have the guts to stand up to them. So now we've got fifty thousand drifters, with nothing better to do, sitting as an assembly of the people. That ought to produce quite a constitution."

Falkenberg shrugged. He might have been about to say something, George thought, but if he were, he changed his mind. They reached the executive dining room and took seats near one wall. Bradford's group had a table across the room from them, and all of Bradford's people looked at them with suspicion.

"You'll get tagged as a traitor for sitting with me, Colonel." Hamner laughed, but his voice was serious. "I think I meant that, you know. Bradford's blaming me for our problems with the techs, and between us he's also insisting that you aren't doing enough to restore order in the city."

Falkenberg ordered coffee. "Do I need to explain to you why we haven't?"

"No." George Hamner's huge hand engulfed a water glass. "God knows you've been given almost no support the last couple of months. Impossible orders, and you've never been allowed to do anything decisive. I see you've stopped the raids on rebel headquarters."

Falkenberg nodded. "We weren't catching anyone. Too many leaks in the Palace. And most of the time the Fourth Battalion had already muddied the waters. If they'd let us do our job instead of having to ask permisson through channels for every operation we undertake, maybe the enemy wouldn't know as much about what we're going to do. Now I've quit asking."

"You've done pretty well with the railroad."

"Yes. That's one success, anyway. Things are pretty quiet out in the country where we're on our own. Odd, isn't it, that the closer we are to the expert supervision of the government, the less effective my men seem to be?"

"But can't you control Cordova's men? They're causing

more people to desert us for the rebels than you can count. I can't believe unrestrained brutality is useful."

"Nor I. Unless there's a purpose to it, force isn't a very effective instrument of government. But surely you know, Mr. Hamner, that I have no control over the Fourth. Mr. Bradford has been expanding it since he took control, and it's now almost as large as the rest of the regiment—and totally under his control, not mine."

"Bradford accused me of being a traitor," Hamner said carefully. "With his own army, he might have something planned. . . ."

"You once thought that of me," Falkenberg said.

"This is very serious," Hamner said. "Ernie Bradford has built an army only he controls, and he's making wild accusations."

Falkenberg smiled grimly. "I wouldn't worry about it too much."

"You wouldn't? No. You wouldn't. But I'm scared, Colonel. I've got my family to think of, and I'm plenty scared." Well, George thought, now it's out in the open; can I trust him not to be Ernie Bradford's man?

"You believe Bradford is planning an illegal move?" Falkenberg asked.

"I don't know." Suddenly George was afraid again. He saw no sympathy in the other man's eyes. And just who can I trust? Who? Anyone?

"Would you feel safer if your family were in our regimental barracks?" Falkenberg asked. "It could be arranged."

"It's about time we had something out," George said at last. "Yes, I'd feel safer with my wife and children under protection. But I'd feel safer yet if you'd level with me."

"About what?" Falkenberg's expression didn't change.

"Those Marines of yours, to begin with," George said. "Those aren't penal battalion men. I've watched them, they're too well disciplined. And the battle banners they carry weren't won in any peanut actions, on this planet or anywhere else. Just who are those men, Colonel?"

John Falkenberg smiled thinly. "I've been wondering when you'd ask. Why haven't you brought this up with President Budreau?"

"I don't know. I think because I trust you more than Bradford, and the President would only ask him. . , besides, if the President dismissed you there'd be nobody able to oppose Ernie. If you will oppose him that is—but you can stand up to him, anyway."

"What makes you think I would?" Falkenberg asked. "I obey the lawful orders of the civilian government—"

"Yeah, sure. Hadley's going downhill so fast another conspiracy more or less can't make any difference anyway. . . you haven't answered my question."

"The battle banners are from the Forty-second CD Marine Regiment," Falkenberg answered slowly. "It was decommissioned as part of the budget cuts."

"Forty-second." Hamner thought for a second. He searched through his mental files to find the information he'd seen on Falkenberg. "That was your regiment."

"Certainly."

"You brought it with you."

"A battalion of it," John Falkenberg agreed. "Their women are waiting to join them when we get settled. When the Forty-second was decommissioned, the men decided to stay together if they could."

"So you brought not only the officers, but the men as well."

"Yes." There was still no change in Falkenberg's expression, although Hamner searched the other man's face closely.

George felt both fear and relief. If those were Falkenberg's men—"What is your game, Colonel? You want more than just pay for your troops. I wonder if I shouldn't be more afraid of you than of Bradford."

Falkenberg shrugged. "Decisions you have to make, Mr. Hamner. I could give you my word that we mean you no harm, but what would that be worth? I will pledge to take care of your family. If you want us to."

There was another shout from the Stadium, louder this time. Bradford and Lieutenant Colonel Cordova left their table, still talking in low tones. The conversation was animated, with violent gestures, as if Cordova were trying to talk Bradford into something. As they left, Bradford agreed.

George watched them leave the room. The mob shouted again, making up his mind for him. "I'll send Laura and the kids over to your headquarters this afternoon."

"Better make it immediately," Falkenberg said calmly.

George frowned. "You mean there's not much time?

Whatever you've got planned, it'll have to be quick, but this afternoon?"

John shook his head. "You seem to think I have some kind of master plan, Mr. Vice President. No. I suggest you get your wife to our barracks before I'm ordered not to undertake her protection, that's all. For the rest, I'm only a soldier in a political situation."

"With Professor Whitlock to advise you," Hamner said. He looked closely at Falkenberg.

"Surprised you with that one, didn't I?" Hamner demanded. "I've seen Whitlock moving around and wondered why he didn't come to the President. He must have fifty political agents in the convention right now."

"You do seem observant," Falkenberg said.

"Sure." Hamner was bitter. "What the hell good does it do me? I don't understand anything that's going on, and I don't trust anybody. I see pieces of the puzzle, but I can't put them together. Sometimes I think I should use what influence I've got left to get *you* out of the picture anyway."

"As you will." Falkenberg's smile was coldly polite. "Whom do you suggest as guards for your family after that? The Chief of Police? Listen."

The Stadium roared again in an angry sound that swelled in volume.

"You win." Hamner left the table and walked slowly back to the council room. His head swirled.

Only one thing stood out clearly. John Christian Falkenberg controlled the only military force on Hadley that could oppose Bradford's people—and the Freedom Party gangsters, who were the original enemies in the first place. Can't forget them just because I'm getting scared of Ernie, George thought.

He turned away from the council room and went downstairs to the apartment he'd been assigned. The sooner Laura was in the Marine barracks, the safer he'd feel.

But am I sending her to my enemies? O God, can I trust anyone at all? Boris said he was an honorable man. Keep remembering that, keep remembering that. Honor. Falkenberg has honor, and Ernie Bradford has none.

And me? What have I got for leaving the Freedom Party and bringing my technicians over to the Progressives? A meaningless title as Second Vice President, and—

The crowd screamed again. "POWER TO THE PEO-PLE!"

George heard and walked faster.

Bradford's grin was back. It was the first thing George noticed as he came into the council chamber. The little man stood at the table with an amused smile. It seemed quite genuine, and more than a little frightening.

"Ah, here is our noble Minister of Technology and Second Vice President," Bradford grinned. "Just in time. Mr. President, that gang out there is threatening the city. I am sure you will all be pleased to know that I've taken steps to end the situation."

"What have you done?" George demanded.

Bradford's smile broadened even more. "At this moment, Colonel Cordova is arresting the leaders of the opposition. Including, Mr. President, the leaders of the Engineers' and Technicians' Association who have joined them. This rebellion will be over within the hour."

Hamner stared at the man. "You fool! You'll have every technician in the city joining the Freedom Party gang! And the techs control the power plants, our last influence over the crowd. You bloody damned fool!"

Bradford spoke with exaggerated politeness. "I thought you would be pleased, George, to see the rebellion end so easily. Naturally I've sent men to secure the power plants. Ah, listen."

The crowd outside wasn't chanting anymore. There was a confused babble, then a welling of sound that turned ugly. No coherent words reached them, only the ugly, angry roars. Then there was a rapid fusillade of shots.

"My God!" President Budreau stared wildly in confusion. "What's happening? Who are they shooting at? Have you started open war?"

"It takes stern measures, Mr. President," Bradford said. "Perhaps too stern for you?" He shook his head slightly. "The time has come for harsh measures, Mr. President. Hadley cannot be governed by weak-willed men. Our future belongs to those who have the will to grasp it!"

George Hamner turned toward the door. Before he could reach it, Bradford called to him. "Please, George." His voice was filled with concern. "I'm afraid you can't leave just yet. It wouldn't be safe for you. I took the liberty of ordering Colonel Cordova's men to, uh, guard this room while my troops restore order."

An uneasy quiet had settled on the Stadium, and they waited for a long time. Then there were screams and more shots.

The sounds moved closer, as if they were outside the Stadium as well as in it. Bradford frowned, but no one said anything. They waited for what seemed a lifetime as the firing continued. Guns, shouts, screams, sirens, and alarms —those and more, all in confusion.

The door burst open. Cordova came in. He now wore the insignia of a full colonel. He looked around the room until he found Bradford. "Sir, could you come outside a moment, please?"

"You will make your report to the Cabinet," President Budreau ordered. Cordova glanced at Bradford. "Now, sir."

Cordova still looked to Bradford. The Vice President nodded slightly.

"Very well, sir," the young officer said. "As directed by the Vice President, elements of the Fourth Battalion proceeded to the Stadium and arrested some fifty leaders of the so-called constitutional convention.

"Our plan was to enter quickly and take the men out through the Presidential box and into the Palace. However, when we attempted to make the arrests we were opposed by armed men, many in the uniforms of household guards. We were told there were no weapons in the Stadium, but this was in error.

"The crowd overpowered my officers and released their prisoners. When we attempted to recover them, we were attacked by the mob and forced to fight our way out of the Stadium."

"Good Lord," Budreau sighed. "How many hurt?"

"The power plants! Did you secure them?" Hamner demanded.

Cordova looked miserable. "No, sir. My men were not admitted. A council of technicians and engineers holds the power plants, and they threaten to destroy them if we attempt forcible entry. We have tried to seal them off from outside support, but I don't think we can keep order with only my battalion. We will need all the constabulary army to—"

"Idiot." Hamner clutched at his left fist with his right, and squeezed until it hurt. A council of technicians. I'll know most of them. My friends. Or they used to be. Will

118

any of them trust me now? At least Bradford didn't control the fusion plants.

"What is the current status outside?" President Budreau demanded. They could still hear firing in the streets.

"Uh, there's a mob barricaded in the market, and another in the theater across from the Palace, sir. My troops are trying to dislodge them." Cordova's voice was apologetic.

"Trying. I take it they aren't likely to succeed." Budreau rose and went to the anteroom door. "Colonel Falkenberg?" he called.

"Yes, sir?" Falkenberg entered the room as the President beckoned.

"Colonel, are you familiar with the situation outside?"

"Yes, Mr. President."

"Damn it, man, can you do something?"

"What does the President suggest I do?" Falkenberg looked at the Cabinet members. "For three months we have attempted to preserve order in this city. We were not able to do so even with the cooperation of the technicians."

"It wasn't my fault—" Lieutenant Colonel Cordova began.

"I did not invite you to speak." Falkenberg's lips were set in a grim line. "Gentlemen, you now have open rebellion and simultaneously have alienated one of the most powerful blocs within your Party. We no longer control either the power plants or the food processing centers. I repeat, what does the President suggest I do?"

Budreau nodded. "A fair enough criticism."

He was interrupted by Bradford. "Drive that mob off the streets! Use those precious troops of yours to fight, that's what you're here for."

"Certainly," Falkenberg said. "Will the President sign a proclamation of martial law?"

Budreau nodded reluctantly. "I suppose I have to."

"Very well," Falkenberg said.

Hamner looked up suddenly. What had he detected in Falkenberg's voice and manner? Something important?

"It is standard for politicians to get themselves into a situation that only the military can get them out of. It is also standard for them to blame the military afterwards," Falkenberg said. "I am willing to accept responsibility for enforcing martial law, but I must have command of all

119

government forces. I will not attempt to restore order when some of the troops are not responsive to my policies."

"No!" Bradford leaped to his feet. The chair crashed to the floor behind him. "I see what you're doing! You're against me too! That's why it was never time to move, never time for me to be President, you want control of this planet for yourself! Well, you won't get away with it, you cheap dictator. Cordova, arrest that man!"

Cordova licked his lips and looked at Falkenberg. Both soldiers were armed. Cordova decided not to chance it. "Lieutenant Hargreave!" he called. The door to the ante-room opened wider.

No one came in. "Hargreave!" Cordova shouted again. He put his hand on the pistol holstered at his belt. "You're under arrest, Colonel Falkenberg."

"Indeed?"

"This is absurd," Budreau shouted. "Colonel Cordova, take your hand off that weapon! I will not have my Cabinet meeting turned into a farce."

For a moment nothing happened. The room was very still, and Cordova looked from Budreau to Bradford, wondering what to do now.

Then Bradford faced the President. "You too, old man? Arrest Mr. Budreau as well, Colonel Cordova. As for you, Mr. Traitor George Hamner, you'll get what's coming to you. I have men all through this Palace. I knew I might have to do this."

"You knew—what is this, Ernest?" President Budreau seemed bewildered, and his voice was plaintive. "What are you doing?"

"Oh, shut up, old man," Bradford snarled. "I suppose you'll have to be shot as well."

"I think we have heard enough," Falkenberg said distinctly. His voice rang through the room although he hadn't shouted. "And I refuse to be arrested."

"Kill him!" Bradford shouted. He reached under his tunic.

Cordova drew his pistol. It had not cleared the holster when there were shots from the doorway. Their sharp barks filled the room, and Hamner's ears rang from the muzzle blast.

Bradford spun toward the door with a surprised look. Then his eyes glazed and he slid to the floor, the half-smile still on his lips. There were more shots and the crash of automatic weapons, and Cordova was flung against the wall of the council chamber. He was held there by the smashing bullets. Bright red blotches spurted across his uniform.

Sergeant Major Calvin came into the room with three Marines in battle dress, leather over bulging body armor. Their helmets were dull in the bright blue-tinted sunlight streaming through the chamber's windows.

Falkenberg nodded and holstered his pistol. "All secure, Sergeant Major?"

"Sir!"

Falkenberg nodded again. "To quote Mr. Bradford, I took the liberty of securing the corridors, Mr. President. Now, sir, if you will issue that proclamation, I'll see to the situation in the streets outside. Sergeant Major."

"Sir!"

"Do you have the proclamation of martial law that Captain Fast drew up?"

"Sir." Calvin removed a rolled document from a pocket of his leather tunic. Falkenberg took it and laid it on the table in front of President Budreau.

"But—" Budreau's tone was hopeless. "All right. Not that there's much chance." He looked at Bradford's body and shuddered. "He was ready to kill me," Budreau muttered. The President seemed confused. Too much had happened, and there was too much to do.

The battle sounds outside were louder, and the council room was filled with the sharp copper odor of fresh blood. Budreau drew the parchment toward himself and glanced at it, then took out a pen from his pocket. He scrawled his signature across it and handed it to Hamner to witness.

"You'd better speak to the President's Guard," Falkenberg said. "They won't know what to do."

"Aren't you going to use them in the street fight?" Hamner asked.

Falkenberg shook his head. "I doubt if they'd fight. They have too many friends among the rebels. They'll protect the Palace, but they won't be reliable for anything else."

"Have we got a chance?" Hamner asked.

Budreau looked up from his reverie at the head of the table. "Yes. Have we?"

"Possibly," Falkenberg said. "Depends on how good the people we're fighting are. If their commander is half as good as I think he is, we won't win this battle."

XI

"GOD DAMN IT, we won't do it!" Lieutenant Martin Latham stared in horror at Captain Fast. "That market's a death trap. These men didn't join to attack across open streets against rioters in safe positions—"

"No. You joined to be glorified police," Captain Fast said calmly. "Now you've let things get out of hand. Who better to put them right again?"

"The Fourth Battalion takes orders from Colonel Cordova, not you." Latham looked around for support. Several squads of the Fourth were within hearing, and he felt reassured.

They stood in a deep indentation of the Palace wall. Just outside and around the corner of the indentation they could hear sporadic firing as the other units of the regiment kept the rebels occupied. Latham felt safe here, but out there—

"No," he repeated. "It's suicide."

"So is refusal to obey orders," Amos Fast said quietly. "Don't look around and don't raise your voice. Now, glance behind me at the Palace walls."

Latham saw them. A flash from a gun barrel; blurs as leather-clad figures settled in on the walls and in the windows overlooking the niche.

"If you don't make the attack, you will be disarmed and tried for cowardice in the face of the enemy," Fast said quietly. "There can be only one outcome of that trial. And only one penalty. You're better off making the assault. We'll support you in that."

"Why are you doing this?" Martin Latham demanded.

"You caused the problem," Fast said. "Now get ready.

When you've entered the market square the rest of the outfit will move up in support."

The assault was successful, but it cost the Fourth heavily. After that came another series of fierce attacks. When they were finished the rioters had been driven from the immediate area of the Palace, but Falkenberg's regiment paid for every meter gained.

Whenever they took a building, the enemy left it blazing. When the regiment trapped one large group of rebels, Falkenberg was forced to abandon the assault to aid in evacuating a hospital that the enemy put to the torch. Within three hours, fires were raging all around the Palace.

There was no one in the council chamber with Budreau and Hamner. The bodies had been removed, and the floor mopped, but it seemed to George Hamner that the room would always smell of death; and he could not keep his eyes from straying from time to time, from staring at the neat line of holes stitched at chest height along the rich wood paneling.

Falkenberg came in. "Your family is safe, Mr. Hamner." He turned to the President. "Ready to report, sir."

Budreau looked up with haunted eyes. The sound of gunfire was faint, but still audible.

"They have good leaders," Falkenberg reported. "When they left the Stadium they went immediately to the police barracks. They took the weapons and distributed them to their allies, after butchering the police."

"They murdered—"

"Certainly," Falkenberg said. "They wanted the police building as a fortress. And we are not fighting a mere mob out there, Mr. President. We have repeatedly run against well-armed men with training. Household forces. I will attempt another assault in the morning, but for now, Mr. President, we don't hold much more than a kilometer around the Palace."

The fires burned all night, but there was little fighting. The regiment held the Palace, with bivouac in the courtyard; and if anyone questioned why the Fourth was encamped in the center of the courtyard with other troops all around them, they did so silently.

Lieutenant Martin Latham might have had an answer for any such questioner, but he lay under Hadley's flag in the honor hall outside the hospital.

In the morning the assaults began again. The regiment moved out in thin streams, infiltrating weak spots, by-passing strong, until it had cleared a large area outside the Palace again. Then it came against another well-fortified position.

An hour later the regiment was heavily engaged against roof-top snipers, barricaded streets, and everywhere burning buildings. Maniples and squads attempted to get through and into the buildings beyond but were turned back.

The Fourth was decimated in repeated assaults against the barricades.

George Hamner had come with Falkenberg and stood in the field headquarters. He watched another platoon assault of the Fourth beaten back. "They're pretty good men," he mused.

"They'll do. Now." Falkenberg said.

"But you've used them up pretty fast."

"Not entirely by choice," Falkenberg said. "The President has ordered me to break the enemy resistance. That squanders soldiers. I'd as soon use the Fourth as blunt the fighting edge of the rest of the regiment."

"But we're not getting anywhere."

"No. The opposition's too good, and there are too many of them. We can't get them concentrated for a set battle, and when we do catch them they set fire to part of the city and retreat under cover of the flames."

A communications corporal beckoned urgently, and Falkenberg went to the low table with its array of electronics. He took the offered earphone and listened, then raised a mike.

"Fall back to the Palace," Falkenberg ordered.

"You're retreating?" Hamner demanded.

Falkenberg shrugged. "I have no choice. I can't hold this thin a perimeter, and I have only two battalions. Plus what's left of the Fourth."

"Where's the Third? The Progressive partisans? My people?"

"Out at the power plants and food centers," Falkenberg answered. "We can't break in without giving the techs time to wreck the place, but we can keep any more rebels from getting in. The Third isn't as well trained as the rest of the regiment—and besides, the techs may trust them."

They walked back through burned-out streets. The

sounds of fighting followed them as the regiment retreated. Civilian workers fought the fires and cared for the wounded and dead.

Hopeless, George Hamner thought. Hopeless. I don't know why I thought Falkenberg would pull some kind of rabbit out of the hat once Bradford was gone. What could he do? What can anyone do?

Worried-looking Presidential Guards let them into the Palace and swung the heavy doors shut behind them. The guards held the Palace, but would not go outside.

President Budreau was in his ornate office with Lieutenant Banners. "I was going to send for you," Budreau said. "We can't win this, can we?"

"Not the way it's going," Falkenberg answered. Hamner nodded agreement.

Budreau nodded rapidly, as if to himself. His face was a mask of lost hopes. "That's what I thought. Pull your men back to barracks, Colonel. I'm going to surrender."

"But you can't," George protested. "Everything we've dreamed of . . . You'll doom Hadley. The Freedom Party can't govern."

"Precisely. And you see it too, don't you, George? How much governing are we doing? Before it came to an open break, perhaps we had a chance. Not now. Bring your men back to the Palace, Colonel Falkenberg. Or are you going to refuse?"

"No, sir. The men are retreating already. They'll be here in half an hour."

Budreau sighed loudly. "I told you the military answer wouldn't work here, Falkenberg."

"We might have accomplished something in the past months if we'd been given the chance."

"You might." The President was too tired to argue. "But putting the blame on poor Ernie won't help. He must have been insane.

"But this isn't three months ago, Colonel. It's not even yesterday. I might have reached a compromise before the fighting started, but I didn't, and you've lost. You're not doing much besides burning down the city. . . at least I can spare Hadley that. Banners, go tell the Freedom Party leaders I can't take anymore."

The Guard officer saluted and left, his face an unreadable mask. Budreau watched him leave the office. His eyes focused far beyond the walls with their Earth decorations.

125

"So you're resigning," Falkenberg said slowly. Budreau nodded.

"Have you resigned, sir?" Falkenberg demanded.

"Yes, blast you. Banners has my resignation."

"And what will you do now?" George Hamner asked. His voice held both contempt and amazement. He had always admired and respected Budreau. And now what had Hadley's great leader left them?

"Banners has promised to get me out of here," Budreau said. "He has a boat in the harbor. We'll sail up the coast and land, then go inland to the mines. There'll be a starship there next week, and I can get out on that with my family. You'd better come with me, George." The President put both hands over his face, then looked up. "There's a lot of relief in giving in, did you know? What will you do, Colonel Falkenberg?"

"We'll manage. There are plenty of boats in the harbor if we need one. But it is very likely that the new government will need trained soldiers."

"The perfect mercenary," Budreau said with contempt. He sighed, then sent his eyes searching around the office, lingering on familiar objects. "It's a relief. I don't have to decide things anymore." He stood and his shoulders were no longer stooped. "I'll get the family. You'd better be moving too, George."

"I'll be along, sir. Don't wait for us. As the Colonel says, there are plenty of boats." He waited until Budreau had left the office, then turned to Falkenberg. "All right, what now?"

"Now we do what we came here to do," Falkenberg said. He went to the President's desk and examined the phones, but rejected them for a pocket communicator. He lifted it and spoke at length.

"Just what are you doing?" Hamner demanded.

"You're not President yet," Falkenberg said. "You won't be until you're sworn in, and that won't happen until I've finished. And there's nobody to accept your resignation, either."

"What the hell?" Hamner looked closely at Falkenberg, but he could not read the officer's expression. "You do have an idea. Let's hear it."

"You're not President yet," Falkenberg said. "Under Budreau's proclamation of martial law, I am to take whatever actions I think are required to restore order in

Refuge. That order is valid until a new President removes it. And at the moment there's no President."

"But Budreau's surrendered! The Freedom Party will elect a President."

"Under Hadley's constitution only the Senate and Assembly in joint session can alter the order of succession. They're scattered across the city and their meeting chambers have been burned."

Sergeant Major Calvin and several of Falkenberg's aides came to the door. They stood, waiting.

"I'm playing guardhouse lawyer," Falkenberg said. "But President Budreau doesn't have the authority to appoint a new President. With Bradford dead, you're in charge here, but not until you appear before a magistrate and take the oath of office."

"This doesn't make sense," Hamner protested. "How long do you think you can stay in control here, anyway?"

"As long as I have to." Falkenberg turned to an aide. "Corporal, I want Mr. Hamner to stay with me and you with him. You will treat him with respect, but he goes nowhere and sees no one without my permission. Understood?"

"Sir!"

"And now what?" Hamner asked.

"And now we wait," John Falkenberg said softly. "But not too long . . ."

George Hamner sat in the council chambers with his back to the stained and punctured wall. He tried to forget those stains, but he couldn't.

Falkenberg was across from him, and his aides sat at the far end of the table. Communications gear had been spread across one side table, but there was no situation map; Falkenberg had not moved his command post here.

From time to time officers brought him battle reports, but Falkenberg hardly listened to them. However, when one of the aides reported that Dr. Whitlock was calling, Falkenberg took the earphones immediately.

George couldn't hear what Whitlock was saying and Falkenberg's end of the conversation consisted of monosyllables. The only thing George was sure of was that Falkenberg was very interested in what his political agent was doing.

The regiment had fought its way back to the Palace and was now in the courtyard. The Palace entrances were held by the Presidential Guard, and the fighting had stopped. The rebels left the guardsmen alone, and an uneasy truce settled across the city of Refuge.

"They're going into the Stadium, sir," Captain Fast reported. "That cheer you heard was when Banners gave 'em the President's resignation."

"I see. Thank you, Captain." Falkenberg motioned for more coffee. He offered a cup to George, but the Vice President didn't want any.

"How long does this go on?" George demanded.

"Not much longer. Hear them cheering?"

They sat for another hour, Falkenberg with outward calm, Hamner with growing tension. Then Dr. Whitlock came to the council room.

The tall civilian looked at Falkenberg and Hamner, then sat easily in the President's chair. "Don't reckon I'll have another chance to sit in the seat of the mighty," he grinned.

"But what is happening?" Hamner demanded.

Whitlock shrugged. "It's 'bout like Colonel Falkenberg figured. Mob's moved right into the Stadium. Nobody wants to be left out now they think they've won. They've rounded up what senators they could find and now they're fixin' to elect themselves a new President."

"But that election won't be valid," Hamner said.

"No, suh, but that don't seem to slow 'em down a bit. They figure they won the right, I guess. And the Guard has already said they're goin' to honor the people's choice." Whitlock smiled ironically.

"How many of my technicians are out there in that mob?" Hamner asked. "They'd listen to me, I know they would."

"They might at that," Whitlock said. "But there's not so many as there used to be. Most of 'em couldn't stomach the burnin' and looting. Still, there's a fair number."

"Can you get them out?" Falkenberg asked.

"Doin' that right now," Whitlock grinned. "One reason I come up here was to get Mr. Hamner to help with that. I got my people goin' round tellin' the technicians they already got Mr. Hamner as President, so why they want somebody else? It's workin' too, but a few words from their leader here might help."

"Right," Falkenberg said. "Well, sir?"

"I don't know what to say," George protested.

Falkenberg went to the wall control panel. "Mr. Vice

128

President, I can't give you orders, but I'd suggest you simply make a few promises. Tell them you will shortly assume command, and that things will be different. Then order them to go home or face charges as rebels. Or ask them to go home as a favor to you. Whatever you think will work."

It wasn't much of a speech, and from the roar outside the crowd did not hear much of it anyway. George promised amnesty for anyone who left the Stadium and tried to appeal to the Progressives who were caught up in the rebellion. When he put down the microphone, Falkenberg seemed pleased.

"Half an hour, Dr. Whitlock?" Falkenberg asked.

"About that," the historian agreed. "All that's leavin' will be gone by then."

"Let's go, Mr. President." Falkenberg was insistent.

"Where?" Hamner asked.

"To see the end of this. Do you want to watch, or would you rather join your family? You can go anywhere you like except to a magistrate—or to someone who might accept your resignation."

"Colonel, this is ridiculous! You can't force me to be President, and I don't understand what's going on."

Falkenberg's smile was grim. "Nor do I want you to understand. Yet. You'll have enough trouble living with yourself as it is. Let's go."

George Hamner followed. His throat was dry, and his guts felt as if they'd knotted themselves into a tight ball.

The First and Second Battalions were assembled in the Palace courtyard. The men stood in ranks. Their synthileather battledress was stained with dirt and smoke from the street fighting. Armor bulged under their uniforms.

The men were silent, and Hamner thought they might have been carved from stone.

"Follow me," Falkenberg ordered. He led the way to the Stadium entrance. Lieutenant Banners stood in the doorway.

"Halt," Banners commanded.

"Really, Lieutenant? Would you fight my troops?" Falkenberg indicated the grim lines behind him.

Lieutenant Banners gulped. Hamner thought the Guard officer looked very young. "No, sir," Banners protested. "But we have barred the doors. The emergency meeting of the Assembly and Senate is electing a new President

129

out there, and we will not permit your mercenaries to interfere."

"They have not elected anyone," Falkenberg said.

"No, sir, but when they do, the Guard will be under his command."

"I have orders from Vice President Hamner to arrest the leaders of the rebellion, and a valid proclamation of martial law," Falkenberg insisted.

"I'm sorry, sir." Banners seemed to mean it. "Our council of officers has decided that President Budreau's surrender is valid. We intend to honor it."

"I see." Falkenberg withdrew. He motioned to his aides, and Hamner joined the group. No one objected.

"Hadn't expected this," Falkenberg said. "It would take a week to fight through those guardrooms." He thought for a moment. "Give me your keys," he snapped at Hamner.

Bewildered, George took them out. Falkenberg grinned widely. "There's another way into there, you know. Major Savage! Take G and H Companies of Second Battalion to secure the Stadium exits. Dig yourselves in and set up all weapons. Arrest anyone who comes out."

"Sir."

"Dig in pretty good, Jeremy. They may be coming out fighting. But I don't expect them to be well organized."

"Do we fire on armed men?"

"Without warning, Major. Without warning. Sergeant Major, bring the rest of the troops with me. Major, you'll have twenty minutes."

Falkenberg led his troops across the courtyard to the tunnel entrance and used Hamner's keys to unlock the doors.

Falkenberg ignored him. He led the troops down the stairway and across, under the field.

George Hamner stayed close to Falkenberg. He could hear the long column of armed men tramp behind him. They moved up stairways on the other side, marching briskly until George was panting. The men didn't seem to notice. Gravity difference, Hamner thought. And training.

They reached the top and deployed along the passageways. Falkenberg stationed men at each exit and came back to the center doors. Then he waited. The tension grew.

"But—"

Falkenberg shook his head. His look demanded silence. He stood, waiting, while the seconds ticked past.

"MOVE OUT!" Falkenberg commanded.

The doors burst open. The armed troopers moved quickly across the top of the Stadium. Most of the mob was below, and a few unarmed men were struck down when they tried to oppose the regiment. Rifle butts swung, then there was a moment of calm. Falkenberg took a speaker from his corporal attendant.

"ATTENTION. ATTENTION. YOU ARE UNDER ARREST BY THE AUTHORITY OF THE MARTIAL LAW PROCLAMATION OF PRESIDENT BUDREAU. LAY DOWN ALL WEAPONS AND YOU WILL NOT BE HARMED. IF YOU RESIST, YOU WILL BE KILLED."

There was a moment of silence, then shouts as the mob realized what Falkenberg had said. Some laughed. Then shots came from the field and the lower seats of the Stadium. Hamner heard the flat snap of a bullet as it rushed past his ear. Then he heard the crack of the rifle.

One of the leaders on the field below had a speaker. He shouted to the others. "ATTACK THEM! THERE AREN'T MORE THAN A THOUSAND OF THEM, WE'RE THIRTY THOUSAND STRONG. ATTACK, KILL THEM!" There were more shots. Some of Falkenberg's men fell. The others stood immobile, waiting for orders.

Falkenberg raised the speaker again. "PREPARE FOR VOLLEY FIRE. MAKE READY. TAKE AIM. IN VOLLEY, FIRE!"

Seven hundred rifles crashed as one.

"FIRE!" Someone screamed, a long drawn-out cry, a plea without words.

"FIRE!"

The line of men clambering up the seats toward them wavered and broke. Men screamed, some pushed back, dove under seats, tried to hide behind their friends, tried to get anywhere but under the unwavering muzzles of the rifles.

"FIRE!"

It was like one shot, very loud, lasting far longer than a rifle shot ought to, but it was impossible to hear individual weapons. "FIRE!"

There were more screams from below. "In the name of God—"

"THE FORTY-SECOND WILL ADVANCE. FIX BAYONETS. FORWARD, MOVE. FIRE. FIRE AT WILL."

Now there was a continuous crackle of weapons. The leather-clad lines moved forward and down, over the stadium seats, flowing down inexorably toward the press below on the field.

"Sergeant Major!"

"SIR!"

"Marksmen and experts will fall out and take station. They will fire on all armed men."

"Sir!"

Calvin spoke into his communicator. Men dropped out of each section and took position behind seats. They began to fire, carefully but rapidly. Anyone below who raised a weapon died. The regiment advanced onward.

Hamner was sick. The screams of wounded could be heard everywhere. God, make it stop, make it stop, he prayed.

"GRENADIERS WILL PREPARE TO THROW." Falkenberg's voice boomed from the speaker. "THROW!"

A hundred grenades arched out from the advancing line. They fell into the milling crowds below. The muffled explosions were masked by screams of terror.

"IN VOLLEY, FIRE!"

The regiment advanced until it made contact with the mob. There was a brief struggle. Rifles fired, and bayonets flashed red. The line halted but momentarily. Then it moved on, leaving behind a ghastly trail.

Men and women jammed in the Stadium exits. Others frantically tried to get out, clambering over the fallen, tearing women out of their way to push past, trampling each other in their scramble to escape. There was a rattle of gunfire from outside. Those in the gates recoiled, to be crushed beneath others trying to get out.

"You won't even let them out!" Hamner screamed at Falkenberg.

"Not armed. And not to escape." The Colonel's face was hard and cold, the eyes narrowed to slits. He watched the slaughter impassively, looking at the entire scene without expression.

"Are you going to kill them all?"

"All who resist."

"But they don't deserve this!" George Hamner felt his voice breaking. "They don't!"

"No one does, George. SERGEANT MAJOR!"

"SIR!"

"Half the marksmen may concentrate on the leaders now."

"SIR!" Calvin spoke quietly into his command set. The snipers concentrated their fire on the Presidential box across from them. Centurions ran up and down the line of hidden troops, pointing out targets. The marksmen kept up a steady fire.

The leather lines of armored men advanced inexorably. They had almost reached the lower tier of seats. There was less firing now, but the scarlet-painted bayonets flashed in the afternoon sun.

Another section fell out of line and moved to guard a tiny number of prisoners at the end of the Stadium. The rest of the line moved on, advancing over seats made slick with blood.

When the regiment reached ground level their progress was slower. There was little opposition, but the sheer mass of people in front of them held up the troopers. There were a few pockets of active resistance, and flying squads rushed there to reinforce the line. More grenades were thrown. Falkenberg watched the battle calmly, and seldom spoke into his communicator. Below, more men died.

A company of troopers formed and rushed up a stairway on the opposite side of the Stadium. They fanned out across the top. Then their rifles leveled, and crashed in another terrible series of volleys.

Suddenly it was over. There was no opposition. There were only screaming crowds. Men threw away weapons to run with their hands in the air. Others fell to their knees to beg for their lives. There was one final volley, then a deathly stillness fell over the Stadium.

But it wasn't quiet, Hamner discovered. The guns were silent, men no longer shouted orders, but there was sound. There were screams from the wounded. There were pleas for help, whimpers, a racking cough that went on and on as someone tried to clear punctured lungs.

Falkenberg nodded grimly. "Now we can find a magistrate, Mr. President. Now."

"I—O my God!" Hamner stood at the top of the

Stadium. He clutched a column to steady his weakened legs. The scene below seemed unreal. There was too much blood, rivers of blood, blood cascading down the steps, blood pouring down stairwells to soak the grassy field below.

"It's over," Falkenberg said gently. "For all of us. The regiment will be leaving as soon as you're properly in command. You shouldn't have any trouble with your power plants. Your technicians will trust you now that Bradford's gone. And without their leaders, the city people won't resist.

"You can ship as many as you have to out to the interior. Disperse them among the loyalists where they won't do you any harm. That amnesty of yours—it's only a suggestion, but I'd renew it."

Hamner turned dazed eyes toward Falkenberg. "Yes. There's been too much slaughter today. Who are you, Falkenberg?"

"A mercenary soldier, Mr. President. Nothing more."

"But—then who are you working for?"

"That's the question nobody asked before. Grand Admiral Lermontov."

"Lermontov? But you were drummed out of the CoDominium! You mean that you were hired—by the admiral? As a mercenary?"

"More or less." Falkenberg nodded coldly. "The Fleet's a little sick of being used to mess up people's lives without having a chance to—to leave things in working order."

"And now you're leaving?"

"Yes. We couldn't stay here, George. Nobody is going to forget today. You couldn't keep us on and build a government that works. I'll take First and Second Battalions, and what's left of the Fourth. There's more work for us."

"And the others?"

"Third will stay on to help you," Falkenberg said. "We put all the married locals, the solid people, in Third, and sent it off to the power plants. They weren't involved in the fighting." He looked across the stadium, then back to Hamner. "Blame it all on us, George. You weren't in command. You can say Bradford ordered this slaughter and killed himself in remorse. People will want to believe that. They'll want to think somebody was punished for—

134

for this." He waved toward the field below. A child was sobbing out there somewhere.

"It had to be done," Falkenberg insisted. "Didn't it? There was no way out, nothing you could do to keep civilization. . . . Dr. Whitlock estimated a third of the population would die when things collapsed. Fleet Intelligence put it higher than that. Now you have a chance."

Falkenberg was speaking rapidly, and George wondered whom he was trying to convince.

"Move them out," Falkenberg said. "Move them out while they're still dazed. You won't need much help for that. They won't resist now. And we got the railroads running for you. Use the railroads and ship people out to the farms. It'll be rough with no preparation, but it's a long time until winter—"

"I know what to do," Hamner interrupted. He leaned against the column, and seemed to gather new strength from the thought. Yes. I do know what to do. Now. "I've known all along what had to be done. Now we can get to it. We won't thank you for it, but—you've saved a whole world, John."

Falkenberg looked at him grimly, then pointed to the bodies below. "Damn you, don't say that!" he shouted. His voice was almost shrill. "I haven't saved anything. All a soldier can do is buy time. I haven't saved Hadley. You have to do that. God help you if you don't."

XII

Crofton's Encyclopedia of Contemporary History and Social Issues (2nd Edition)

MERCENARY FORCES

Perhaps the most disturbing development arising from CoDominium withdrawal from most distant colony worlds (see Independence Movements) has been the rapid growth of purely mercenary military units. The trend was predictable and perhaps inevitable, although the extent has exceeded expectations.

Many of the former colony worlds do not have planetary governments. Consequently, these new nations do not possess sufficient population or industrial resources to maintain large and effective national military forces. The disbanding of numerous CoDominium Marine units left a surplus of trained soldiers without employment, and it was inevitable that some of them would band together into mercenary units.

The colony governments are thus faced with a cruel and impossible dilemma. Faced with mercenary troops specializing in violence, they have had little choice but to reply in kind. A few colonies have broken this cycle by creating their own national armies, but have then been unable to pay for them.

Thus, in addition to the purely private mercenary organizations such as Falkenberg's Mercenary Legion, there are now national forces hired out to reduce expenses to their parent governments. A few former colonies have found this practice so lucrative that the export of mercenaries has become their principal source of income, and the recruiting and training of soldiers their major industry.

The CoDominium Grand Senate has attempted to maintain its presence in the former colonial areas through promulgation of the so-called Laws of War (*q.v.*), which purport to regulate the weapons and tactics mercenary units may employ. Enforcement of these regulations is sporadic. When the Senate orders Fleet intervention to enforce the Laws of War the suspicion inevitably arises that other CoDominium interests are at stake, or that one or more Senators have undisclosed reasons for their interest.

Mercenary units generally draw their recruits from the same sources as the CoDominium Marines, and training stresses loyalty to comrades and commanders rather than to any government. The extent to which mercenary commanders have successfully separated their troops from all normal social intercourse is both surprising and alarming.

The best-known mercenary forces are described in separate articles. See: *Covenant; Friedland; Xanadu; Falkenberg's Mercenary Legion; Nouveau Legion Etrangere; Katanga Gendarmerie; Moolman's Commandos . . .*

FALKENBERG'S MERCENARY LEGION

Purely private military organization formed from the former Forty-second CoDominium Line Marines under Colonel John Christian Falkenberg III. Falkenberg was cashiered from the CoDominium Fleet under questionable circumstances, and his regiment disbanded shortly thereafter. A large proportion of former Forty-second officers and men chose to remain with Falkenberg.

Falkenberg's Legion appears to have been first employed by the government of the then newly independent former colony of Hadley (*q.v.*) for suppression of civil disturbances. There have been numerous complaints that excessive violence was used by both sides in the unsuccessful rebellion following CoDominium withdrawal, but the government of Hadley has expressed satisfaction with Falkenberg's efforts there.

Following its employment on Hadley Falkenberg's Legion took part in numerous small wars of defense and conquest on at least five planets, and in the process gained a reputation as one of the best-trained and most effective small military units in existence. It was then engaged by the CoDominium Governor on the CD prison planet of Tanith.

This latter employment caused great controversy in the Grand Senate, as Tanith remains under CD control. However, Grand Admiral Lermontov pointed out that his budget did not permit his stationing regular Marine forces on Tanith owing to other commitments mandated by the Grand Senate; after lengthy debate the employment was approved as an alternative to raising a new regiment of CD Marines.

At last report Falkenberg's Legion remains on Tanith. Its contract with the Governor there is said to have expired.

Tanith's bright image had replaced Earth's on Grand Admiral Lermontov's view screen. The planet might have been Earth: it had bright clouds obscuring the outlines of land and sea, and they swirled in typical cyclonic patterns.

A closer look showed differences. The sun was yellow: Tanith's star was not as hot as Sol, but Tanith was closer to it. There were fewer mountains, and more swamplands steaming in the yellow-orange glare.

Despite its miserable climate, Tanith was an important world. It was first and foremost a convenient dumping ground for Earth's disinherited. There was no better way to deal with criminals than to send them off to hard—and useful—labor on another planet. Tanith received them all: the rebels, the criminals, the malcontents, victims of administrative hatred; all the refuse of a civilization that could no longer afford misfits.

Tanith was also the main source of borloi, which the World Pharmaceutical Society called "the perfect intoxicating drug." Given large supplies of borloi the lid could be kept on the Citizens in their Welfare Islands. The happiness the drug induced was artificial, but it was none the less real.

"And so I am trading in drugs," Lermontov told his visitor. "It is hardly what I expected when I became Grand Admiral."

"I'm sorry, Sergei." Grand Senator Martin Grant had aged; in ten years he had come to look forty years older. "The fact is, though, you're better off with Fleet ownership of some of the borloi plantations than you are relying on what I can get for you out of the Senate."

Lermontov nodded in disgust. "It must end, Martin. Somehow, somewhere, it must end. I cannot keep a fighting service together on the proceeds of drug sales—drugs grown by slaves! Soldiers do not make good slavemasters."

Grant merely shrugged.

"Yes, it is easy to think, is it not?" The admiral shook his head in disgust. "But there are vices natural to the soldier and the sailor. We have those, in plenty, but they are not vices that corrupt his ability as a fighting man. Slaving is a vice that corrupts everything it touches."

"If you feel that way, what can I say?" Martin Grant asked. "I can't give you an alternative."

"And I cannot let go," Lermontov said. He punched viciously at the console controls and Tanith faded from the screen. Earth, bluer and to Lermontov far more lovely, swam out of the momentary blackness. "They are fools down there," Sergei Lermontov muttered. "And we are no better. Martin, I ask myself again and again, why can we not control—anything? Why are we caught like chips in a rushing stream? Men can guide their destinies. I know that. So why are we so helpless?"

"You don't ask yourself more often than I do," Senator Grant said. His voice was low and weary. "At least we still try. Hell, you've got more power than I have. You've got the Fleet, and you've got the secret funds you get from Tanith—Christ, Sergei, if you can't do something with that—"

"I can urinate on fires," Lermontov said. "And little else." He shrugged. "So, if that is all I can do, then I will continue to make water. Will you have a drink?"

"Thanks."

Lermontov went to the sideboard and took out bottles. His conversations with Grand Senator Grant were never heard by anyone else, not even his orderlies who had been with him for years.

"Prosit."

"Prosit!"

They drank. Grant took out a cigar. "By the way, Sergei, what are you going to do with Falkenberg now that the trouble on Tanith is finished?"

Lermontov smiled coldly. "I was hoping that you would have a solution to that. I have no more funds—"

"The Tanith money—"

"Needed elsewhere, just to keep the Fleet together," Lermontov said positively.

"Then Falkenberg'll just have to find his own way. Shouldn't be any problem, with his reputation," Grant said. "And even if it is, he's got no more troubles than we have."

XIII

2093 A.D.

HEAT BEAT DOWN on sodden fields. Two hours before the noon of Tanith's fifteen plus hours of sunshine the day was already hot; but all of Tanith's days are hot. Even in midwinter the jungle steams in late afternoon.

The skies above the regiment's camp were yellow-gray. The ground sloped off to the west into inevitable swamp, where Weem's Beasts snorted as they burrowed deeper into protective mud. In the camp itself the air hung hot and wet, heavy, with a thick smell of yeast and decay.

The regiment's camp was an island of geometrical precision in the random tumble of jungles and hilltops. Each yellow rammed-earth barrack was set in an exact relationship with every other, each company set in line from its centurion's hut at one end to the senior platoon sergeant's at the other.

A wide street separated Centurion's Row from the Company Officers Line, and beyond that was the shorter Field Officers Line, the pyramid narrowing inevitably until at its apex stood a single building where the colonel lived. Other officers lived with their ladies, and married enlisted men's quarters formed one side of the compound; but the colonel lived alone.

The visitor stood with the colonel to watch a mustering ceremony evolved in the days of Queen Anne's England when regimental commanders were paid according to the strength of their regiments, and the Queen's muster masters had to determine that each man drawing pay could indeed pass muster—or even existed.

The visitor was an amateur historian and viewed the parade with wry humor. War had changed and men no longer marched in rigid lines to deliver volleys at word of command—but colonels were again paid according to the forces they could bring into battle.

"Report!" The adjutant's command carried easily across the open parade field to the rigidly immobile blue and gold squares.

"First Battalion, B Company on patrol. Battalion present or accounted for, sir!"

"Second Battalion present or accounted for, sir." "Third Battalion present or accounted for, sir!"

"Fourth Battalion, four men absent without leave, sir."

"How embarrassing," the visitor said *sotto voce*. The colonel tried to smile but made a bad job of it.

"Artillery present or accounted for, sir!" "Scout Troop all present, sir!" "Sappers all present, sir!"

"Weapons Battalion, Aviation Troop on patrol. Battalion present or accounted for, sir!"

"Headquarters Company present or on guard, sir!"

The adjutant returned each salute, then wheeled crisply to salute the colonel. "Regiment has four men absent without leave, sir."

Colonel Falkenberg returned the salute. "Take your post."

Captain Fast pivoted and marched to his place. "Pass in review!"

"Sound off!"

The band played a military march that must have been old in the twentieth century as the regiment formed column to march around the field. As each company reached the reviewing stand and men snapped their heads in unison, guidons and banners lowered in salute, and officers and centurions whirled sabers with flourishes.

The visitor nodded to himself. No longer very appropriate. In the eighteenth century, demonstrations of the men's ability to march in ranks, and of the non-coms and officers to use a sword with skill, were relevant to battle capabilities. Not now. Still, it made an impressive ceremony.

"Attention to orders!" The sergeant major read from his clipboard. Promotions, duty schedules, the daily activities of the regiment, while the visitor sweated.

"Very impressive, Colonel," he said. "Our Washingtonians couldn't look that sharp on their best day."

John Christian Falkenberg nodded coldly. "Implying that they mightn't be as good in the field, Mr. Secretary? Would you like another kind of demonstration?"

142

Howard Bannister shrugged. "What would it prove, Colonel? You need employment before your regiment goes to hell. I can't imagine chasing escapees on the CoDominium prison planet has much attraction for good soldiers."

"It doesn't. When we first came things weren't that simple."

"I know that too. The Forty-second was one of the best outfits of the CD Marine—I've never understood why it was disbanded instead of one of the others. I'm speaking of your present situation with your troops stuck here without transport—surely you're not intending to make Tanith your lifetime headquarters?"

Sergeant Major Calvin finished the orders of the day and waited patiently for instructions. Colonel Falkenberg studied his bright-uniformed men as they stood rigidly in the blazing noon of Tanith. A faint smile might have played across his face for a moment. There were few of the four thousand whose names and histories he didn't know.

Lieutenant Farquhar was a party hack forced on him when the Forty-second was hired to police Hadley. He became a good officer and elected to ship out after the action. Private Alcazar was a brooding giant with a raging thirst, the slowest man in K Company, but he could lift five times his own mass and hide in any terrain. Dozens, thousands of men, each with his own strengths and weaknesses, adding up to a regiment of mercenary soldiers with no chance of going home, and an unpleasant future if they didn't get off Tanith.

"Sergeant Major."

"Sir!"

"You will stay with me and time the men. Trumpeter, sound Boots and Saddles, On Full Kits, and Ready to Board Ship."

"Sir!" The trumpeter was a grizzled veteran with corporal's stripes. He lifted the gleaming instrument with its blue and gold tassels, and martial notes poured across the parade ground. Before they died away the orderly lines dissolved into masses of running men.

There was less confusion than Howard Bannister had expected. It seemed an incredibly short time before the first men fell back in. They came from their barracks in small groups, some in each company, then more, a rush, and finally knots of stragglers. Now in place of bright

143

colors there was the dull drab of synthetic leather bulging over Nemourlon body armor. The bright polish was gone from the weapons. Dress caps were replaced by bulging combat helmets, shining boots by softer leathers. As the regiment formed Bannister turned to the colonel.

"Why trumpets? I'd think that's rather out of date."

Falkenberg shrugged. "Would you prefer shouted orders? You must remember, Mr. Secretary, mercenaries live in garrison as well as in combat. Trumpets remind them that they're soldiers."

"I suppose."

"Time, Sergeant Major," the adjutant demanded.

"Eleven minutes, eighteen seconds, sir."

"Are you trying to tell me the men are ready to ship out now?" Bannister asked. His expression showed polite disbelief.

"It would take longer to get the weapons and artillery battalion equipment together, but the infantry could board ship right now."

"I find that hard to believe—of course the men know this is only a drill."

"How would they know that?"

Bannister laughed. He was a stout man, dressed in expensive business clothes with cigar ashes down the front. Some of the ash floated free when he laughed. "Well, you and the sergeant major are still in parade uniform."

"Look behind you," Falkenberg said.

Bannister turned. Falkenberg's guards and trumpeter were still in their places, their blue and gold dress contrasting wildly with the grim synthi-leathers of the others who had formed up with them. "The headquarters squad has our gear," Falkenberg explained. "Sergeant Major."

"Sir!"

"Mr. Bannister and I will inspect the troops."

"Sir!" As Falkenberg and his visitor left the reviewing stand Calvin fell in with the duty squad behind him.

"Pick a couple at random," Falkenberg advised. "It's hot out here. Forty degrees anyway."

Bannister was thinking the same thing. "Yes. No point in being too hard on the men. It must be unbearable in their armor."

"I wasn't thinking of the men," Falkenberg said.

The Secretary for War chose L Company of Third Battalion for review. The men all looked alike, except for size. He looked for something to stand out—a strap not

144

buckled, something to indicate an individual difference—but he found none. Bannister approached a scarred private who looked forty years old. With regeneration therapy he might have been half that again. "This one."

"Fall out, Wiszorik!" Calvin ordered. "Lay out your kit."

"Sir!" Private Wiszorik might have smiled thinly, but if he did Bannister missed it. He swung the packframe easily off his shoulders and stood it on the ground. The headquarters squad helped him lay out his nylon shelter cloth, and Wiszorik emptied the pack, placing each item just so.

Rifle: a New Aberdeen seven-mm semi-automatic, with ten-shot clip and fifty-round box magazine, both full and spotlessly clean like the rifle. A bandolier of cartridges. Five grenades. Nylon belt with bayonets, canteen, spoon, and stainless cup that served as a private's entire mess kit. Great-cloak and poncho, string net underwear, layers of clothing—

"You'll note he's equipped for any climate," Falkenberg commented. "He'd expect to be issued special gear for a non-Terran environment, but he can live on any inhabitable world with what he's got."

"Yes." Bannister watched interestedly. The pack hadn't seemed heavy, but Wiszorik kept withdrawing gear from it. First aid kit, chemical warfare protection drugs and equipment, concentrated field rations, soup and beverage powders, a tiny gasoline-burning field stove—"What's that?" Bannister asked. "Do all the men carry them?"

"One to each maniple, sir," Wiszorik answered.

"His share of five men's community equipment," Falkenberg explained. "A monitor, three privates, and a recruit make up the basic combat unit of this outfit, and we try to keep the maniples self-sufficient."

More gear came from the pack. Much of it was light alloys or plastic, but Bannister wondered about the total weight. Trowel, tent pegs, nylon cordage, a miniature cutting torch, more group equipment for field repairs to both machinery and the woven Nemourlon armor, night sights for the rifle, a small plastic tube half a meter long and eight centimeters in diameter—"And that?" Bannister asked.

"Anti-aircraft rocket," Falkenberg told him. "Not effective against fast jets, but it'll knock out a chopper ninety-five percent of the time. Has some capability against

145

tanks, too. We don't like the men too dependent on heavy weapons units."

"I see. Your men seem well equipped, Colonel," Bannister commented. "It must weight them down badly."

"Twenty-one kilograms in standard g field," Falkenberg answered. "More here, less by a lot on Washington. Every man carries a week's rations, ammunition for a short engagement, and enough equipment to live in the field."

"What's the little pouch on his belt?" Bannister asked interestedly.

Falkenberg shrugged. "Personal possessions. Probably everything he owns. You'll have to ask Wiszorik's permission if you want to examine that."

"Never mind. Thank you, Private Wiszorik." Howard Bannister produced a brightly colored bandanna from an inner pocket and mopped his brow. "All right, Colonel. You're convincing—or your men are. Let's go to your office and talk about money."

As they left, Wiszorik and Sergeant Major Calvin exchanged knowing winks, while Monitor Hartzinger breathed a sigh of relief. Just suppose that visiting panjandrum had picked Recruit Latterby! Hell, the kid couldn't find his arse with both hands.

XIV

FALKENBERG'S OFFICE WAS hot. It was a large room, and a
ceiling fan tried without success to stir up a breeze. Everything was damp from Tanith's wet jungle air. Howard
Bannister thought he saw fungus growing in the narrow
space between a file cabinet and the wall.

In contrast to the room itself, the furniture was elabo-
rate. It had been handcarved and was the product of hundreds of hours' labor by soldiers who had little else but
time to give their commanding officer. They'd taken Sergeant Major Calvin into a conspiracy, getting him to talk
Falkenberg into going on an inspection tour while they
scrapped his functional old field gear and replaced it with
equipment as light and useful, but handcarved with battle
scenes.

The desk was large and entirely bare. To one side a
table, in easy reach, was covered with papers. On the other
side a two-meter star cube portrayed the known stars with
inhabited planets. Communication equipment was built
into a spindly legged sideboard that also held whiskey.
Falkenberg offered his visitor a drink.

"Could we have something with ice?"

"Certainly." Falkenberg turned toward his sideboard
and raised his voice, speaking with a distinct change in
tone. "Orderly, two gin and tonics, with much ice, if you
please. Will that be satisfactory, Mr. Secretary?"

"Yes, thank you." Bannister wasn't accustomed to electronics being so common. "Look, we needn't spar about. I
need soldiers and you need to get off this planet. It's as
simple as that."

"Hardly," Falkenberg replied. "You've yet to mention
money."

Howard shrugged. "I don't have much. Washington has

147

damned few exports. Franklin's dried those up with the blockade. Your transport and salaries will use up most of what we've got. But you already know this, I suppose—I'm told you have access to Fleet Intelligence sources."

Falkenberg shrugged. "I have my ways. You're prepared to put our return fare on deposit with Dayan, of course."

"Yes." Bannister was startled. "Dayan? You do have sources. I thought our negotiations with New Jerusalem were secret. All right—we have arrangements with Dayan to furnish transportation. It took all our cash, so everything else is contingency money. We can offer you something you need, though. Land, good land, and a permanent base that's a lot more pleasant than Tanith. We can also offer—well, the chance to be part of a free and independent nation, though I'm not expecting that to mean much to you."

Falkenberg nodded. "That's why you—excuse me." He paused as the orderly brought in a tray with tinkling glasses. The trooper wore battledress, and his rifle was slung across his shoulder.

"Will you be wanting the men to perform again?" Falkenberg asked.

Bannister hesitated. "I think not."

"Orderly, ask Sergeant Major to sound recall. Dismissed." He looked back to Bannister. "Now. You chose us because you've nothing to offer. The New Democrats on Friedland are happy enough with their base, as are the Scots on Covenant. Xanadu wants hard cash before they throw troops into action. You could find some scrapings on Earth, but we're the only first-class outfit down on its luck at the moment—what makes you think we're *that* hard up, Mr. Secretary? Your cause on Washington is lost, isn't it?"

"Not for us." Howard Bannister sighed. Despite his bulk he seemed deflated. "All right. Franklin's mercenaries have defeated the last organized field army we had. The resistance is all guerrilla operations, and we both know that won't win. We need an organized force to rally around, and we haven't got one." *Dear God, we haven't got one.* Bannister remembered rugged hills and forests, weathered mountains with snow on their tops, and in the valleys were ranches with the air crisp and cool. He remembered plains golden with mutated wheat and the swaying tassels of Washington's native corn plant rippling in

148

the wind. The Patriot army marched again to the final battle.

They'd marched with songs in their hearts. The cause was just and they faced only mercenaries after defeating Franklin's regular army. Free men against hirelings in one last campaign.

The Patriots entered the plains outside the capital city, confident that the mercenaries could never stand against them—and the enemy didn't run. The humorless Covenant Scots regiments chewed through their infantry, while Friedland armor squadrons cut across the flank and far into the rear, destroying their supply lines and capturing the headquarters. Washington's army had not so much been defeated as dissolved, turned into isolated groups of men whose enthusiasm was no match for the iron discipline of the mercenaries. In three weeks they'd lost everything gained in two years of war.

But yet—the planet was still only thinly settled. The Franklin Confederacy had few soldiers and couldn't afford to keep large groups of mercenaries on occupation duty. Out in the mountains and across the plains the settlements were seething, and ready to revolt again. It would only take a tiny spark to arouse them.

"We've a chance, Colonel. I wouldn't waste our money and risk my people's lives if I didn't think so. Let me show you. I've a map in my gear."

"Show me on this one." Falkenberg opened a desk drawer to reveal a small input panel. He touched keys and the translucent gray of his desk top dissolved into colors. A polar projection of Washington formed.

There was only one continent, an irregular mass squatting at the top of the planet. From 25° North to the South Pole there was nothing but water. The land above that was cut by huge bays and nearly land-locked seas. Towns showed as a network of red dots across a narrow band of land jutting down to the 30° to 50° level.

"You sure don't have much land to live on," Falkenberg observed. "A strip a thousand kilometers wide by four thousand long—why Washington, anyway?"

"Original settlers had ancestors in Washington state. The climate's similar too. Franklin's the companion planet. It's got more industry than we do, but even less agricultural land. Settled mostly by Southern U.S. people—they call themselves the Confederacy. Washington's a secondary colony from Franklin."

149

Falkenberg chuckled. "Dissidents from a dissident colony. You must be damned independent chaps."

"So independent that we're not going to let Franklin run our lives! They treat us like a wholly owned subsidiary, and we are not going to take it!"

"You'll take it if you can't get somebody to fight for you," Falkenberg reminded him brutally. "Now, you are offering us transport out, a deposit against our return, minimum troop pay, and land to settle on?"

"Yes, that's right. You can use the return deposit to transport your non-combatants later. Or cash it in. But it's all the money we can offer, Colonel." And be damned to you. You don't care at all, but I have to deal with you. For now.

"Yeah." Falkenberg regarded the map sourly. "Are we facing nukes?"

"They've got some but so do we. We concealed ours in Franklin's capital to make it a standoff."

"Uh-huh." Falkenberg nodded. The situation wasn't that unusual. The CD Fleet still tried to enforce the ban for that matter. "Do they still have those Covenant Highlanders that whipped you last time?"

Bannister winced at the reminder. "God damn it, good men were killed in that fight, and you've got no right to—"

"Do they still have the Covenanters, Mr. Secretary?" Falkenberg repeated.

"Yes. Plus a brigade of Friedland armor and another ten thousand Earth mercenaries on garrison duty."

Falkenberg snorted. No one thought much of Earth's cannon fodder. The best Earth recruits joined the growing national armies. Bannister nodded agreement. "Then there are about eight thousand Confederate troops, native Franklin soldiers who'd be no match for our Washingtonians."

"You hope. Don't play Franklin down. They're putting together the nucleus of a damned good fighting force, Mr. Bannister—as you know. It is my understanding that they have plans for further conquests once they've consolidated their hold on New Washington."

Bannister agreed carefully. "That's the main reason we're so desperate, Colonel. We won't buy peace by giving in to the Confederacy because they're set to defy the CoDominium when they can build a fleet. I don't understand why the CD Navy hasn't put paid to Franklin's little scheme, but it's obvious Earth isn't going to do anything.

In a few years the Confederates will have their fleet and be as strong as Xanadu or Danube, strong enough to give the CD a *real* fight."

"You're too damn isolated," Falkenberg replied. "The Grand Senate won't even keep the Fleet up to enough strength to protect what the CD's already got—let alone find the money to interfere in your sector. The short-sighted bastards run around putting out fires, and the few Senators who look ten years ahead don't have any influence." He shook his head suddenly. "But that's not our problem. Okay, what about landing security? I don't have any assault boats, and I doubt you've the money to hire those from Dayan."

"It's tough," Bannister admitted. "But blockade runners can get through. Tides on New Washington are enormous, but we know our coasts. The Dayan captain can put you down at night here, or along there . . ." The rebel war secretary indicated a number of deep bays and fiords on the jagged coast, bright blue spatters on the desk map. "You'll have about two hours of slack water. That's all the time you'd have anyway before the Confederate spy satellites detect the ship."

XV

Roger Hastings drew his pretty brunette wife close to him and leaned against the barbecue pit. It made a nice pose and the photographers took several shots. They begged for more, but Hastings shook his head. "Enough, boys, enough! I've only been sworn in as mayor of Allansport—you'd think I was Governor General of the whole planet!"

"But give us a statement," the reporters begged. "Will you support the Confederacy's rearmament plans? I understand the smelter is tooling up to produce naval armament alloys—"

"I said *enough*," Roger commanded. "Go have a drink." The reporters reluctantly scattered. "Eager chaps," Hastings told his wife. "Pity there's only the one little paper."

Juanita laughed. "You'd make the capital city *Times* if there was a way to get the pictures there. But it was a fair question, Roger. What are you going to do about Franklin's war policies? What will happen to Harley when they start expanding the Confederacy?" The amusement died from her face as she thought of their son in the army.

"There isn't much I can do. The mayor of Allansport isn't consulted on matters of high policy. Damn it, sweetheart, don't you start in on me too. It's too nice a day."

Hastings' quarried stone house stood high on a hill above Nanaimo Bay. The city of Allansport sprawled across the hills below them, stretching almost to the high water mark running irregularly along the sandy beaches washed by endless surf. At night they could hear the waves crashing.

They held hands and watched the sea beyond the island that formed Allansport Harbor. "Here it comes!" Roger said. He pointed to a wall of rushing water two meters high. The tide bore swept around the end of Waada Island, then curled back toward the city.

"Pity the poor sailors," Juanita said.

Roger shrugged. "The packet ship's anchored well enough."

They watched the hundred-and-fifty-meter cargo vessel tossed about by the tidal force. The tide bore caught her nearly abeam and she rolled dangerously before swinging on her chains to head into the flowing tide water. It seemed nothing could hold her, but those chains had been made in Roger's foundries, and he knew their strength.

"It has been a nice day." Juanita sighed. Their house was on one of the large greensward commons running up the hill from Allansport, and the celebrations had spilled out of their yard, across the greens, and into their neighbors' yards as well. Portable bars manned by Roger's campaign workers dispensed an endless supply of local wines and brandies.

To the west New Washington's twin companion, Franklin, hung in its eternal place. When sunset brought New Washington's twenty hours of daylight to an end it passed from a glowing ball in the bright day sky to a gibbous sliver in the darkness, then rapidly widened. Reddish shadows danced on Franklin's cloudy face.

Roger and Juanita stood in silent appreciation of the stars, the planet, the sunset. Allansport was a frontier town on an unimportant planet, but it was home and they loved it.

The inauguration party had been exhaustingly successful. Roger gratefully went to the drawing room while Juanita climbed the stairs to put their sleepy children to bed. As manager of the smelter and foundry, Roger had a home that was one of the finest on all the Ranier Peninsula. It stood tall and proud—a big stone Georgian mansion with wide entry hall and paneled rooms. Now, he was joined by Martine Ardway in his favorite, the small conversation-sized drawing room.

"Congratulations again, Roger," Colonel Ardway boomed. "We'll all be behind you." The words were more than the usual inauguration day patter. Although Ardway's son Johann was married to Roger's daughter, the Colonel had opposed Hastings' election, and Ardway had a large following among the hard-line Loyalists in Allansport. He was also commander of the local militia. Johann held a captain's commission. Roger's own boy Harley was only a lieutenant, but in the Regulars.

"Have you told Harley about your winning?" Ardway asked.

"Can't. The communications to Vancouver are out. As a matter of fact, all our communications are out right now."

Ardway nodded phlegmatically. Allansport was the only town on a peninsula well over a thousand kilometers from the nearest settlements. New Washington was so close to its red dwarf sun that loss of communications was standard through much of the planet's fifty-two standard-day year. An undersea cable to Preston Bay had been planned when the rebellion broke out, and now that it was over work could start again.

"I mean it about being with you," Ardway repeated. "I still think you're wrong, but there can't be more than one policy about this. I just hope it works."

"Look, Martine, we can't go on treating the rebels like traitors. We need 'em too much. There aren't many rebels here, but if I enforce the confiscation laws it'll cause resentment in the East. We've had enough bloody war." Roger stretched and yawned. "Excuse me. It's been a hard day and it's a while since I was a rock miner. There was once a time when I could dig all day and drink all night."

Ardway shrugged. Like Hastings, he had once been a miner, but unlike the mayor he hadn't kept in shape. He wasn't fat, but he had become a large, balding, round man with a paunch that spilled over his wide garrison belt. It spoiled his looks when he wore military uniform, which he did whenever possible. "You're in charge, Roger. I won't get in your way. Maybe you can even get the old rebel families on your side against this stupid imperialistic venture Franklin's pushing. God knows we've enough problems at home without looking for more. I think. What in hell's going on out there?"

Someone was yelling in the town below. "Good God, were those shots?" Roger asked. "We better find out." Reluctantly he pushed himself up from the leather easy chair. "Hello—hello—what's this? The phone is out, Martine. Dead."

"Those *were* shots," Colonel Ardway said. "I don't like this—rebels? The packet came in this afternoon, but you don't suppose there were rebels on board her? We better go down and see to this. You sure the phone's dead?"

154

"Very dead," Hastings said quietly. "Lord, I hope it's not a new rebellion. Get your troops called out, though."

"Right." Ardway took a pocket communicator from his belt pouch. He spoke into it with increasing agitation. "Roger, there is something wrong! I'm getting nothing but static. Somebody's jamming the whole communications band."

"Nonsense. We're near periastron. The sunspots are causing it." Hastings sounded confident, but he was praying silently. Not more war. It wouldn't be a threat to Allansport and the Peninsula—there weren't more than a handful of rebels out here, but they'd be called on for troops to go east and fight in rebel areas like Ford Heights and the Columbia Valley. It was so damn rotten! He remembered burning ranches and plantations during the last flareup.

"God damn it, don't those people know they lose more in the wars than Franklin's merchants are costing them?" But he was already speaking to an empty room. Colonel Ardway had dashed outside and was calling to the neighbors to fall out with military equipment.

Roger followed him outside. To the west Franklin flooded the night with ten thousand times Luna's best efforts on Earth. There were soldiers coming up the broad street from the main section of town.

"Who in hell—those aren't rebels," Hastings shouted. They were men in synthi-leather battledress, and they moved too deliberately. Those were Regulars.

There was a roar of motors. A wave of helicopters passed overhead. Roger heard ground effects cars on the greensward, and at least two hundred soldiers were running purposefully up the street toward his house. At each house below a knot of five men fell out of the open formation.

"Turn out! Militia turn out! Rebels!" Colonel Ardway was shouting. He had a dozen men, none in armor, and their best weapons were rifles.

"Take cover! Fire at will!" Ardway screamed. His voice carried determination but it had an edge of fear. "Roger, get the hell inside, you damn fool!"

"But—" The advancing troops were no more than a hundred meters away. One of Ardway's militia fired an automatic rifle from the house next door. The leather-clad troops scattered and someone shouted orders.

Fire lashed out to rake the house. Roger stood in his

155

front yard, dazed, unbelieving, as under Franklin's bright reddish light the nightmare went on. The troops advanced steadily again and there was no more resistance from the militia.

It all happened so quickly. Even as Roger had that thought, the leather lines of men reached him. An officer raised a megaphone.

"I CALL ON YOU TO SURRENDER IN THE NAME OF THE FREE STATES OF WASHINGTON. STAY IN YOUR HOMES AND DO NOT TRY TO RESIST. ARMED MEN WILL BE SHOT WITHOUT WARNING."

A five-man detachment ran past Roger Hastings and through the front door of his home. It brought him from his daze. "Juanita!" He screamed and ran toward his house.

"HALT! HALT OR WE FIRE! YOU MAN, HALT!"

Roger ran on heedlessly.

"SQUAD FIRE."

"BELAY THAT ORDER!"

As Roger reached the door he was grabbed by one of the soldiers and flung against the wall. "Hold it right there," the trooper said grimly. "Monitor, I have a prisoner."

Another soldier came into the broad entryway. He held a clipboard and looked up at the address of the house, checking it against his papers. "Mr. Roger Hastings?" he asked.

Roger nodded dazedly. Then he thought better of it. "No. I'm—"

"Won't do," the soldier said. "I've your picture, Mr. Mayor." Roger nodded again. Who was this man? There had been many accents, and the officer with the clipboard had yet another. "Who are you?" he demanded.

"Lieutenant Jaimie Farquhar of Falkenberg's Mercenary Legion, acting under authority of the Free States of Washington. You're under military detention, Mr. Mayor."

There was more firing outside. Roger's house hadn't been touched. Everything looked so absolutely ordinary. Somehow that added to the horror.

A voice called from upstairs. "His wife and kids are up here, Lieutenant."

"Thank you, Monitor. Ask the lady to come down, please. Mr. Mayor, please don't be concerned for your

156

family. We do not make war on civilians." There were more shots from the street.

A thousand questions boiled in Roger's mind. He stood dazedly trying to sort them into some order. "Have you shot Colonel Ardway? Who's fighting out there?"

"If you mean the fat man in uniform, he's safe enough. We've got him in custody. Unfortunately, some of your militia have ignored the order to surrender, and it's going to be hard on them."

As if in emphasis there was the muffled blast of a grenade, then a burst from a machine pistol answered by the slow deliberate fire of an automatic rifle. The battle noises swept away across the brow of the hill, but sounds of firing and shouted orders carried over the pounding surf.

Farquhar studied his clipboard. "Mayor Hastings and Colonel Ardway. Yes, thank you for identifying him. I've orders to take you both to the command post. Monitor!"

"Sir!"

"Your maniple will remain here on guard. You will allow no one to enter this house. Be polite to Mrs. Hastings, but keep her and the children here. If there is any attempt at looting you will prevent it. This street is under the protection of the Regiment. Understood?"

"Sir!"

The slim officer nodded in satisfaction. "If you'll come with me, Mr. Mayor, there's a car on the greensward." As Roger followed numbly he saw the hall clock. He had been sworn in as mayor less than eleven hours ago.

The Regimental Command Post was in the city council meeting chambers, with Falkenberg's office in a small connecting room. The council room itself was filled with electronic gear and bustled with runners, while Major Savage and Captain Fast controlled the military conquest of Allansport. Falkenberg watched the situation develop in the maps displayed on his desk top.

"It was so fast!" Howard Bannister said. The pudgy secretary of war shook his head in disbelief. "I never thought you could do it."

Falkenberg shrugged. "Light infantry can move, Mr. Secretary. But it cost us. We had to leave the artillery train in orbit with most of our vehicles. I can equip with captured stuff, but we're a bit short on transport." He watched

157

lights flash confusedly for a second on the display before the steady march of red lights blinking to green resumed.

"But now you're without artillery," Bannister said. "And the Patriot army's got none."

"Can't have it both ways. We had less than an hour to offload and get the Dayan boats off planet before the spy satellites came over. Now we've got the town and nobody knows we've landed. If this goes right the first the Confederates'll know about us is when their spy snooper stops working."

"We had some luck," Bannister said. "Boat in harbor, communications out to the mainland—"

"Don't confuse luck with decision factors," Falkenberg answered. "Why would I take an isolated hole full of Loyalists if there weren't some advantages?" Privately he knew better. The telephone exchange taken by infiltrating scouts, the power plant almost unguarded and falling to three minutes' brief combat—it was all luck you could count on with good men, but it was luck. "Excuse me." He touched a stud in response to a low humming note. "Yes?"

"Train coming in from the mines, John Christian," Major Savage reported. "We have the station secured, shall we let it go past the block outside town?"

"Sure, stick with the plan, Jerry. Thanks." The miners coming home after a week's work on the sides of Ranier Crater were due for a surprise.

They waited until all the lights changed to green. Every objective was taken. Power plants, communications, homes of leading citizens, public buildings, railway station and airport, police station . . . Allansport and its eleven thousand citizens were under control. A timer display ticked off the minutes until the spy satellite would be overhead.

Falkenberg spoke to the intercom. "Sergeant Major, we have twenty-nine minutes to get this place looking normal for this time of night. See to it."

"Sir!" Calvin's unemotional voice was reassuring.

"I don't think the Confederates spend much time examining pictures of the boondocks anyway," Falkenberg told Bannister. "But it's best not to take any chances." Motors roared as ground cars and choppers were put under cover. Another helicopter flew overhead looking for telltales.

"As soon as that thing's past get the troops on the packet ship," Falkenberg ordered. "And send in Captain

Svoboda, Mayor Hastings, and the local militia colonel—Ardway, wasn't it?"

"Yes, sir," Calvin answered. "Colonel Martine Ardway. I'll see if he's up to it, Colonel."

"Up to it, Sergeant Major? Was he hurt?"

"He had a pistol, Colonel. Twelve millimeter thing, big slug, slow bullet, couldn't penetrate armor but he bruised hell out of two troopers. Monitor Badnikov laid him out with a rifle butt. Surgeon says he'll be all right."

"Good enough. If he's able to come I want him here."

"Sir."

Falkenberg turned back to the desk and used the computer to produce a planetary map. "Where would the supply ship go from here, Mr. Bannister?"

The secretary traced a course. "It would—and will—stay inside this island chain. Nobody but a suicide takes ships into open water on this planet. With no land to interrupt them the seas go sixty meters in storms." He indicated a route from Allansport to Cape Titan, then through an island chain in the Sea of Mariners. "Most ships stop at Preston Bay to deliver metalshop goods for the ranches up on Ford Heights Plateau. The whole area's Patriot territory and you could liberate it with one stroke."

Falkenberg studied the map, then said, "No. So most ships stop there—do some go directly to Astoria?" He pointed to a city eighteen hundred kilometers east of Preston Bay.

"Yes, sometimes—but the Confederates keep a big garrison in Astoria, Colonel. Much larger than the one in Preston Bay. Why go twenty-five hundred kilometers to fight a larger enemy force when there's good Patriot country at half the distance?"

"For the same reason the Confederates don't put much strength at Preston Bay. It's isolated. The Ford Heights ranches are scattered—look, Mr. Secretary, if we take Astoria we have the key to the whole Columbia River Valley. The Confederates won't know if we're going north to Doak's Ferry, east to Grand Forks and on into the capital plains, or west to Ford Heights. If I take Preston Bay first they'll know what I intend because there's only one thing a sane man could do from there."

"But the Columbia Valley people aren't reliable! You won't get good recruits—"

They were interrupted by a knock. Sergeant Major Calvin ushered in Roger Hastings and Martine Ardway. The

159

militiaman had a lump over his left eye, and his cheek was bandaged.

Falkenberg stood to be introduced and offered his hand, which Roger Hastings ignored. Ardway stood rigid for a second, then extended his own. "I won't say I'm pleased to meet you, Colonel Falkenberg, but my compliments on an operation well conducted."

"Thank you, Colonel. Gentlemen, please be seated. You have met Captain Svoboda, my Provost?" Falkenberg indicated a lanky officer in battledress who'd come in with them. "Captain Svoboda will be in command of this town when the Forty-second moves out."

Ardway's eyes narrowed with interest. Falkenberg smiled. "You'll see it soon enough, Colonel. Now, the rules of occupation are simple. As mercenaries, gentlemen, we are subject to the CoDominium's Laws of War. Public property is seized in the name of the Free States. Private holdings are secure, and any property requisitioned will be paid for. Any property used to aid resistance, whether directly or as a place to make conspiracy, will be instantly confiscated."

Ardway and Hastings shrugged. They'd heard all this before. At one time the CD tried to suppress mercenaries. When that failed the Fleet rigidly enforced the Grand Senate's Laws of War, but now the Fleet was weakened by budget cuts and a new outbreak of U.S.–Soviet hatred. New Washington was isolated and it might be years before CD Marines appeared to enforce rules the Grand Senate no longer cared about.

"I have a problem, gentlemen," Falkenberg said. "This city is Loyalist, and I must withdraw my regiment. There aren't any Patriot soldiers yet. I'm leaving enough force to complete the conquest of this peninsula, but Captain Svoboda will have few troops in Allansport itself. Since we cannot occupy the city, it can legitimately be destroyed to prevent it from becoming a base against me."

"You can't!" Hastings protested, jumping to his feet, shattering a glass ashtray. "I was sure all that talk about preserving private property was a lot of crap!" He turned to Bannister. "Howard, I told you last time all you'd succeed in doing was burning down the whole goddamn planet! Now you import soldiers to do it for you! What in God's name can you get from this war?"

"Freedom," Bannister said proudly. "Allansport is a nest of traitors anyway."

160

"Hold it," Falkenberg said gently.

"Traitors!" Bannister repeated. "You'll get what you deserve, you—"

"TENSH-HUT!" Sergeant Major Calvin's command startled them. "The Colonel said you was to hold it."

"Thank you," Falkenberg said quietly. The silence was louder than the shouts had been. "I said I could burn the city, not that I intended to. However, since I won't I must have hostages." He handed Roger Hastings a computer typescript. "Troops are quartered in homes of these persons. You will note that you and Colonel Ardway are at the top of my list. All will be detained, and anyone who escapes will be replaced by members of his family. Your property and ultimately your lives are dependent on your cooperation with Captain Svoboda until I send a regular garrison here. Is this understood?"

Colonel Ardway nodded grimly. "Yes, sir. I agree to it."

"Thank you," Falkenberg said. "And you, Mr. Mayor?"

"I understand."

"And?" Falkenberg prompted.

"And what? You want me to like it? What kind of sadist are you?"

"I don't care if you like it, Mr. Mayor. I am waiting for you to agree."

"He doesn't understand, Colonel," Martine Ardway said. "Roger, he's asking if you agree to serve as a hostage for the city. The others will be asked as well. If he doesn't get enough to agree he'll burn the city to the ground."

"Oh." Roger felt a cold knife of fear. What a hell of a choice.

"The question is," Falkenberg said, "will you accept the responsibilities of the office you hold and keep your damn people from making trouble?"

Roger swallowed hard. *I wanted to be mayor so I could erase the hatreds of the rebellion.* "Yes. I agree."

"Excellent. Captain Svoboda."

"Sir."

"Take the mayor and Colonel Ardway to your office and interview the others. Notify me when you have enough hostages to ensure security."

"Yes, sir. Gentlemen?" It was hard to read his expression as he showed them to the door. The visor of his helmet was up, but Svoboda's angular face remained in shadow. As he escorted them from the room the intercom buzzed.

161

"The satellite's overhead," Major Savage reported. "All correct, John Christian. And we've secured the passengers off that train."

The office door closed. Roger Hastings moved like a robot across the bustling city council chamber room, only dimly aware of the bustle of headquarters activities around him. The damn war, the fools, the bloody damned fools—couldn't they ever leave things alone?

XVI

A DOZEN MEN in camouflage battledress led a slim pretty girl across hard-packed sands to the water's edge. They were glad to get away from the softer sands above the highwater mark nearly a kilometer from the pounding surf. Walking in that had been hell, with shifting powder sands infested with small burrowing carnivores too stupid not to attack a booted man.

The squad climbed wordlessly into the waiting boat while their leader tried to assist the girl. She needed no help. Glenda Ruth wore tan nylon coveralls and an equipment belt, and she knew this planet and its dangers better than the soldiers. Glenda Ruth Horton had been taking care of herself for twenty-four of her twenty-six years.

White sandy beaches dotted with marine life exposed by the low tide stretched in both directions as far as they could see. Only the boat and its crew showed that the planet had human life. When the coxswain started the boat's water jet the whirr sent clouds of tiny sea birds into frantic activity.

The fast packet *Maribell* lay twelve kilometers offshore, well beyond the horizon. When the boat arrived deck cranes dipped to seize her and haul the flat-bottomed craft to her davits. Captain Ian Frazer escorted Glenda Ruth to the chart room.

Falkenberg's battle staff waited there impatiently, some sipping whiskey, others staring at charts whose information they had long since absorbed. Many showed signs of seasickness: the eighty-hour voyage from Allansport had been rough, and it hadn't helped that the ship pushed along at thirty-three kilometers an hour, plowing into big swells among the islands.

Ian saluted, then took a glass from the steward and

offered it to Glenda Ruth. "Colonel Falkenberg, Miss Horton. Glenda Ruth is the Patriot leader in the Columbia Valley. Glenda Ruth, you'll know Secretary Bannister."

She nodded coldly as if she did not care for the rebel minister, but she put out her hand to Falkenberg and shook his in a thoroughly masculine way. She had other masculine gestures, but even with her brown hair tucked neatly under a visored cap no one would mistake her for a man. She had a heart-shaped face and large green eyes, and her weathered tan might have been envied by the great ladies of the CoDominium.

"My pleasure, Miss Horton," Falkenberg said perfunctorily. "Were you seen?"

Ian Frazer looked pained. "No, sir. We met the rebel group and it seemed safe enough, so Centurion Michaels and I borrowed some clothing from the ranchers and let Glenda Ruth take us to town for our own look." Ian moved to the chart table.

"The fort's up here on the heights." Frazer pointed to the coastal chart. "Typical wall and trench system. Mostly they depend on the Friedlander artillery to control the city and river mouth."

"What's in there, Ian?" Major Savage asked.

"Worst thing is artillery," the Scout Troop commander answered. "Two batteries of 105's and a battery of 155's, all self-propelled. As near as we can figure it's a standard Friedland detached battalion."

"About six hundred Friedlanders, then," Captain Rottermill said thoughtfully. "And we're told there's a regiment of Earth mercenaries. Anything else?"

Ian glanced at Glenda Ruth. "They moved in a squadron of Confederate Regular Cavalry last week," she said. "Light armored cars. We think they're due to move on, because there's nothing for them to do here, but nobody knows where they're going."

"That is odd," Rottermill said. "There's not a proper petrol supply for them here—where would they go?"

Glenda Ruth regarded him thoughtfully. She had little use for mercenaries. Freedom was something to be won, not bought and paid for. But they needed these men, and at least this one had done his homework. "Probably to the Snake Valley. They've got wells and refineries there." She indicated the flatlands where the Snake and Columbia merged at Doak's Ferry six hundred kilometers to the north. "That's Patriot country and cavalry could be useful to supplement the big fortress at the Ferry."

"Damn bad luck all the same, Colonel," Rottermill said. "Nearly three thousand men in that damned fortress and we've not a lot more. How's the security, Ian?"

Frazer shrugged. "Not tight. The Earth goons patrol the city, doing MP duty, checking papers. No trouble avoiding them."

"The Earthies make up most of the guard details too," Glenda Ruth added. "They've got a whole rifle regiment of them."

"We'll not take that place by storm, John Christian," Major Savage said carefully. "Not without losing half the regiment."

"And just what are your soldiers for?" Glenda Ruth demanded. "Do they fight sometimes?"

"Sometimes." Falkenberg studied the sketch his scout commander was making. "Do they have sentries posted, Captain?"

"Yes, sir. Pairs in towers and walking guards. There are radar dishes every hundred meters, and I expect there are body capacitance wires strung outside as well."

"I told you," Secretary Bannister said smugly. There was triumph in his voice, in contrast to the grim concern of Falkenberg and his officers. "You'll have to raise an army to take that place. Ford Heights is our only chance, Colonel. Astoria's too strong for you."

"No!" Glenda Ruth's strong, low-pitched voice commanded attention. "We've risked everything to gather the Columbia Valley Patriots. If you don't take Astoria now, they'll go back to their ranches. I was opposed to starting a new revolution, Howard Bannister. I don't think we can stand another long war like the last one. But I've organized my father's friends, and in two days I'll command a fighting force. If we scatter now I'll never get them to fight again."

"Where is your army—and how large is it?" Falkenberg asked.

"The assembly area is two hundred kilometers north of here. I have six hundred riflemen now and another five thousand coming. A force that size can't hide!" She regarded Falkenberg without enthusiasm. They needed a strong organized nucleus to win, but she was trusting her friends' lives to a man she'd never met. "Colonel, my ranchers can't face Confederate Regulars or Friedland

165

armor without support, but if you take Astoria we'll have a base we can hold."

"Yes." Falkenberg studied the maps as he thought about the girl. She had a more realistic appreciation of irregular forces than Bannister—but how reliable was she? "Mr. Bannister, we can't take Astoria without artillery even with your Ford Heights ranchers. I need Astoria's guns, and the city's the key to the whole campaign anyway. With it in hand there's a chance to win this war quickly."

"But it can't be done!" Bannister insisted.

"Yet it must be done," Falkenberg reminded him. "And we do have surprise. No Confederate knows we're on this planet and won't for—" he glanced at his pocket computer—"twenty-seven hours, when Weapons Detachment knocks down the snooper. Miss Horton, have you made trouble for Astoria lately?"

"Not for months," she said. Was this mercenary, this man Falkenberg, different? "I only came this far south to meet you."

Captain Frazer's sketch of the fort lay on the table like a death warrant. Falkenberg watched in silence as the scout drew in machine-gun emplacements along the walls.

"I forbid you to risk the revolution on some mad scheme!" Bannister shouted. "Astoria's far too strong. You said so yourself."

Glenda Ruth's rising hopes died again. Bannister was giving the mercenaries a perfect out.

Falkenberg straightened and took a brimming glass from the steward. "Who's junior man here?" He looked around the steel-riveted chart room until he saw an officer near the bulkhead. "Excellent. Lieutenant Fuller was a prisoner on Tanith, Mr. Bannister. Until we caught him—Mark, give us a toast."

"A toast, Colonel?"

"Montrose's toast, Mister. Montrose's toast."

Fear clutched Bannister's guts into a hard ball. Montrose! And Glenda Ruth stared uncomprehendingly, but there was reborn hope in her eyes . . .

"Aye aye, Colonel." Fuller raised his glass. "He either fears his fate too much, or his desserts are small, who dares not put it to the touch, to win or lose it all."

Bannister's hands shook as the officers drank. Falkenberg's wry smile, Glenda Ruth's answering look of comprehension and admiration—they were all crazy! The lives of all the Patriots were at stake, and the man and the girl, both of them, they were insane!

Maribell swung to her anchors three kilometers offshore from Astoria. The fast-moving waters of the Columbia swept around her toward the ocean some nine kilometers downstream, where waves crashed in a line of breakers five meters high. Getting across the harbor bar was a tricky business, and even in the harbor itself the tides were too fierce for the ship to dock.

Maribell's cranes hummed as they swung cargo lighters off her decks. The air-cushion vehicles moved gracelessly across the water and over the sandy beaches to the corrugated aluminum warehouses, where they left cargo containers and picked up empties.

In the fortress above Astoria the officer of the guard dutifully logged the ship's arrival into his journal. It was the most exciting event in two weeks. Since the rebellion had ended there was little for his men to do.

He turned from the tower to look around the encampment. Blasted waste of good armor, he thought. No point in having self-propelled guns as harbor guards. The armor wasn't used, since the guns were in concrete revetments. The lieutenant had been trained in mobile war, and though he could appreciate the need for control over the mouth of New Washington's largest river, he didn't like this duty. There was no glory in manning an impregnable fortress.

Retreat sounded and all over the fort men stopped to face the flags. The Franklin Confederacy colors fluttered down the staff to the salutes of the garrison. Although as guard officer he wasn't supposed to, the lieutenant saluted as the trumpets sang.

Over by the guns men stood at attention, but *they* didn't salute. Friedland mercenaries, they owed the Confederacy no loyalty that hadn't been bought and paid for. The lieutenant admired them as soldiers, but they were not likable. It was worth knowing them, though, since nobody else could handle armor like them. He had managed to make friends with a few. Someday, when the Confederacy was stronger, they would dispense with mercenaries, and until then he wanted to learn all he could. There were rich planets in this sector of space, planets that Franklin could add to the Confederacy now that the rebellion was over. With the CD Fleet weaker every year, opportunities at the edges of inhabited space grew, but only for those ready for them.

When retreat ended he turned back to the harbor. An ugly cargo lighter was coming up the broad roadway to the fort. He frowned, puzzled, and climbed down from the tower.

When he reached the gate the lighter had halted there. Its engine roared, and it was very difficult to understand the driver, a broad-shouldered seaman-stevedore who was insisting on something.

"I got no orders," the Earth mercenary guardsman was protesting. He turned to the lieutenant in relief. "Sir, they say they have a shipment for us on that thing."

"What is it?" the lieutenant shouted. He had to say it again to be heard over the roar of the motors. "What is the cargo?"

"Damned if I know," the driver said cheerfully. "Says on the manifest 'Astoria Fortress, attention supply officer.' Look, Lieutenant, we got to be moving. If the captain don't catch the tide he can't cross the harbor bar tonight and he'll skin me for squawrk bait! Where's the supply officer?"

The lieutenant looked at his watch. After retreat the men dispersed rapidly and supply officers kept short hours. "There's nobody to offload," he shouted.

"Got a crane and crew here," the driver said. "Look, just show me where to put this stuff. We got to sail at slack water."

"Put it out here," the lieutenant said.

"Right. You'll have a hell of a job moving it though." He turned to his companion in the cab. "O.K., Charlie, dump it!"

The lieutenant thought of what the supply officer would say when he found he'd have to move the ten-by-five-meter containers. He climbed into the bed of the cargo lighter. In the manifest pocket of each container was a ticket reading "COMMISSARY SUPPLIES."

"Wait," he ordered. "Private, open the gates. Driver, take this over there." He indicated a warehouse near the center of the camp. "Offload at the big doors."

"Right. Hold it, Charlie," Sergeant Major Calvin said cheerfully. "The lieutenant wants the stuff inside." He gave his full attention to driving the ungainly GEM.

The lighter crew worked the crane efficiently, stacking

the cargo containers by the warehouse doors. "Sign here," the driver said.

"I—perhaps I better get someone to inventory the cargo."

"Aw, for Christ's sake," the driver protested. "Look, you can see the seals ain't broke—here, I'll write it in. 'Seals intact, but cargo not inspected by recip—' How you spell 'recipient,' Lieutenant?"

"Here, I'll write it for you." He did, and signed with his name and rank. "Have a good voyage?"

"Naw. Rough out there, and getting worse. We got to scoot, more cargo to offload."

"Not for us!"

"Naw, for the town. Thanks, Lieutenant." The GEM pivoted and roared away as the guard lieutenant shook his head. What a mess. He climbed into the tower to write the incident up in the day book. As he wrote he sighed. One hour to dark, and three until he was off duty. It had been a long, dull day.

Three hours before dawn the cargo containers silently opened, and Captain Ian Frazer led his scouts onto the darkened parade ground. Wordlessly they moved toward the revetted guns. One squad formed ranks and marched toward the gates, rifles at slope arms.

The sentries turned. "What the hell?" one said. "It's not time for our relief, who's there?"

"Can it," the corporal of the squad said. "We got orders to go out on some goddam perimeter patrol. Didn't you get the word?"

"Nobody tells me anythin'—uh." The sentry grunted as the corporal struck him with a leather bag of shot. His companion turned quickly, but too late. The squad had already reached him.

Two men stood erect in the starlight at the posts abandoned by the sentries. Astoria was far over the horizon from Franklin, and only a faint red glow to the west indicated the companion planet.

The rest of the squad entered the guardhouse. They moved efficiently among the sleeping relief men, and when they finished the corporal took a communicator from his belt. "Laertes."

On the other side of the parade ground, Captain Frazer led a group of picked men to the radar control center. There was a silent flurry of bayonets and rifle butts. When

169

the brief struggle ended Ian spoke into his communicator. "Hamlet."

There was no answer, but he hadn't expected one.

Down in the city other cargo containers opened in darkened warehouses. Armed men formed into platoons and marched through the dockside streets. The few civilians who saw them scurried for cover; no one had much use for the Earthling mercenaries the Confederates employed.

A full company marched up the hill to the fort. On the other side, away from the city, the rest of the regiment crawled across plowed fields, heedless of radar alarms but careful of the sentries on the walls above. They passed the first line of capacitance wires and Major Savage held his breath. Ten seconds, twenty. He sighed in relief and motioned the troops to advance.

The marching company reached the gate. Sentries challenged them while others in guard towers watched in curiosity. When the gates swung open the tower guards relaxed. The officer of the watch must have had special orders . . .

The company moved into the armored car park. Across the parade ground a sentry peered into the night. Something out there? "Halt! Who's there?" There was only silence.

"See something, Jack?" his companion asked.

"Dunno—look out there. By the bushes. Somethin'— My God, Harry! The field's full of men! CORPORAL OF THE GUARD! Turn out the Guard!" He hesitated before taking the final step, but he was sure enough to risk his sergeant's scathing displeasure. A stabbing finger hit the red alarm button, and lights blazed around the camp perimeter. The sirens hooted, and he had time to see a thousand men in the field near the camp; then a burst of fire caught him, and he fell.

The camp erupted into confusion. The Friedland gunners woke first. They wasted less than a minute before their officers realized the alarm was real. Then the gunners boiled out of the barracks to save their precious armor, but from each revetment, bursts of machine-gun fire cut into them. Gunners fell in heaps as the rest scurried for cover. Many had not brought personal weapons in their haste to serve the guns, and they lost time going back for them.

Major Savage's men reached the walls and clambered over. Alternate sections kept the walls under a ripple of fire, and despite their heavy battle armor the men climbed easily in Washington's lower gravity. Officers sent them to the parade ground where they added their fire to that of the men in the revetments. Hastily set machine guns isolated the artillery emplacements with a curtain of fire.

That artillery was the fort's main defense. Once he was certain it was secure, Major Savage sent his invaders by waves into the camp barracks. They burst in with grenades and rifles ready, taking whole companies before their officers could arrive with the keys to their weapons racks. Savage took the Confederate Regulars that way, and only the Freidlanders had come out fighting; but their efforts were directed toward their guns, and there they had no chance.

Meanwhile the Earth mercenaries, never very steady troops at best, called for quarter; many had not fired a shot. The camp defenders fought as disorganized groups against a disciplined force whose communications worked perfectly.

At the fortress headquarters building the alarms woke Commandant Albert Morris. He listened in disbelief to the sounds of battle, and although he rushed out half-dressed, he was too late. His command was engulfed by nearly four thousand screaming men. Morris stood a moment in indecision, torn by the desire to run to the nearest barracks and rally what forces he could, but he decided his duty was in the communications room. The Capital must be told. Desperately he ran to the radio shack.

Everything seemed normal inside, and he shouted orders to the duty sergeant before he realized he had never seen the man before. He turned to face a squad of leveled rifles. A bright light stabbed from a darker corner of the room.

"Good morning, sir," an even voice said.

Commandant Morris blinked, then carefully raised his hands in surrender. "I've no sidearms. Who the hell are you, anyway?"

"Colonel John Christian Falkenberg, at your service. Will you surrender this base and save your men?"

Morris nodded grimly. He'd seen enough outside to know the battle was hopeless. His career was finished too, no matter what he did, and there was no point in letting the Freidlanders be slaughtered. "Surrender to whom?"

The light flicked off and Morris saw Falkenberg. There was a grim smile on the Colonel's lips. "Why, to the Great

Jehovah and the Free States of Washington, Commandant. . . ."

Albert Morris, who was no historian, did not understand the reference. He took the public address mike the grim troopers handed him. Fortress Astoria had fallen.

Twenty-three hundred kilometers to the west at Allansport, Sergeant Sherman White slapped the keys to launch three small solid rockets. They weren't very powerful birds, but they could be set up quickly, and they had the ability to loft a hundred kilos of tiny steel cubes to one hundred forty kilometers. White had very good information on the Confederate satellite's ephemeris; he'd observed it for its past twenty orbits.

The target was invisible over the horizon when Sergeant White launched his interceptors. As it came overhead the small rockets had climbed to meet it. Their radar fuses sought the precise moment, then they exploded in a cloud of shot that rose as it spread. It continued to climb, halted, and began to fall back toward the ground. The satellite detected the attack and beeped alarms to its masters. Then it passed through the cloud at fourteen hundred meters per second relative to the shot. Four of the steel cubes were in its path.

XVII

Falkenberg studied the manuals on the equipment in the Confederate command car as it raced northward along the Columbia Valley road toward Doak's Ferry. Captain Frazer's scouts were somewhere ahead with the captured cavalry equipment and behind Falkenberg the regiment was strung out piecemeal. There were men on motorcycles, in private trucks, horse-drawn wagons, and on foot.

There'd be more walking soon. The captured cavalry gear was a lucky break, but the Columbia Valley wasn't technologically developed. Most local transport was by animal power, and the farmers relied on the river to ship produce to the deepwater port at Astoria. The river boats and motor fuel were the key to the operation. There wasn't enough of either.

Glenda Ruth Horton had surprised Falkenberg by not arguing about the need for haste, and her ranchers were converging on all the river ports, taking heavy casualties in order to seize boats and fuel before the scattered Confederate occupation forces could destroy them. Meanwhile Falkenberg had recklessly flung the regiment northward.

"Fire fight ahead," his driver said. "Another of them one battery posts."

"Right." Falkenberg fiddled with the unfamiliar controls until the map came into sharper focus, then activated the comm circuit.

"Sir," Captain Frazer answered. "They've got a battery of 105's and an MG Company in there. More than I can handle."

"Right. Pass it by. Let Miss Horton's ranchers keep it under siege. Found any more fuel?"

Frazer laughed unpleasantly. "Colonel, you can adjust the carburetors in these things to handle a lot, but Christ,

173

they bloody well won't run on paraffin. There's not even farm machinery out here! We're running on fumes now, and damned low-grade fumes at that."

"Yeah." The Confederates were getting smarter. For the first hundred kilometers they took fueling stations intact, but now, unless the Patriots were already in control, the fuel was torched before Frazer's fast-moving scouts arrived. "Keep going as best you can, Captain."

"Sir. Out."

"We got some reserve fuel with the guns," Sergeant Major Calvin reminded him. The big RSM sat in the turret of the command caravan and at frequent intervals fondled the thirty-mm cannon there. It wasn't much of a weapon, but it had been a long time since the RSM was gunner in an armored vehicle. He was hoping to get in some fighting.

"No. Those guns have to move east to the passes. They're sure to send a reaction force from the capital, Top Soldier."

But would they? Falkenberg wondered. Instead of moving northwest from the capital to reinforce the fortress at Doak's Ferry, they might send troops by sea to retake Astoria. It would be a stupid move, and Falkenberg counted on the Confederates acting intelligently. As far as anyone knew, the Astoria Fortress guns dominated the river mouth.

A detachment of Weapons Battalion remained there with antiaircraft rockets to keep reconnaissance at a distance, but otherwise Astoria was held only by a hastily raised Patriot force stiffened with a handful of mercenaries. The Friedlander guns had been taken out at night.

If Falkenberg's plan worked, by the time the Confederates knew what they faced, Astoria would be strongly held by Valley Patriot armies, and other Patriot forces would have crossed the water to hold Allansport. It was a risky battle plan, but it had one merit: it was the only one that could succeed.

Leading elements of the regiment covered half the six hundred kilometers north to Doak's Ferry in ten hours. Behind Falkenberg's racing lead groups the main body of the regiment moved more ponderously, pausing to blast out pockets of resistance where that could be quickly done, otherwise bypassing them for the Patriot irregulars to starve into submission. The whole Valley was rising, and the further north Falkenberg went the greater the number of Patriots he encountered. When they reached the four-hundred-kilometer point, he sent Glenda Ruth Horton eastward toward the passes to join Major Savage and the Friedland artillery. Like the regiment, the ranchers moved by a variety of means: helicopters, GEM's, trucks, mules, and on foot.

"Real boot straps," Hiram Black said. Black was a short, wind-browned rancher commissioned colonel by the Free States Council and sent with Falkenberg to aid in controlling rebel forces. Falkenberg liked the man's dry humor and hard realism. "General Falkenberg, we got the damnedest collection in the history of warfare."

"Yes." There was nothing more to say. In addition to the confused transport situation, there was no standardization of weapons: they had hunting pieces, weapons taken from the enemy, the regiment's own equipment, and stockpiles of arms smuggled in by the Free States before Falkenberg's arrival. "That's what computers are for," Falkenberg said.

"Crossroad coming up," the driver warned. "Hang on." The crossing was probably registered by the guns of an untaken post eight kilometers ahead. Frazer's cavalry had blinded its hilltop observation radars before passing it by, but the battery would have had brief sights of the command car.

The driver suddenly halted. There was a sharp whistle, and an explosion rocked the caravan. Shrapnel rattled off the armored sides. The car bounded into life and accelerated.

"Ten credits you owe me, Seregant Major," the driver said. "Told you they'd expect me to speed up."

"Think I wanted to win the bet, Carpenter?" Calvin asked.

They drove through rolling hills covered with the golden tassels of corn plants. Genetic engineering had made New Washington's native grain one of the most valuable food crops in space. Superficially similar to Earth maize, this corn had a growing cycle of two local years. Toward the end of the cycle hydrostatic pressures built up until it exploded, but if harvested in the dry period New Washington corn was high-protein dehydrated food energy, palatable when cooked in water, and good fodder for animals as well.

"Ought to be getting past the opposition now," Hiram

Black said. "Expect the Feddies'll be pulling back to the fort at Doak's Ferry from here on."

His estimate was confirmed a half hour later when Falkenberg's comm set squawked into action. "We're in a little town called Madselin, Colonel," Frazer said. "Used to be a garrison here, but they're running up the road. There's a citizen's committee to welcome us."

"To hell with the citizen's committee," Falkenberg snapped. "Pursue the enemy!"

"Colonel, I'd be very pleased to do so, but I've no petrol at all."

Falkenberg nodded grimly. "Captain Frazer, I want the scouts as far north as they can get. Isn't there *any* transport?"

There was a long silence. "Well, sir, there are bicycles . . ."

"Then use bicycles, by God! Use whatever you have to, Captain, but until you are stopped by the enemy you will continue the advance, bypassing concentrations. Snap at their heels. Ian, they're scared. They don't know what's chasing them, and if you keep the pressure on they won't stop to find out. Keep going, laddie. I'll bail you out if you get in trouble."

"Aye, aye, Colonel. See you in Doak's Ferry."

"Correct. Out."

"Can you keep that promise, General?" Hiram Black asked.

Falkenberg's pale blue eyes stared through the rancher. "That depends on how reliable your Glenda Ruth Horton is, Colonel Black. Your ranchers are supposed to be gathering along the Valley. With that threat to their flanks the Confederates will not dare form a defense line south of Doak's Ferry. If your Patriots don't show up then it's another story entirely." He shrugged. Behind him the Regiment was strung out along three hundred kilometers of roads, its only flank protection its speed and the enemy's uncertainties. "It's up to her in more ways than one," Falkenberg continued. "She said the main body of Friedland armor was in the capital area."

Hiram Black sucked his teeth in a very unmilitary way. "General, if Glenda Ruth's sure of something, you can damn well count on it."

Sergeant Major Calvin grunted. The noise spoke his thoughts better than words. It was a hell of a thing when the life of the Forty-second had to depend on a young colonial girl.

"How did she come to command the Valley ranchers, anyway?" Falkenberg asked.

"Inherited it," Black answered. "Her father was one hell of a man, General. Got himself killed in the last battle of the first revolution. She'd been his chief of staff. Old Josh trusted her more'n he did most of his officers. So would I, if I was you, General."

"I already do." To Falkenberg the regiment was more than a mercenary force. Like any work of art, it was an instrument perfectly forged—its existence and perfection its own reason for existence.

But unlike any work of art, because the regiment was a military unit, it had to fight battles and take casualties. The men who died in battle were mourned. They weren't the regiment, though, and it would exist when every man now in it was dead. The Forty-second had faced defeat before and might find it again—but this time the regiment itself was at hazard. Falkenberg was gambling not merely their lives, but the Forty-second itself.

He studied the battle maps as they raced northward. By keeping the enemy off balance, one regiment could do the work of five. Eventually, though, the Confederates would no longer retreat. They were falling back on their fortress at Doak's Ferry, gathering strength and concentrating for a battle that Falkenberg could never win. Therefore that battle must not be fought until the ranchers had concentrated. Meanwhile, the regiment must bypass Doak's Ferry and turn east to the mountain passes, closing them before the Friedland armor and Covenant Highlanders could debauch onto the western plains.

"Think you'll make it?" Hiram Black asked. He watched as Falkenberg manipulated controls to move symbols across the map tank in the command car. "Seems to me the Friedlanders will reach the pass before you can."

"They will," Falkenberg said. "And if they get through, we're lost." He twirled a knob, sending a bright blip representing Major Savage with the artillery racing diagonally from Astoria to Hillyer Gap, while the main force of the regiment continued up the Columbia, then turned east to the mountains, covering two legs of a triangle. "Jerry Savage could be there first, but he won't have enough force to stop them." Another set of symbols crawled across the map. Instead of a distinctly formed body, this was a series of rivulets coming together at the pass. "Miss Horton has also promised to be there with reinforcements and supplies—enough to hold in the first battle, anyway. If they delay the Friedlanders long enough for the rest of us to get there, we'll own the entire agricultural area of New Washington. The revolution will be better than half over."

"And what if she can't get there—or they can't hold the Friedlanders and Covenant boys?" Hiram Black asked.

Sergeant Major Calvin grunted again.

XVIII

HILLYER GAP WAS a six-kilometer-wide hilly notch in the high mountain chain. The Aldine Mountains ran roughly northwest to southeast, and were joined at their midpoint by the southward stretching Temblors. Just at the join was the Gap that connected the capital city plain to the east with the Columbia Valley to the west.

Major Jeremy Savage regarded his position with satisfaction. He not only had the twenty-six guns taken from the Friedlanders at Astoria, but another dozen captured in scattered outposts along the lower Columbia, and all were securely dug in behind hills overlooking the Gap. Forward of the guns were six companies of infantry, Second Battalion and half of Third, with a thousand ranchers behind in reserve.

"We won't be outflanked, anyway," Centurion Bryant observed. "Ought to hold just fine, sir."

"We've a chance," Major Savage agreed. "Thanks to Miss Horton. You must have driven your men right along."

Glenda Ruth shrugged. Her irregulars had run low on fuel one hundred eighty kilometers west of the Gap, and she'd brought them on foot in one forced march of thirty hours, after sending her ammunition supplies ahead with the last drops of gasoline. "I just came on myself, Major. Wasn't a question of driving them, the men followed right enough."

Jeremy Savage looked at her quickly. The slender girl was not very pretty at the moment, with her coveralls streaked with mud and grease, her hair falling in strings from under her cap, but he'd rather have seen her just then than the current Miss Universe. With her troops and ammunition supplies he had a chance to hold this position.

"I suppose they did at that." Centurion Bryant turned away quickly with something caught in his throat.

"Can we hold until Colonel Falkenberg gets here?" Glenda Ruth asked. "I expect them to send everything they've got."

"We sincerely hope they do," Jeremy Savage answered. "It's our only chance, you know. If that armor gets onto open ground . . ."

"There's no other way onto the plains, Major," she replied "The Temblors go right on down to the Matson swamplands, and nobody's fool enough to risk armor there. Great Bend's Patriot country. Between the swamps and the Patriot irregulars it'd take a week to cross the Matson. If they're comin' by land, they're comin' through here."

"And they'll be coming," Savage finished for her. "They'll want to relieve the Doak's Ferry fortress before we can get it under close siege. At least that was John Christian's plan, and he's usually right."

Glenda Ruth used her binoculars to examine the road. There was nothing out there—yet. "This colonel of yours. What's in this for him? Nobody gets rich on what we can pay."

"I should think you'd be glad enough we're here," Jeremy said.

"Oh, I'm glad all right. In two hundred forty hours Falkenberg's isolated every Confederate garrison west of the Temblors. The capital city forces are the only army left to fight—you've almost liberated the planet in one campaign."

"Luck," Jeremy Savage murmured. "Lots of it, all good."

"Heh." Glenda Ruth was contemptuous. "I don't believe in that, no more do you. Sure, with the Confederates scattered out on occupation duty anybody who could get troops to move fast enough could cut the Feddies up before they got into big enough formations to resist. The fact is, Major, nobody believed that could be done except on maps. Not with real troops—and he did it. That's not luck, that's genius."

Savage shrugged. "I wouldn't dispute that."

"No more would I. Now answer this—just what is a real military genius doing commanding mercenaries on a jerkwater agricultural planet? A man like that should be Lieutenant General of the CoDominium."

"The CD isn't interested in military genius, Miss Horton. The Grand Senate wants obedience, not brilliance."

"Maybe. I hadn't heard Lermontov was a fool, and they made him Grand Admiral. O.K., the CoDominium had no use for Falkenberg. But why Washington, Major? With that regiment you could take anyplace but Sparta and give the Brotherhoods a run for it there." She swept the horizon with the binoculars, and Savage could not see her eyes.

This girl disturbed him. No other Free State official questioned the good fortune of hiring Falkenberg. "The regimental council voted to come here because we were sick of Tanith, Miss Horton."

"Sure." She continued to scan the bleak foothills in front of them. "Look, I'd better get some rest if we've got a fight coming—and we do. Look just at the horizon on the left side of the road." As she turned away Centurion Bryant's communicator buzzed. The outposts had spotted the scout elements of an armored task force.

As Glenda Ruth walked back to her bunker, her head felt as if it would begin spinning. She had been born on New Washington and was used to the planet's forty-hour rotation period, but lack of sleep made her almost intoxicated even so.

Walking on pillows, she told herself. That had been Harley Hastings' description of how they felt when they didn't come in until dawn.

Is Harley out there with the armor? she wondered. She hoped not. It would never have worked, but he's such a good boy. Too much of a boy though, trying to act like a man. While it's nice to be treated like a lady sometimes, he could never believe I could do anything for myself at all. . . .

Two ranchers stood guard with one of Falkenberg's corporals at her bunker. The corporal came to a rigid present; the ranchers called a greeting. Glenda Ruth made a gesture, halfway between a wave and a return of the corporal's salute and went inside. The contrast couldn't have been greater, she thought. Her ranchers weren't about to make themselves look silly, with present arms, and salutes, and the rest of it.

She stumbled inside and wrapped herself in a thin blanket without undressing. Somehow the incident outside bothered her. Falkenberg's men were military professionals. All of them. What were they doing on New Washington?

Howard Bannister asked them here. He even offered them land for a permanent settlement and he had no right to do that. There's no way to control a military force like that without keeping a big standing army, and the cure is worse than the disease.

But without Falkenberg the revolution's doomed.

And what happens if we win it? What will Falkenberg do after it's over? Leave? I'm afraid of him because he's not the type to just leave.

And, she thought, to be honest Falkenberg's a very attractive man. I liked just the way he toasted. Howard gave him the perfect out, but he didn't take it.

She could still remember him with his glass lifted, an enigmatic smile on his lips—and then he went into the packing crates himself, along with Ian and his men.

But courage isn't anything special. What we need here is loyalty, and that he's never promised at all . . .

There was no one to advise her. Her father was the only man she'd ever really respected. Before he was killed, he'd tried to tell her that winning the war was only a small part of the problem. There were countries on Earth that had gone through fifty bloody revolutions before they were lucky enough to have a tyrant gain control and stop them. Revolution's the easy part, as her father used to say. Ruling afterwards—that's something else entirely.

As she fell asleep she saw Falkenberg in a dream. What if Falkenberg wouldn't let them keep their revolution? His hard features softened in a swirling mist. He was wearing military uniform and sat at a desk, Sergeant Major Calvin at his side.

"These can live. Kill those. Send these to the mines," Falkenberg ordered.

The big sergeant moved tiny figures that looked like model soldiers, but they weren't all troops. One was her father. Another was a group of her ranchers. And they weren't models at all. They were real people reduced to miniatures whose screams could barely be heard as the stern voice continued to pronounce their dooms . . .

Brigadier Wilfred von Mellenthin looked up the hill toward the rebel troop emplacements, then climbed back down into his command caravan to wait for his scouts to report. He had insisted that the Confederacy send his armor

182

west immediately after the news arrived that Astoria had fallen, but the General Staff wouldn't let him go.

Fools, he thought. The staff said it was too big a risk. Von Mellenthin's Friedlander armored task force was the Confederacy's best military unit, and it couldn't be risked in a trap.

Now the General Staff was convinced that they faced only one regiment of mercenaries. One regiment, and that must have taken heavy casualties in storming Astoria. So the staff said. Von Mellenthin studied the map table and shrugged.

Someone was holding the Gap, and he had plenty of respect for the New Washington ranchers. Given rugged terrain like that in front of him, they could put up a good fight. A good enough fight to blunt his force. But, he decided, it was worth it. Beyond the Gap was open terrain, and the ranchers would have no chance there.

The map changed and flowed as he watched. Scouts reported, and Von Mellenthin's staff officers checked the reports, correlated the data, and fed it onto his displays. The map showed well-dug-in infantry, far more of it than von Mellenthin had expected. That damned Falkenberg. The man had an uncanny ability to move troops.

Von Mellenthin turned to the Chief of Staff. "Horst, do you think he has heavy guns here already?"

Oberst Carnap shrugged. *"Weiss nicht,* Brigadier. Every hour gives Falkenberg time to dig in at the Gap, and we have lost many hours."

"Not Falkenberg," von Mellenthin corrected. "He is now investing the fortress at Doak's Ferry. We have reports from the commandant there. Most of Falkenberg's force must be far to the west."

He turned back to his maps. They were as complete as they could be without closer observation.

As if reading his mind, Carnap asked, "Shall I send scouting forces, Brigadier?"

Von Mellenthin stared at the map as if it might tell him one more detail, but it would not. "No. We got through with everything," he said in sudden decision. "Kick their arses, don't pee on them."

"Jawohl." Carnap spoke quietly into the command circuit. Then he looked up again. "It is my duty to point out the risk, Brigadier. We will take heavy losses if they have brought up artillery."

"I know. But if we fail to get through now, we may

never relieve the fortress in time. Half the war is lost when Doak's Ferry is taken. Better heavy casualties immediately than a long war. I will lead the attack myself. You will remain with the command caravan."

"*Jawohl*, Brigadier."

Von Mellenthin climbed out of the heavy caravan and into a medium tank. He took his place in the turret, then spoke quietly to the driver. "Forward."

The armor brushed the infantry screens aside as if they had not been there. Von Mellenthin's tanks and their supporting infantry cooperated perfectly to pin down and root out the opposition. The column moved swiftly forward to cut the enemy into disorganized fragments for the following Covenanter infantry to mop up.

Von Mellenthin was chewing up the blocking force piecemeal as his brigade rushed deeper into the Gap. It was all too easy, and he thought he knew why.

The sweating tankers approached the irregular ridge at the very top of the pass. Suddenly a fury of small arms and mortar fire swept across them. The tanks moved on, but the infantry scrambled for cover. Armor and infantry were separated for a moment, and at that instant his lead tanks reached the minefields.

Brigadier von Mellenthin began to worry. Logic told him the minefields couldn't be wide or dense, and if he punched through he would reach the soft headquarters areas of his enemies. Once there his tanks would make short work of the headquarters and depots, the Covenanter infantry would secure the pass, and his brigade could charge across the open fields beyond.

But—if the defenders had better transport than the General Staff believed, and thus had thousands of mines, he was dooming his armor.

"Evaluation," he demanded. The repeater screen in his command tank swam, then showed the updated maps. His force was bunched up, and his supporting infantry was pinned and taking casualties. "Recommendation?"

"Send scouting forces," Oberst Carnap's voice urged.

Von Mellenthin considered it for a moment. Compromises in war are often worse than either course of action. A small force could be lost without gaining anything. Divided forces can be defeated in detail. He had only moments to reach a decision. "Boot, don't spatter," he said. "We go forward."

They reached the narrowest part of the Gap. His force

now bunched together even more, and his drivers, up to now automatically avoiding terrain features that might be registered by artillery, had to approach conspicuous landmarks. Brigadier von Mellenthin gritted his teeth.

The artillery salvo was perfectly delivered. The brigade had less than a quarter-minute warning as the radars picked up the incoming projectiles. Then the shells exploded all at once, dropping among his tanks to brush away the last of the covering infantry.

As the barrage lifted, hundreds of men appeared from the ground itself. A near perfect volley of infantry-carried anti-tank rockets slammed into his tanks. Then the radars showed more incoming mail—and swam in confusion.

"*Ja,* that too," von Mellenthin muttered. His counter-battery screens showed a shower of gunk.

The defenders were firing chaff, hundreds of thousands of tiny metal chips which slowly drifted to the ground. Neither side could use radar to aim indirect fire, but von Mellenthin's armor was under visual observation, while the enemy guns had never been precisely located.

Another time-on-target salvo landed. "Damned good shooting," von Mellenthin muttered to his driver. There weren't more than five seconds between the first and the last shell's arrival.

The brigade was being torn apart on this killing ground. The lead elements ran into more minefields. Defending infantry crouched in holes and ditches, tiny little groups that his covering infantry could sweep aside in a moment if it could get forward, but the infantry was cut off by the barrages falling behind and around the tanks.

There was no room to maneuver and no infantry support, the classic nightmare of an armor commander. The already rough ground was strewn with pits and ditches. High explosive anti-tank shells fell all around his force. There were not many hits yet, but any disabled tanks could be pounded to pieces, and there was nothing to shoot back at. The lead tanks were under steady fire, and the assault slowed.

The enemy expended shells at a prodigal rate. Could they keep it up? If they ran out of shells it was all over. Von Mellenthin hesitated. Every moment kept his armor in hell.

Doubts undermined his determination. Only the Confederate General Staff told him he faced no more than

Falkenberg's Legion, and the staff had been wrong before. Whatever was out there had taken Astoria before the commandant could send a single message. At almost the same moment the observation satellite was killed over Allansport. Every fortress along the Columbia was invested within hours. Surely not even Falkenberg could do that with no more than one regiment!

What was he fighting? If he faced a well-supplied force with transport enough to continue this bombardment for hours, not minutes, the brigade was lost. His brigade, the finest armor in the worlds, lost to the faulty intelligence of these damned colonials!

"Recall the force. Consolidate at Station Hildebrand." The orders flashed out, and the tanks fell back, rescuing the pinned infantry and covering their withdrawal. When the brigade assembled east of the Gap von Mellenthin had lost an eighth of his tanks, and he doubted if he would recover any of them.

XIX

THE HONOR GUARD presented arms as the command caravan unbuttoned. Falkenberg acknowledged their salutes and strode briskly into the staff bunker. "Tensh-Hut!" Sergeant Major Calvin commanded.

"Carry on, gentlemen. Major Savage, you'll be pleased to know I've brought the regimental artillery. We landed it yesterday. Getting a bit thin, wasn't it?"

"That it was, John Christian," Jeremy Savage answered grimly. "If the battle had lasted another hour we'd have been out of everything. Miss Horton, you can relax now— the colonel said carry on."

"I wasn't sure," Glenda Ruth huffed. She glanced outside where the honor guard was dispersing and scowled in disapproval. "I'd hate to be shot for not bowing properly."

Officers and troopers in the CP tensed, but nothing happened. Falkenberg turned to Major Savage. "What were the casualties, Major?"

"Heavy, sir. We have 283 effectives remaining in Second Battalion."

Falkenberg's face was impassive. "And how many walking wounded?"

"Sir, that includes the walking wounded."

"I see." Sixty-five percent casualties, not including the walking wounded. "And Third?"

"I couldn't put together a corporal's guard from the two companies. The survivors are assigned to headquarters duties."

"What's holding the line out there, Jerry?" Falkenberg demanded.

"Irregulars and what's left of Second Battalion, Colonel. We are rather glad to see you, don't you know?"

Glenda Ruth Horton had a momentary struggle with herself. Whatever she might think about all the senseless militaristic rituals Falkenberg was addicted to, honesty demanded that she say something. "Colonel, I owe you an apology. I'm sorry I implied that your men wouldn't fight at Astoria."

"The question is, Miss Horton, will yours? I have two batteries of the Forty-second's artillery, but I can add nothing to the line itself. My troops are investing Doak's Ferry, my cavalry and First Battalion are on Ford Heights, and the regiment will be scattered for three more days. Are you saying your ranchers can't do as well as my mercenaries?"

She nodded unhappily. "Colonel, we could never have stood up to that attack. The Second's senior Centurion told me many of his mortars were served by only one man before the battle ended. We'll never have men that steady."

Falkenberg looked relieved. "Centurion Bryant survived, then."

"Why—yes."

"Then the Second still lives." Falkenberg nodded to himself in satisfaction.

"But we can't stop another attack by that armor!" Glenda Ruth protested.

"But maybe we won't have to," Falkenberg said. "Miss Horton, I'm betting that von Mellenthin won't risk his armor until the infantry has cleared a hole. From his view he's tried and run into something he can't handle. He doesn't know how close it was.

"Meanwhile, thanks to your efforts in locating transport, we have the artillery partly resupplied. Let's see what we can do with what we've got."

Three hours later they looked up from the maps. "That's it, then," Falkenberg said.

"Yes." Glenda Ruth looked over the troop dispositions. "Those forward patrols are the key to it all," she said carefully.

"Of course." He reached into his kit bag. "Have a drink?"

"Now?" But why not? "Thank you, I will." He poured two mess cups partly full of whiskey and handed her one. "I can't stay long, though," she said.

He shrugged and raised the glass. "A willing foe. But not too willing," he said.

She hesitated a moment, then drank. "It's a game to you, isn't it?"

"Perhaps. And to you?"

"I hate it. I hate all of it. I didn't want to start the rebellion again." She shuddered. "I've had enough of killing and crippled men and burned farms—"

"Then why are you here?" he asked. There was no mockery in his voice—and no contempt. The question was genuine.

"My friends asked me to lead them, and I couldn't let them down."

"A good reason," Falkenberg said.

"Thank you." She drained the cup. "I've got to go now. I have to get into my battle armor."

"That seems reasonable, although the bunkers are well built."

"I won't be in a bunker, Colonel. I'm going on patrol with my ranchers."

Falkenberg regarded her critically. "I wouldn't think that wise, Miss Horton. Personal courage in a commanding officer is an admirable trait, but—"

"I know." She smiled softly. "But it needn't be demonstrated because it is assumed, right? Not with us. I can't order the ranchers, and I don't have years of tradition to keep them—that's the reason for all the ceremonials, isn't it?" she asked in surprise.

Falkenberg ignored the question. "The point is, the men follow you. I doubt they'd fight as hard for me if you're killed."

"Irrelevant, Colonel. Believe me, I don't want to take this patrol out, but if I don't take the first one, there may never be another. We're not used to holding lines, and it's taking some doing to keep my troops steady."

"And so you have to shame them into going out."

She shrugged. "If I go, they will."

"I'll lend you a Centurion and some headquarters guards."

"No. Send the same troops with me that you'll send with any other Patriot force." She swayed for a moment. Lack of sleep and the whiskey and the knot of fear in her guts combined for a moment. She held the edge of the desk for a second while Falkenberg looked at her.

"Oh damn," she said. Then she smiled slightly. "John

Christian Falkenberg, don't you see why it has to be this way?"

He nodded. "I don't have to like it. All right, get your final briefing from the sergeant major in thirty-five minutes. Good luck, Miss Horton."

"Thank you." She hesitated, but there was nothing more to say.

The patrol moved silently through low scrub brush. Something fluttered past her face; a flying squirrel, she thought. There were a lot of gliding creatures on New Washington.

The low hill smelled of toluenes from the shells and mortars that had fallen there in the last battle. The night was pitch dark, with only Franklin's dull red loom at the far western horizon, so faint that it was sensed, not seen. Another flying fox chittered past, darting after insects and screeching into the night.

A dozen ranchers followed in single file. Behind them came a communications maniple from the Forty-second's band. Glenda wondered what they did with their instruments when they went onto combat duty, and wished she'd asked. The last man on the trail was a Sergeant Hruska, who'd been sent along by Sergeant Major Calvin at the last minute. Glenda Ruth had been glad to see him, although she felt guilty about having him along.

And that's silly, she told herself. Men think that way. I don't have to. I'm not trying to prove anything.

The ranchers carried rifles. Three of Falkenberg's men did also. The other two had communications gear, and Sergeant Hruska had a submachine gun. It seemed a pitifully small force to contest ground with Covenant Highlanders.

They passed through the final outposts of her nervous ranchers and moved into the valleys between the hills. Glenda Ruth felt completely alone in the silence of the night. She wondered if the others felt it too. Certainly the ranchers did. They were all afraid. What of the mercenaries? she wondered. They weren't alone, anyway. They were with comrades who shared their meals and their bunkers.

As long as one of Falkenberg's men was alive, there would be someone to care about those lost. And they do care, she told herself. Sergeant Major Calvin, with his gruff dismissal of casualty reports. "Bah. Another trooper," he'd said when they told him an old messmate had bought it in the fight with the armor. Men.

She tried to imagine the thoughts of a mercenary soldier, but it was impossible. They were too alien.

Was Falkenberg like the rest of them?

They were nearly a kilometer beyond the lines when she found a narrow gulley two meters deep. It meandered down the hillsides along the approaches to the outposts behind her, and any attacking force assaulting her sector would have to pass it. She motioned the men into the ditch.

Waiting was hardest of all. The ranchers continually moved about, and she had to crawl along the gulley to whisper them into silence. Hours went by, each an agony of waiting. She glanced at her watch to see that no time had elapsed since the last time she'd looked, and resolved not to look again for a full fifteen minutes.

After what seemed fifteen minutes, she waited for what was surely another ten, then looked to see that only eleven minutes had passed altogether. She turned in disgust to stare into the night, blinking against the shapes that formed; shapes that couldn't be real.

Why do I keep thinking about Falkenberg? And why did I call him by his first name?

The vision of him in her dream still haunted her as well. In the starlit gloom she could almost see the miniature figures again. Falkenberg's impassive orders rang in her ears. "Kill this one. Send this one to the mines." He could do that, she thought. He could—

The miniatures were joined by larger figures in battle armor. With a sudden start she knew they were real. Two men stood motionless in the draw below her.

She touched Sergeant Hruska and pointed. The trooper looked carefully and nodded. As they watched, more figures joined the pair of scouts, until soon there were nearly fifty of them in the fold of the hill two hundred meters away. They were too far for her squad's weapons to have much effect, and a whispered command sent Hruska crawling along the gulley to order the men to stay down and be silent.

The group continued to grow. She couldn't see them all, and since she could count nearly a hundred she must be observing the assembly area of a full company. Were these the dreaded Highlanders? Memories of her father's defeat came unwanted, and she brushed them away. They were only hired men—but they fought for glory, and somehow that was enough to make them terrible.

After a long time the enemy began moving toward her. They formed a V-shape with the point aimed almost directly at her position, and she searched for the ends of the formation. What she saw made her gasp.

Four hundred meters to her left was another company of soldiers in double file. They moved silently and swiftly up the hill, and the lead elements were already far beyond her position. Frantically she looked to the right, focusing the big electronic light-amplifying glasses—and saw another company of men half a kilometer away. A full High-lander Battalion was moving right up her hill in an inverted M, and the group in front of her was the con-necting sweep to link the assault columns. In minutes they would be among the ranchers in the defense line.

Still she waited, until the dozen Highlanders of the point were ten meters from her. She shouted commands. "Up and at them! Fire!" From both ends of her ditch the mercenaries' automatic weapons chattered, then their fire was joined by her riflemen. The point was cut down to a man, and Sergeant Hruska directed fire on the main body, while Glenda Ruth shouted into her communicator.

"Fire Mission. Flash Uncle Four!"

There was a moment's delay which seemed like years. "Flash Uncle Four." Another long pause. "On the way," an unemotional voice answered. She thought it sounded like Falkenberg, but she was too busy to care.

"Reporting," she said. "At least one battalion of light infantry in assault columns is moving up Hill 905 along ridges Uncle and Zebra."

"They're shifting left." She looked up to see Hruska. The non-com pointed to the company in front of her posi-tion. Small knots of men curled leftward. They hugged the ground and were visible only for seconds.

"Move some men to that end of the gulley," she ordered. It was too late to shift artillery fire. Anyway, if the High-landers ever got to the top of the ridge, the ranchers wouldn't hold them. She held her breath and waited.

There was the scream of incoming artillery, then the night was lit by bright flashes. VT shells fell among the distant enemy on the left flank. "Pour it on!" she shouted into the communicator. "On target!"

"Right. On the way."

She was sure it was Falkenberg himself at the other

end. Catlike she grinned in the dark. What was a colonel doing as a telephone orderly? Was he worried about her? She almost laughed at the thought. Certainly he was, the ranchers would be hard to handle without her.

The ridge above erupted in fire. Mortars and grenades joined the artillery pounding the leftward assault column. Glenda Ruth paused to examine the critical situation to the right. The assault force five hundred meters away was untouched and continued to advance toward the top of the ridge. It was going to be close.

She let the artillery hold its target another five minutes while her riflemen engaged the company in front of her, then took up the radio again. The right-hand column had nearly reached the ridges, and she wondered if she had waited too long.

"Fire mission. Flash Zebra Nine."

"Zebra Nine," the emotionless voice replied. There was a short delay, then, "On the way." The fire lifted from the left flank almost immediately, and two minutes later began to fall five hundred meters to the right.

"They're flanking us, Miss," Sergeant Hruska reported. She'd been so busy directing artillery at the assaults against the ridge line that she'd actually forgotten her twenty men were engaged in a fire fight with over a hundred enemies. "Shall we pull back?" Hruska asked.

She tried to think, but it was impossible in the noise and confusion. The assault columns were still moving ahead, and she had the only group that could observe the entire attack. Every precious shell had to count. "No. We'll hold on here."

"Right, Miss." The sergeant seemed to be enjoying himself. He moved away to direct the automatic weapons and rifle fire. How long can we hold? Glenda Ruth wondered.

She let the artillery continue to pound the right-hand assault force for twenty minutes. By then the Highlanders had nearly surrounded her and were ready to assault from the rear. Prayerfully she lifted the radio again.

"Fire Mission. Give me everything you can on Jack Five—and for God's sake don't go over. We're at Jack Six."

"Flash Jack Five," the voice acknowledged immediately. There was a pause. "On the way." They were the most beautiful words she'd ever heard.

Now they waited. The Highlanders rose to charge. A

wild sound filled the night. MY GOD, PIPES! she thought. But even as the infantry moved the pipes were drowned by the whistle of artillery. Glenda Ruth dove to the bottom of the gulley and saw that the rest of her command had done the same.

The world erupted in sound. Millions of tiny fragments at enormous velocity filled the night with death. Cautiously she lifted a small periscope to look behind her.

The Highlander company had dissolved. Shells were falling among dead men, lifting them to be torn apart again and again as the radar-fused shells fell among them. Glenda Ruth swallowed hard and swept the glass around. The left assault company had reformed and were turning back to attack the ridge. "Fire Flash Uncle Four," she said softly.

"Interrogative."

"FLASH UNCLE FOUR!"

"Uncle Four. On the way."

As soon as the fire lifted from behind them her men returned to the lip of the gulley and resumed firing, but the sounds began to die away.

"We're down to the ammo in the guns now, Miss," Hruska reported. "May I have your spare magazines?"

She realized with a sudden start that she had yet to fire a single shot.

The night wore on. Whenever the enemy formed up to assault her position he was cut apart by the merciless artillery. Once she asked for a box barrage all around her gulley—by that time the men were down to three shots in each rifle, and the automatic weapons had no ammo at all. The toneless voice simply answered, "On the way."

An hour before dawn nothing moved on the hill.

XX

THE THIN NOTES of a military trumpet sounded across the barren hills of the Gap. The ridges east of Falkenberg's battle line lay dead, their foliage cut to shreds by shell fragments, the very earth thrown into crazyquilt craters partly burying the dead. A cool wind blew through the Gap, but it couldn't dispel the smells of nitro and death.

The trumpet sounded again. Falkenberg's glasses showed three unarmed Highlander officers carrying a white flag. An ensign was dispatched to meet them, and the young officer returned with a blindfolded Highlander major.

"Major MacRae, Fourth Covenant Infantry," the officer introduced himself after the blindfold was removed. He blinked at the bright lights of the bunker. "You'll be Colonel Falkenberg."

"Yes. What can we do for you, Major?"

"I've orders to offer a truce for burying the dead. Twenty hours, Colonel, if that's agreeable."

"No. Four days and nights—one hundred sixty hours, Major," Falkenberg said.

"A hundred sixty hours, Colonel?" The burly Highlander regarded Falkenberg suspiciously. "You'll want that time to complete your defenses."

"Perhaps. But twenty hours is not enough time to transfer the wounded men. I'll return all of yours—under parole, of course. It's no secret I'm short of medical supplies, and they'll receive better care from their own surgeons."

The Highlander's face showed nothing, but he paused. "You wouldn't tell me how many there be?" He was silent for a moment, then speaking very fast, he said, "The time you set is within my discretion, Colonel." He held out a bulky dispatch case. "My credentials and instructions.

195

'Twas a bloody battle, Colonel. How many of my laddies have ye killed?"

Falkenberg and Glenda Ruth glanced at each other. There is a bond between those who have been in combat together, and it can include those of the other side. The Covenant officer stood impassively, unwilling to say more, but his eyes pleaded with them.

"We counted four hundred and nine bodies, Major," Glenda Ruth told him gently. "And—" she looked at Falkenberg, who nodded. "We brought in another three hundred seventy wounded." The usual combat ratio is four men wounded to each killed; nearly sixteen hundred Covenanters must have been taken out of action in the assault. Toward the end the Highlanders were losing men in their efforts to recover their dead and wounded.

"Less than four hundred," the major said sadly. He stood to rigid attention. "Hae your men search the ground well, Colonel. There's aye more o' my lads out there." He saluted and waited for the blindfold to be fixed again. "I thank you, Colonel."

As the mercenary officer was led away Falkenberg turned to Glenda Ruth with a wistful smile. "Try to bribe him with money and he'd challenge me, but when I offer him his men back—" He shook his head sadly.

"Have they really given up?" Glenda Ruth asked.

"Yes. The truce finishes it. Their only chance was to break through before we brought up more ammunition and reserves, and they know it."

"But why? In the last revolution they were so terrible, and now—why?"

"It's the weakness of mercenaries," Falkenberg explained crisply. "The fruits of victory belong to our employers, not us. Friedland can't lose her armor and Covenant can't lose her men, or they've nothing more to sell."

"But they fought before!"

"Sure, in a fluid battle of maneuver. A frontal assault is always the most costly kind of battle. They tried to force the passage, and we beat them fairly. Honor is satisfied. Now the Confederacy will have to bring up its own Regulars if they want to force a way through the Gap. I don't think they'll squander men like that, and anyway it takes time. Meanwhile we've got to go to Allansport and deal with a crisis."

"What's wrong there?" she asked.

"This came in regimental code this morning." He handed her a message flimsy.

FALKENBERG FROM SVOBODA BREAK PA-
TRIOT ARMY LOOTING ALLANSPORT STOP
REQUEST COURT OF INQUIRY INVESTIGATE
POSSIBLE VIOLATIONS OF LAWS OF WAR
STOP EXTREMELY INADVISABLE FOR ME TO
COMPLY WITH YOUR ORDERS TO JOIN REGI-
MENT STOP PATRIOT ARMY ACTIONS PRO-
VOKING SABOTAGE AND REVOLT AMONG
TOWNSPEOPLE AND MINERS STOP MY SECU-
RITY FORCES MAY BE REQUIRED TO HOLD
THE CITY STOP AWAIT YOUR ORDERS STOP
RESPECTFULLY ANTON SVOBODA BREAK
BREAK MESSAGE ENDSXXX

She read it twice. "My God, Colonel—what's going on there?"

"I don't know," he said grimly. "I intend to find out. Will you come with me as a representative of the Patriot Council?"

"Of course—but shouldn't we send for Howard Bannister? The Council elected him President."

"If we need him we'll get him. Sergeant Major."

"Sir!"

"Put Miss Horton's things on the troop carrier with mine. I'll take the Headquarters Guard platoon to Allansport."

"Sir. Colonel, you'll want me along."

"Will I? I suppose so, Sergeant Major. Get your gear aboard."

"Sir."

"It's probably already there, of course. Let's move out."

The personnel carrier took them to a small airfield where a jet waited. It was one of forty on the planet, and it would carry a hundred men; but it burned fuel needed for ammunition transport. Until the oil fields around Doak's Ferry could be secured it was fuel they could hardly afford.

The plane flew across Patriot-held areas, staying well away from the isolated Confederate strongpoints remaining west of the Gap. Aircraft had little chance of surviving in a combat environment when any infantryman could carry target-seeking rockets, while trucks could carry equipment to defeat airborne countermeasures. They crossed the Columbia Valley and turned southwest over the broad forests of Ford Heights Plateau, then west again to avoid Preston Bay where pockets of Confederates remained after the fall of the main fortress.

"You do the same thing, don't you?" Glenda Ruth said suddenly. "When we assaulted Preston Bay you let my people take the casualties."

Falkenberg nodded. "For two reasons. I'm as reluctant to lose troops as the Highlanders—and without the regiment you'd not hold the Patriot areas a thousand hours. You need us as an intact force, not a pile of corpses."

"Yes." It was true enough, but those were her friends who'd died in the assault. Would the outcome be worth it? Would Falkenberg *let* it be worth it?

Captain Svoboda met them at the Allansport field. "Glad to see you, sir. It's pretty bad in town."

"Just what happened, Captain?" Svoboda looked critically at Glenda Ruth, but Falkenberg said, "Report."

"Yes, sir. When the provisional governor arrived I turned over administration of the city as ordered. At that time the peninsula was pacified, largely due to the efforts of Mayor Hastings, who wants to avoid damage to the city. Hastings believes Franklin will send a large army from the home planet and says he sees no point in getting Loyalists killed and the city burned in resistance that won't change the final outcome anyway."

"Poor Roger—he always tries to be reasonable, and it never works," Glenda Ruth said. "But Franklin will send troops."

"Possibly," Falkenberg said. "But it takes time for them to mobilize and organize transport. Continue, Captain Svoboda."

"Sir. The Governor posted a list of proscribed persons whose property was forfeit. If that wasn't enough, he told his troops that if they found any Confederate government property, they could keep half its value. You'll see the results when we get to town, Colonel. There was looting and fire that my security forces and the local fire people only barely managed to control."

"Oh, Lord," Glenda Ruth murmured. "Why?"

Svoboda curled his lip. "Looters often do that, Miss Horton. You can't let troops sack a city and not expect damage. The outcome was predictable, Colonel. Many townspeople took to the hills, particularly the miners. They've taken several of the mining towns back."

Captain Svoboda shrugged helplessly. "The railway is cut. The city itself is secure, but I can't say how long. You only left me one hundred fifty troops to control eleven thousand people, which I did with hostages. The Governor brought another nine hundred men and that's not enough to rule *their* way. He's asked Preston Bay for more soldiers."

"Is that where the first group came from?" Glenda Ruth asked.

"Yes, Miss. A number of them, anyway."

"Then its understandable if not excusable, Colonel," she said. "Many ranches on Ford Heights were burned out by Loyalists in the first revolution. I suppose they think they're paying the Loyalists back."

Falkenberg nodded. "Sergeant Major!"

"Sir!"

"Put the Guard in battle armor and combat weapons. Captain, we are going to pay a call on your provisional governor. Alert your men."

"Colonel!" Glenda Ruth protested. "You—what are you going to do?"

"Miss Horton, I left an undamaged town, which is now a nest of opposition. I'd like to know why. Let's go, Svoboda."

City Hall stood undamaged among burned-out streets. The town smelled of scorched wood and death, as if there'd been a major battle fought in the downtown area. Falkenberg sat impassive as Glenda Ruth stared unbelievingly at what had been the richest city outside the capital area.

"I tried, Colonel," Svoboda muttered. He blamed himself anyway. "I'd have had to fire on the Patriots and arrest the governor. You were out of communication, and I didn't want to take that responsibility without orders. Should I have, sir?"

Falkenberg didn't answer. Possible violations of mercenary contracts were always delicate situations. Finally he said, "I can hardly blame you for not wanting to involve the regiment in war with our sponsors."

The Patriot irregular guards at City Hall protested as Falkenberg strode briskly toward the Governor's office. They tried to bar the way, but when they saw his forty guardsmen in battle armor they moved aside.

The governor was a broad-shouldered former rancher who'd done well in commodities speculation. He was a skilled salesman, master of the friendly grip on the elbow and pat on the shoulder, the casual words in the right places, but he had no experience in military command. He glanced nervously at Sergeant Major Calvin and the grimfaced guards outside his office as Glenda introduced Falkenberg.

"Governor Jack Silana," she said. "The governor was active in the first revolution, and without his financial help we'd never have been able to pay your passage here, Colonel."

"I see." Falkenberg ignored the governor's offered hand. "Did you authorize more looting, Governor?" he asked. "I see some's still going on."

"Your mercenaries have all the tax money," Silana protested. He tried to grin. "My troops are being ruined to pay you. Why shouldn't the Fedsymps contribute to the war? Anyway, the real trouble began when a town girl insulted one of my soldiers. He struck her. Some townspeople interfered, and his comrades came to help. A riot started and someone called out the garrison to stop it—"

"And you lost control," Falkenberg said.

"The traitors got no more than they deserve anyway! Don't think *they* didn't loot cities when they won, Colonel. These men have seen ranches burned out, and they know Allansport's a nest of Fedsymp traitors."

"I see." Falkenberg turned to his Provost. "Captain, had you formally relinquished control to Governor Silana before this happened?"

"Yes, sir. As ordered."

"Then it's none of the regiment's concern. Were any of our troops involved?"

Svoboda nodded unhappily. "I have seven troopers and Sergeant Magee in arrest, sir. I've held summary court on six others myself."

"What charges are you preferring against Magee?" Falkenberg had personally promoted Magee once. The man had a mean streak, but he was a good soldier.

"Looting. Drunk on duty. Theft. And conduct prejudicial."

"And the others?"

"Three rapes, four grand theft, and one murder, sir. They're being held for a court. I also request an inquiry into my conduct as commander."

"Granted. Sergeant Major."

"Sir!"

"Take custody of the prisoners and convene a General Court. What officers have we for an investigation?"

"Captain Greenwood's posted for light duty only by the surgeon, sir."

"Excellent. Have him conduct a formal inquiry into Captain Svoboda's administration of the city."

"Sir."

"What will happen to those men?" Glenda Ruth asked.

"The rapists and murderer will be hanged if convicted. Hard duty for the rest."

"You'd hang your own men?" she asked. She didn't believe it, and her voice showed it.

"I cannot allow rot in my regiment," Falkenberg snapped. "In any event the Confederacy will protest this violation of the Laws of War to the CD."

Governor Silana laughed. "We protested often enough in the last revolution, and nothing came of it. I think we can chance it."

"Perhaps. I take it you will do nothing about this?"

"I'll issue orders for the looting to stop."

"Haven't you done so already?"

"Well, yes, Colonel—but the men, well, they're about over their mad now, I think."

"If previous orders haven't stopped it, more won't. You'll have to be prepared to punish violators. Are you?"

"I'll be damned if I'll hang my own soldiers to protect traitors!"

"I see. Governor, how do you propose to pacify this area?"

"I've sent for reinforcements—"

"Yes. Thank you. If you'll excuse us, Governor, Miss Horton and I have an errand." He hustled Glenda Ruth out of the office. "Sergeant Major, bring Mayor Hastings and Colonel Ardway to Captain Svoboda's office."

"They shot Colonel Ardway," Svoboda said. "The mayor's in the city jail."

"Jail?" Falkenberg muttered.

"Yes, sir. I had the hostages in the hotel, but Governor Silana—"

"I see. Carry on, Sergeant Major."

"Sir!"

* * *

"What do you want now, you bloody bastard?" Hastings demanded ten minutes later. The mayor was haggard, with several days' growth of stubble, and his face and hands showed the grime of confinement without proper hygiene facilities.

"One thing at a time, Mr. Mayor. Any trouble, Sergeant Major?"

Calvin grinned. "Not much, sir. The officer didn't want no problems with the Guard—Colonel, they got all them hostages crammed into cells."

"What have you done with my wife and children?" Roger Hastings demanded frantically. "I haven't heard anything for days."

Falkenberg looked inquiringly at Svoboda but got only a headshake. "See to the mayor's family, Sergeant Major. Bring them here. Mr. Hastings, do I understand that you believe this is my doing?"

"If you hadn't taken this city . . ."

"That was a legitimate military operation. Have you charges to bring against my troops?"

"How would I know?" Hastings felt weak. He hadn't been fed properly for days, and he was sick with worry about his family. As he leaned against the desk he saw Glenda Ruth for the first time. "You too, eh?"

"It was none of my doing, Roger." He had almost become her father-in-law. She wondered where young Lieutenant Harley Hastings was. Although she'd broken their engagement long ago, their disagreements had mostly been political, and they were still friends. "I'm sorry."

"It was your doing, you and the damned rebels. Oh, sure, you don't like burning cities and killing civilians, but it happens all the same—and you started the war. You can't shed the responsibility."

Falkenberg interrupted him. "Mr. Mayor, we have mutual interests still. This peninsula raises little food, and your people cannot survive without supplies. I'm told over a thousand of your people were killed in the riots, and nearly that many are in the hills. Can you get the automated factories and smelters operating with what's left?"

"After all this you expect me to—I won't do one damn thing for you, Falkenberg!"

"I didn't ask if you would, only if it could be done."

"What difference does it make?"

"I doubt you want to see the rest of your people starving, Mr. Mayor. Captain, take the mayor to your quarters and get him cleaned up. By the time you've done that, Sergeant Major Calvin will know what happened to his family." Falkenberg nodded dismissal and turned to Glenda Ruth. "Well, Miss Horton? Have you seen enough?"

"I don't understand."

"I am requesting you to relieve Silana of his post and return administration of this city to the regiment. Will you do it?"

Good Lord! she thought. "I haven't the authority."

"You've got more influence in the Patriot army than anyone else. The Council may not like it, but they'll take it from you. Meanwhile, I'm sending for the Sappers to rebuild this city and get the foundries going."

Everything moves so fast. Not even Joshua Horton had made things happen like this man. "Colonel, what is your interest in Allansport?"

"It's the only industrial area we control. There will be no more military supplies from off planet. We hold everything west of the Temblors. The Matson Valley is rising in support of the revolution, and we'll have it soon. We can follow the Matson to Vancouver and take that— and then what?"

"Why—then we take the capital city! The revolution's over!"

"No. That was the mistake you made last time. Do you really think your farmers, even with the Forty-second, can move onto level, roaded ground and fight set-piece battles? We've no chance under those conditions."

"But—" He was right. She'd always known it. When they defeated the Friedlanders at the Gap she'd dared hope, but the capital plains were not Hillyer Gap. "So it's back to attrition."

Falkenberg nodded. "We do hold all the agricultural areas. The Confederates will begin to feel the pinch soon enough. Meanwhile we chew around the edges. Franklin will have to let go—there's no profit in keeping colonies that cost money. They may try landing armies from the home world, but they'll not take us by surprise and they don't have *that* big an army. Eventually we'll wear them down."

She nodded sadly. It would be a long war after all, and she'd have to be in it, always raising fresh troops as the ranchers began to go home again—it would be tough enough holding what they had when people realized what they were in for. "But how do we pay your troops in a long war?"

"Perhaps you'll have to do without us."

"You know we can't. And you've always known it. What do you want?"

"Right now I want you to relieve Silana. Immediately."

"What's the hurry? As you say, it's going to be a long war."

"It'll be longer if more of the city is burned." He almost told her more, and cursed himself for the weakness of temptation. She was only a girl, and he'd known thousands of them since Grace left him all those years ago. The bond of combat wouldn't explain it, he'd known other girls who were competent officers, many of them—so why was he tempted at all? "I'm sorry," he said gruffly. "I must insist. As you say, you can't do without us."

Glenda Ruth had grown up among politicians and for four years had been a revolutionary leader herself. She knew Falkenberg's momentary hesitation was important, and that she'd never find out what it meant.

What was under that mask? Was there a man in there making all those whirlwind decisions? Falkenberg dominated every situation he fell into, and a man like that wanted more than money. The vision of Falkenberg seated at a desk pronouncing dooms on her people haunted her still.

And yet. There was more. A warrior leader of warriors who had won the adoration of uneducated privates—and men like Jeremy Savage as well. She'd never met anyone like him.

"I'll do it." She smiled and walked across the room to stand next to him. "I don't know why, but I'll do it. Have you got any friends, John Christian Falkenberg?"

The question startled him. Automatically he answered. "Command can have no friends, Miss Horton."

She smiled again. "You have one now. There's a condition to my offer. From now on, you call me Glenda Ruth. Please?"

A curious smile formed on the soldier's face. He regarded her with amusement, but there was something more as well. "It doesn't work, you know."

"What doesn't work?"

"Whatever you're trying. Like me, you've command responsibilities. It's lonely, and you don't like that. The reason command has no friends, Glenda Ruth, is not merely to spare the commander the pain of sending friends to their death. If you haven't learned the rest of it, learn it now, because some day you'll have to betray either your friends or your command, and that's a choice worth avoiding."

What am I doing? Am I trying to protect the revolution by getting to know him better—or is he right, I've no friends either, and he's the only man I ever met who could be— She let the thought fade out, and laid her hand on his for a brief second. "Let's go tell Governor Silana, John Christian. And let the little girl worry about her own emotions, will you? She knows what she's doing."

He stood next to her. They were very close and for a moment she thought he intended to kiss her. "No, you don't."

She wanted to answer, but he was already leaving the room and she had to hurry to catch him.

XXI

"I say we only gave the Fedsymp traitors what they deserved!" Jack Silana shouted. There was a mutter of approval from the delegates, and open cheers in the bleachers overlooking the gymnasium floor. "I have great respect for Glenda Ruth, but she is not old Joshua," Silana continued. "Her action in removing me from a post given by President Bannister was without authority. I demand that the Council repudiate it." There was more applause as Silana took his seat.

Glenda Ruth remained at her seat for a moment. She looked carefully at each of the thirty men and women at the horseshoe table, trying to estimate just how many votes she had. Not a majority, certainly, but perhaps a dozen. She wouldn't have to persuade more than three or four to abandon the Bannister-Silana faction, but what then? The bloc she led was no more solid than Bannister's coalition. Just who would govern the Free States?

More men were seated on the gymnasium floor beyond the council table. They were witnesses, but their placement at the focus of the Council's attention made it look as if Falkenberg and his impassive officers might be in the dock. Mayor Hastings sat with Falkenberg, and the illusion was heightened by the signs of harsh treatment he'd received. Some of his friends looked even worse.

Beyond the witnesses the spectators chattered among themselves as if this were a basketball game rather than a solemn meeting of the supreme authority for three-quarters of New Washington. A gymnasium didn't seem a very dignified place to meet anyway, but there was no larger hall in Astoria Fortress.

Finally she stood. "No, I am not my father," she began. "He would have had Jack Silana shot for his actions!"

"Give it to 'em, Glenda Ruth!" someone shouted from the balcony.

Howard Bannister looked up in surprise. "We will have order here!"

"Hump it, you Preston Bay bastard!" the voice replied. The elderly rancher was joined by someone below. "Damn right, Ford Heights don't control the Valley!" There were cheers at that.

"Order! Order!" Bannister's commands drowned the shouting as the technicians turned up the amplifiers to full volume. "Miss Horton, you have the floor."

"Thank you. What I was trying to say is that we did not start this revolution to destroy New Washington! We must live with the Loyalists once it is over, and—"

"Fedsymp! She was engaged to a Feddie soldier!" "Shut up and let her talk!" "Order! ORDER!"

Falkenberg sat motionless as the hall returned to silence, and Glenda Ruth tried to speak again. "Bloody noisy lot," Jeremy Savage murmured.

Falkenberg shrugged. "Victory does that to politicians."

Glenda Ruth described the conditions she'd seen in Allansport. She told of the burned-out city, hostages herded into jail cells—

"Serves the Fedsymps right!" someone interrupted, but she managed to continue before her supporters could answer.

"Certainly they are Loyalists. Over a third of the people in the territory we control are. Loyalists are a majority in the capital city. Will it help if we persecute their friends here?"

"We won't ever take the capital the way we're fighting!" "Damn right! Time we moved on the Feddies." "Send the mercenaries in there, let 'em earn the taxes we pay!"

This time Bannister made little effort to control the crowd. They were saying what he had proposed to the Council, and one reason he supported Silana was because he needed the governor's merchant bloc with him on the war issue. After the crowd had shouted enough about renewing the war, Bannister used the microphone to restore order and let Glenda Ruth speak.

The Council adjourned for the day without deciding anything. Falkenberg waited for Glenda Ruth and walked out with her. "I'm glad we didn't get a vote today," she told him. "I don't think we'd have won."

"Noisy beggars," Major Savage observed again.

"Democracy at work," Falkenberg said coldly. "What do you need to convince the Council that Silana is unfit as a governor?"

"That's not the real issue, John," she answered. "It's really the war. No one is satisfied with what's being done."

"I should have thought we were doing splendidly," Savage retorted. "The last Confederate thrust into the Matson ran into your ambush as planned."

"Yes, that was brilliant," Glenda Ruth said.

"Hardly. It was the only possible attack route," Falkenberg answered. "You're very quiet, Mayor Hastings." They had left the gymnasium and were crossing the parade ground to the barracks where the Friedlanders had been quartered. Falkenberg's troops had it now, and they kept the Allansport officials with them.

"I'm afraid of that vote," Hastings said. "If they send Silana back, we'll lose everything."

"Then support me!" Falkenberg snapped. "My engineers already have the automated factories and mills in reasonable shape. With some help from you they'd be running again. Then I'd have real arguments against Silana's policies."

"But that's treason," Hastings protested. "You need the Allansport industry for your war effort. Colonel, it's a hell of a way to thank you for rescuing my family from that butcher, but I can't do it."

"I suppose you're expecting a miracle to save you?" Falkenberg asked.

"No. But what happens if you win? How long will you stay on the Ranier Peninsula? Bannister's people will be there one of these days—Colonel, my only chance is for the Confederacy to bring in Franklin troops and crush the lot of you!"

"And you'll be ruled from Franklin," Glenda Ruth said. "They won't give you as much home rule as you had last time."

"I know," Roger said miserably. "But what can I do? This revolt ruined our best chance. Franklin might have been reasonable in time—I was going to give good government to everyone. But you finished that."

"All of Franklin's satraps weren't like you, Roger," Glenda Ruth said. "And don't forget their war policies! They'd have got us sucked into their schemes and eventually we'd have been fighting the CoDominium itself. Colonel Falkenberg can tell you what it's like to be victim of a CD punitive expedition!"

"Christ, I don't know what to do," Roger said unhappily.

Falkenberg muttered something which the others didn't catch, then said, "Glenda Ruth, if you will excuse me, Major Savage and I have administrative matters to discuss. I would be pleased if you'd join me for dinner in the Officers' Mess at nineteen hundred hours."

"Why—thank you, John. I'd like to, but I must see the other delegates tonight. We may be able to win that vote tomorrow."

Falkenberg shrugged. "I doubt it. If you can't win it, can you delay it?"

"For a few days, perhaps—why?"

"It might help, that's all. If you can't make dinner, the regiment's officers are entertaining guests in the mess until quite late. Will you join us when you're done with politics?"

"Thank you. Yes, I will." As she crossed the parade ground to her own quarters, she wished she knew what Falkenberg and Savage were discussing. It wouldn't be administration—did it matter what the Council decided?

She looked forward to seeing John later, and the anticipation made her feel guilt. What is there about the man that does this to me? He's handsome enough, broad shoulders and thoroughly military—nonsense. I am damned if I'll believe in some atavistic compulsion to fall in love with warriors, I don't care what the anthropologists say. So why do I want to be with him? She pushed the thought away. There was something more important to think about. What would Falkenberg do if the Council voted against him? And beyond that, what would she do when he did it?

Falkenberg led Roger Hastings into his office. "Please be seated, Mr. Mayor."

Roger sat uncomfortably. "Look, Colonel, I'd like to help, but—"

"Mayor Hastings, would the owners of the Allansport industries rather have half of a going concern, or all of nothing?"

"What's that supposed to mean?"

"I will guarantee protection of the foundries and smelters in return for a half interest in them." When Hastings looked up in astonishment, Falkenberg continued. "Why not? Silana will seize them anyway. If my regiment is part owner, I may be able to stop him."

"It wouldn't mean anything if I granted it," Hastings protested. "The owners are on Franklin."

"You are the ranking Confederate official for the entire Ranier Peninsula," Falkenberg said carefully. "Legal or not, I want your signature on this grant." He handed Roger a sheaf of papers.

Hastings read them carefully. "Colonel, this also confirms a land grant given by the rebel government! I can't do that!"

"Why not? It's all public land—and that *is* in your power. The document states that in exchange for protection of lives and property of the citizens of Allansport you are awarding certain lands to my regiment. It notes that you don't consider a previous grant by the Patriot Government to be valid. There's no question of treason—you do want Allansport protected against Silana, don't you?"

"Are you offering to doublecross the Patriots?"

"No. My contract with Bannister specifically states that I cannot be made party to violations of the Laws of War. This document hires me to enforce them in an area already pacified. It doesn't state who might violate them."

"You're skating on damned thin ice, Colonel. If the Council ever saw this paper they'd hang you for treason!" Roger read it again. "I see no harm in signing, but I tell you in advance the Confederacy won't honor it. If Franklin wins this they'll throw you off this planet—if they don't have you shot."

"Let me worry about the future, Mr. Mayor. Right now *your* problem is protecting your people. You can help with that by signing."

"I doubt it," Hastings said. He reached for a pen. "So long as you know there isn't a shadow of validity to this because I'll be countermanded from the home world—" he scrawled his name and title across the papers and handed them back to Falkenberg.

Glenda Ruth could hear the regimental party across the wide parade ground. As she approached with Hiram Black they seemed to be breasting their way upstream through waves of sound, the crash of drums, throbbing, wailing bagpipes, mixed with off-key songs from intoxicated male baritones.

It was worse inside. As they entered a flashing saber

swept within inches of her face. A junior captain saluted and apologized in a stream of words. "I was showing Oberleutnant Marcks a new parry I learned on Sparta, Miss. Please forgive me?" When she nodded the captain drew his companion to one side and the saber whirled again.

"That's a Friedland officer—all the Friedlanders are here," Glenda Ruth said. Hiram Black nodded grimly. The captured mercenaries wore dress uniform, green and gold contrasting with the blue and gold of Falkenberg's men. Medals flashed in the bright overhead lights. She looked across the glittering room and saw the colonel at a table on the far side.

Falkenberg and his companion stood when she reached the table after a perilous journey across the crowded floor. Pipers marched past pouring out more sound.

Falkenberg's face was flushed, and she wondered if he were drunk. "Miss Horton, may I present Major Oscar von Thoma," he said formally. "Major von Thoma commands the Friedland artillery battalion."

"I—" She didn't know what to say. The Friedlanders were enemies, and Falkenberg was introducing her to the officer as his guest. "My pleasure," she stammered. "And this is Colonel Hiram Black."

Von Thoma clicked his heels. The men stood stiffly until she was seated next to Falkenberg. That kind of chivalry had almost vanished, but somehow it seemed appropriate here. As the stewards brought glasses von Thoma turned to Falkenberg. "You ask too much," he said. "Besides, you may have fired the lands from the barrels by then."

"If we have we'll reduce the price," Falkenberg said cheerfully. He noted Glenda Ruth's puzzled expression. "Major von Thoma has asked if he can buy his guns back when the campaign is ended. He doesn't care for my terms."

Hiram Black observed drily, "Seems to me the Council's goin' to want a say in fixin' that price, General Falkenberg."

Falkenberg snorted contemptuously. "No."

He is drunk, Glenda Ruth thought. It doesn't show much, but—do I know him that well already?

"Those guns were taken by the Forty-second without Council help. I will see to it that they aren't used against Patriots, and the Council has no further interest in the matter." Falkenberg turned to Glenda Ruth. "Will you win the vote tomorrow?"

"There won't be a vote tomorrow."

"So you can't win," Falkenberg muttered. "Expected that. What about the war policy vote?"

"They'll be debating for the next two days—" she looked nervously at Major von Thoma. "I don't want to be impolite, but should we discuss that with him at the table?"

"I understand." Von Thoma got unsteadily to his feet. "We will speak of this again, Colonel. It has been my pleasure, Miss Horton. Colonel Black." He bowed stiffly to each and went to the big center table where a number of Friedland officers were drinking with Falkenberg's.

"John, is this wise?" she asked. "Some of the Councillors are already accusing you of not wanting to fight—"

"Hell, they're callin' him a traitor," Black interrupted. "Soft on Fedsymps, consortin' with the enemy—they don't even like you recruitin' new men to replace your losses." Black hoisted a glass of whiskey and drained it at one gulp. "I wish some of 'em had been ridin' up the Valley with us! Glenda Ruth, that was some ride. And when Captain Frazer runs out of fuel, Falkenberg tells him, cool as you please, to use bicycles!" Black chuckled in rememberance.

"I'm serious!" Glenda Ruth protested. "John, Bannister hates you. I think he always has." The stewards brought whiskey for Falkenberg. "Wine or whiskey, Miss?" one asked.

"Wine—John, please, they're going to order you to attack the capital!"

"Interesting." His features tightened suddenly, and his eyes became alert. Then he relaxed and let the whiskey take effect. "If we obey those orders I'll need Major von Thoma's good offices to get *my* equipment back. Doesn't Bannister know what will happen if we let them catch us on those open plains?"

"Howie Bannister knows his way 'round a conspiracy better'n he does a battlefield, General," Black observed. "We give him the secretary of war title 'cause we thought he'd drive a hard bargain with you, but he's not much on battles."

"I've noticed," Falkenberg said. He laid his hand on Glenda Ruth's arm and gently stroked it. It was the first time he'd ever touched her, and she sat very still. "This is supposed to be a party," Falkenberg laughed. He looked up and caught the mess president's eye. "Lieutenant, have Pipe Major give us a song!"

The room was instantly still. Glenda Ruth felt the warmth of Falkenberg's hand. The soft caress promised much more, and she was suddenly glad, but there was a stab of fear as well. He'd spoken so softly, yet all those people had stopped their drinking, the drums ceased, the pipes, everything, at his one careless nod. Power like that was frightening.

The burly Pipe Major selected a young tenor. One pipe and a snare drum played as he began to sing. "Oh Hae ye nae heard o' the false Sakeld, Hae ye nae heard o' the keen Lord Scroop? For he ha' ta'en the Kinmont Willie, to Haribee for to hang him up . . ."

"John, please listen," she pleaded.

> "They hae ta'en the news to the Bold Bacleugh,
> in Branksome Ha where he did lay,
> that Lord Scroop has ta'en the Kinmont Willie,
> between the hours of night and day.
>
> He has ta'en the table wi' his hand,
> he has made the red wine spring on hie.
> Now Christ's curse be on my head, he said,
> but avenged of Lord Scroop I will be."

"John, really."

"Perhaps you should listen," he said gently. He raised his glass as the young voice rose and the tempo gathered.

> "O is my basnet a widow's curch?
> Or my lance the wand o' the willow tree?
> And is my hand a lady's lilly hand,
> That this English lord should lightly me?"

The song ended. Falkenberg signaled to the steward. "We'll have more to drink," he said. "And no more talk of politics."

They spent the rest of the evening enjoying the party. Both the Friedlanders and Falkenberg's mercenary officers were educated men, and it was a very pleasant evening for Glenda Ruth to have a room full of warriors

213

competing to please her. They taught her the dances and wild songs of a dozen cultures, and she drank far too much.

Finally he stood. "I'll see you back to your quarters," Falkenberg told her.

"All right." She took his arm, and they went through the thinning crowd. "Do you often have parties like this?" she asked.

"When we can." They reached the door. A white-coated private appeared from nowhere to open it for them. He had a jagged scar across his face that ran down his neck until it disappeared into his collar, and she thought she would be afraid to meet him anywhere else.

"Good night, Miss," the private said. His voice had a strange quality, almost husky, as if he were very concerned about her.

They crossed the parade ground. The night was clear, and the sky was full of stars. The sounds of the river rushing by came faintly up to the old fortress.

"I didn't want it ever to end," she said.

"Why?"

"Because—you've built an artificial world in there. A wall of glory to shut out the realities of what we do. And when it ends we go back to the war." And back to whatever you meant when you had that boy sing that sinister old border ballad.

"That's well put. A wall of glory. Perhaps that's what we do."

They reached the block of suites assigned to the senior officers. Her door was next to his. She stood in front of it, reluctant to go inside. The room would be empty, and tomorrow there was the Council, and—she turned to him and said bitterly, "Does it have to end? I was happy for a few minutes. Now—"

"It doesn't have to end, but do you know what you're doing?"

"No." She turned away from her own door and opened his. He followed, but didn't go inside. She stood in the doorway for a moment, then laughed. "I was going to say something silly. Something like, 'Let's have a last drink.' But I wouldn't have meant that, and you'd have known it, so what's the point of games?"

"There is no point to games. Not between us. Games are for soldiers' girls and lovers."

"John—my God, John, are you as lonely as I am?"

"Yes. Of course."

"Then we can't let the party end. Not while there's a single moment it can go on." She went inside his room.

After a few moments he followed and closed the door.

During the night she was able to forget the conflict between them, but when she left his quarters in the morning the ballad returned to haunt her.

She knew she must do something, but she couldn't warn Bannister. The Council, the revolution, independence, none of them had lost their importance; but though she would serve those causes she felt apart from them.

"I'm a perfect fool," she told herself. But fool or not, she could not warn Bannister. Finally she persuaded the President to meet John away from the shouting masses of the Council Chamber.

Bannister came directly to the point. "Colonel, we can't keep a large army in the field indefinitely. Miss Horton's Valley ranchers may be willing to pay these taxes, but most of our people can't."

"Just what did you expect when you began this?" Falkenberg asked.

"A long war," Bannister admitted. "But your initial successes raised hopes, and we got a lot of supporters we hadn't expected. They demand an end."

"Fair-weather soldiers." Falkenberg snorted. "Common enough, but why did you let them gain so much influence in your Council?"

"Because there were a lot of them."

And they all support you for President, Glenda Ruth thought. While my friends and I were out at the front, you were back here organizing the newcomers, grabbing for power . . . you're not worth the life of one of those soldiers. John's or mine.

"After all, this is a democratic government," Bannister said.

"And thus quite unable to accomplish anything that takes sustained effort. Can you afford this egalitarian democracy of yours?"

"You were not hired to restructure our government!" Bannister shouted.

Falkenberg activated his desktop map. "Look. We have the plains ringed with troops. The irregulars can hold the passes and swamps practically forever. Any real threat of a breakthrough can be held by my regiment in mobile reserve. The Confederates can't get at us—but we can't risk a battle in the open with them."

"So what can we do?" Bannister demanded. "Franklin is sure to send reinforcements. If we wait, we lose."

"I doubt that. They've no assault boats either. They can't land in any real force on our side of the line, and what good does it do them to add to their force in the capital? Eventually we starve them out. Franklin itself must be hurt by the loss of the corn shipments. They won't be able to feed their army forever."

"A mercenary paradise," Bannister muttered. "A long war and no fighting. Damn it, you've got to attack while we've still got troops! I tell you, our support is melting away."

"If we put our troops out where von Mellenthin's armor can get at them with room to maneuver, they won't melt, they'll burn."

"You tell him, Glenda Ruth," Bannister said. "He won't listen to me."

She looked at Falkenberg's impassive face and wanted to cry. "John, he may be right. I know my people, they can't hold on forever. Even if they could, the Council is going to insist . . ."

His look didn't change. There's nothing I can say, she thought, nothing I know that he doesn't, because he's right but he's wrong too. These are only civilians in arms. They're not iron men. All the time my people are guarding those passes their ranches are going to ruin.

Is Howard right? Is this a mercenary paradise, and you're not even trying? But she didn't want to believe that.

Unwanted, the vision she'd had that lonely night at the pass returned. She fought it with the memory of the party, and afterwards . . .

"Just what the hell are you waiting on, *Colonel* Falkenberg?" Bannister demanded.

Falkenberg said nothing, and Glenda Ruth wanted to cry; but she did not.

XXII

THE COUNCIL HAD not voted six days later. Glenda Ruth
used every parliamentary trick her father had taught her
during the meetings, and after they adjourned each day
she hustled from delegate to delegate. She made promises
she couldn't keep, exploited old friends and made new
ones, and every morning she was sure only that she could
delay a little longer.

She wasn't sure herself why she did it. The war vote was
linked to the reappointment of Silana as governor in Allansport, and she did know that the man was incompetent;
but mostly, after the debates and political meetings, Falkenberg would come for her, or send a junior officer to escort
her to his quarters—and she was glad to go. They seldom
spoke of politics, or even talked much at all. It was enough
to be with him—but when she left in the mornings, she was
afraid again. He'd never promised her anything.

On the sixth night she joined him for a late supper.
When the orderlies had taken the dinner cart she sat mood-
ily at the table. "This is what you meant, isn't it?" she
asked.

"About what?"

"That I'd have to betray either my friends or my
command—but I don't even know if you're my friend.
John, what am I going to do?"

Very gently he laid his hand against her cheek. "You're
going to talk sense—and keep them from appointing
Silana in Allansport."

"But what are we waiting for?"

He shrugged. "Would you rather it came to an open
break? There'll be no stopping them if we lose this vote.
The mob's demanding your arrest right now—for the past

217

three days Calvin has had the Headquarters Guard on full alert in case they're fool enough to try it."

She shuddered, but before she could say more he lifted her gently to her feet and pressed her close to him. Once again her doubts vanished but she knew they'd be back. Who was she betraying? And for what?

The crowd shouted before she could speak. "Mercenary's whore!" someone called. Her friends answered with more epithets, and it was five minutes before Bannister could restore order.

How long can I keep it up? At least another day or so, I suppose. Am I his whore? If I'm not, I don't know what I am. He's never told me. She carefully took papers from her briefcase, but there was another interruption. A messenger strode quickly, almost running, across the floor to hand a flimsy message to Howard Bannister. The pudgy President glanced at it, then began to read more carefully.

The hall fell silent as everyone watched Bannister's face. The President showed a gamut of emotions: surprise, bewilderment, then carefully controlled rage. He read the message again and whispered to the messenger, who nodded. Bannister lifted the microphone.

"Councillors, I have—I suppose it would be simpler to read this to you. 'PROVISIONAL GOVERNMENT FREE STATES OF WASHINGTON FROM CDSN CRUISER INTREPID BREAK BREAK WE ARE IN RECEIPT OF DOCUMENTED COMPLAINT FROM CONFEDERATE GOVERNMENT THAT FREE STATES ARE IN VIOLATION OF LAWS OF WAR STOP THIS VESSEL ORDERED TO INVESTIGATE STOP LANDING BOAT ARRIVES ASTORIA SIXTEEN HUNDRED HOURS THIS DAY STOP PROVISIONAL GOVERNMENT MUST BE PREPARED TO DISPATCH ARMISTICE COMMISSION TO MEET WITH DELEGATES FROM CONFEDERACY AND CODOMINIUM INVESTIGATING OFFICERS IMMEDIATELY UPON ARRIVAL OF LANDING BOAT STOP COMMANDING OFFICERS ALL MERCENARY FORCES ORDERED TO BE PRESENT TO GIVE EVIDENCE STOP BREAK BREAK JOHN GRANT CAPTAIN CODOMINIUM SPACE NAVY BREAK MESSAGE ENDS'"

There was a moment of hushed silence, then the gymnasium erupted in sound. "Investigate us?" "Goddamn CD is—" "Armistice hell!"

Falkenberg caught Glenda Ruth's eye. He gestured toward the outside and left the hall. She joined him minutes later. "I really ought to stay, John. We've got to decide what to do."

"What you decide has just become unimportant," Falkenberg said. "Your Council doesn't hold as many cards as it used to."

"John, what will they do?"

He shrugged. "Try to stop the war now that they're here. I suppose it never occurred to Silana that a complaint from Franklin industrialists is more likely to get CD attention than a similar squawk from a bunch of farmers . . ."

"You expected this! Was this what you were waiting for?"

"Something like this."

"You know more than you're saying! John, why won't you tell me? I know you don't love me, but haven't I a right to know?"

He stood at stiff attention in the bright reddish-tinted sunlight for a long time. Finally he said, "Glenda Ruth, nothing's certain in politics and war. I once promised something to a girl, and I couldn't deliver it."

"But—"

"We've each command responsibilities—and each other. Will you believe me when I say I've tried to keep you from having to choose—and keep myself from the same choice? You'd better get ready. A CD Court of Inquiry isn't in the habit of waiting for people, and they're due in little more than an hour."

The Court was to be held aboard *Intrepid*. The four-hundred-meter bottle-shaped warship in orbit around New Washington was the only neutral territory available. When the Patriot delegates were piped aboard, the Marines in the landing dock gave Bannister the exact honors they'd given the Confederate Governor General, then hustled the delegation through gray steel corridors to a petty officer's lounge reserved for them.

"Governor General Forrest of the Confederacy is already aboard, sir," the Marine sergeant escort told them. "Captain would like to see Colonel Falkenberg in his cabin in ten minutes."

Bannister looked around the small lounge. "I suppose it's bugged," he said. "Colonel, what happens now?"

Falkenberg noted the artificially friendly tone Bannister had adopted. "The Captain and his advisors will hear each of us privately. If you want witnesses summoned, he'll take care of that. When the Court thinks the time proper, he'll bring both parties together. The CD usually tries to get everyone to agree rather than impose some kind of settlement."

"And if we can't agree?"

Falkenberg shrugged. "They might let you fight it out. They might order mercenaries off planet and impose a blockade. They could even draw up their own settlement and order you to accept it."

"What happens if we just tell them to go away? What can they do?" Bannister demanded.

Falkenberg smiled tightly. "They can't conquer the planet because they haven't enough Marines to occupy it —but there's not a lot else they can't do, Mr. President. There's enough power aboard this cruiser to make New Washington uninhabitable.

"You don't have either planetary defenses or a fleet. I'd think a long time before I made Captain Grant angry —and on that score, I've been summoned to his cabin." Falkenberg saluted. There was no trace of mockery in the gesture, but Bannister grimaced as the soldier left the lounge.

Falkenberg was conducted past Marine sentries to the captain's cabin. The orderly opened the door and let him in, then withdrew.

John Grant was a tall, thin officer with premature graying hair that made him look older than he was. As Falkenberg entered, Grant stood and greeted him with genuine warmth. "Good to see you, John Christian." He extended his hand and looked over his visitor with pleasure. "You're keeping fit enough."

"So are you, Johnny." Falkenberg's smile was equally genuine. "And the family's well?"

"Inez and the kids are fine. My father's dead."

"Sorry to hear that."

Captain Grant brought his chair from behind his desk and placed it facing Falkenberg's. Unconsciously he dogged it into place. "It was a release for him, I think. Single-passenger flier accident."

Falkenberg frowned, and Grant nodded. "Coroner said

accident," the Captain said. "But it could have been suicide. He was pretty broken up about Sharon. But you
don't know that story, do you? No matter. My kid sister's
fine. They've got a good place on Sparta."

Grant reached to his desk to touch a button. A steward
brought brandy and glasses. The Marine set up a col-
lapsible table between them, then left.

"The Grand Admiral all right?" Falkenberg asked.

"He's hanging on." Grant drew in a deep breath and
let it out quickly. "Just barely, though. Despite everything
Uncle Martin could do the budget's lower again this year.
I can't stay here long, John. Another patrol, and it's getting harder to cover these unauthorized missions in the
log. Have you accomplished your job?"

"Yeah. Went quicker than I thought. I've spent the last
hundred hours wishing we'd arranged to have you arrive
sooner." He went to the screen controls on the cabin bulkhead.

"Got that complaint signaled by a merchantman as we
came in," Grant said. "Surprised hell out of me. Here,
let me get that, they've improved the damned thing and
it's tricky." He played with the controls until New Washington's inhabited areas showed on the screen. "O.K.?"

"Right." Falkenberg spun dials to show the current
military situation on the planet below. "Stalemate," he
said. "As it stands. But once you order all mercenaries off
planet, we won't have much trouble taking the capital
area."

"Christ, John, I can't do anything as raw as that! If
the Friedlanders go, you have to go as well. Hell, you've
accomplished the mission. The rebels may have a hell of a
time taking the capital without you, but it doesn't really
matter who wins. Neither one of 'em's going to build a
fleet for a while after this war's over. Good work."

Falkenberg nodded. "That was Sergei Lermontov's plan.
Neutralize this planet with minimum CD investment and
without destroying the industries. Something came up,
though, Johnny, and I've decided to change it a bit. The
regiment's staying."

"But I—"

"Just hold on," Falkenberg said. He grinned broadly.
"I'm not a mercenary within the meaning of the act.
We've got a land grant, Johnny. You can leave us as set-
tlers, not mercenaries."

"Oh, come off it." Grant's voice showed irritation. "A

221

land grant by a rebel government not in control? Look, nobody's going to look *too* close at what I do, but Franklin can buy one Grand Senator anyway. I can't risk it, John. Wish I could."

"What if the grant's confirmed by the local Loyalist government?" Falkenberg asked impishly.

"Well, then it'd be O.K.—how in hell did you manage *that?*" Grant was grinning again. "Have a drink and tell me about it." He poured for both of them. "And where do you fit in?"

Falkenberg looked up at Grant and his expression changed to something like astonishment. "You won't believe this, Johnny."

"From the look on your face you don't either."

"Not sure I do. Johnny, I've got a girl. A soldier's girl, and I'm going to marry her. She's leader of most of the rebel army. There are a lot of politicians around who think they count for something, but—" He made a sharp gesture with his right hand.

"Marry the queen and become king, uh?"

"She's more like a princess. Anyway, the Loyalists aren't going to surrender to the rebels without a fight. That complaint they sent was quite genuine. There's no rebel the Loyalists will trust, not even Glenda Ruth."

Grant nodded comprehension. "Enter the soldier who enforced the Laws of War. He's married to the princess and commands the only army around. What's your *real* stake here, John Christian?"

Falkenberg shrugged. "Maybe the princess won't leave the kingdom. Anyway. Lermontov's trying to keep the balance of power. God knows, somebody's got to. Fine. The Grand Admiral looks ten years ahead—but I'm not sure the CoDominium's going to *last* ten years, Johnny."

Grant slowly nodded agreement. His voice fell and took on a note of awe. "Neither am I. It's worse just in the last few weeks. The Old Man's going out of his mind. One thing, though. There are some Grand Senators trying to hold it together. Some of them have given up the Russki-American fights to stand together against their own governments."

"Enough? Can they do it?"

"I wish I knew." Grant shook his head in bewilderment. "I always thought the CoDominium was the one stable thing on old Earth," he said wonderingly. "Now it's all we can do to hold it together. The nationalists keep winning, John, and nobody knows how to stop them." He drained his glass. "The Old Man's going to hate losing you."

"Yeah. We've worked together a long time." Falkenberg looked wistfully around the cabin. Once he'd thought this would be the high point of his life, to be captain of a CD warship. Now he might never see one again.

Then he shrugged. "There's worse places to be, Johnny," Falkenberg said. "Do me a favor, will you? When you get back to Luna Base, ask the admiral to see that all copies of that New Washington mineral survey are destroyed. I'd hate for somebody to learn there really is something here worth grabbing."

"O.K. You're a long way from anything, John."

"I know. But if things break up around Earth, this may be the best place to be. Look, Johnny, if you need a safe base some day, we'll be here. Tell the Old Man that."

"Sure." Grant gave Falkenberg a twisted grin. "Can't get over it. Going to marry the girl, are you? I'm glad for both of you."

"Thanks."

"King John I. What kind of government will you set up, anyway?"

"Hadn't thought. Myths change. Maybe people are ready for monarchy again at that. We'll think of something, Glenda Ruth and I."

"I just bet you will. She must be one hell of a girl."

"She is that."

"A toast to the bride, then." They drank, and Grant refilled their glasses. Then he stood. "One last, eh? To the CoDominium."

Falkenberg stood and raised his glass. They drank the toast while below them New Washington turned, and a hundred parsecs away Earth armed for her last battle.